CHA MEL EON

SARAH HOLDING

Matador
9 Priory Business Park,
Wistow Road, Kibworth Beauchamp,
Leicestershire. LE8 0RX
Tel: 0116 279 2299
Email: books@troubador.co.uk
Web: www.troubador.co.uk/matador
Twitter: @matadorbooks

ISBN 978 1838593 698

Cover design by Firehorse
British Library Cataloguing in Publication Data.
A catalogue record for this book is available from the British Library.

Printed and bound in the UK by TJ International, Padstow, Cornwall
Typeset in 11pt Minion Pro by Troubador Publishing Ltd, Leicester, UK

Matador is an imprint of Troubador Publishing Ltd

To my soulmate, Eric,
with love and thanks for thirty-five years of adventures
and doubtless many more.

To journey without being changed, is to be a nomad.
To change without journeying is to be a chameleon.
To journey and to be transformed by the journeying
is to be a pilgrim.

Mark Nepo, The Exquisite Risk

CONTENTS

My Lord Atlas,

Our preparations are proceeding slowly. The Hall of Records will soon be completed and sealed under the great leonine statue and, thanks to the Builders, the three pyramids are beginning to take shape on the great plateau, in alignment with Orion's Belt, just as you instructed. I believe there is now a good chance New Atlantis will be ready in time for your People to relocate here before the Earth Changes begin in earnest.

According to my divinations, we have already reached the tipping point for the Kingdom of Atlantis and are rapidly approaching the end sequence. With each day that passes, there will be ever more violent climatic, seismic, volcanic and meteoric activity, and you will soon exhaust all possible means of preventing or holding off the Kingdom's demise. There is no denying that our day of reckoning is approaching, just as the Emerald Tablets prophesised. There is very little time left to evacuate Atlantis, and I recommend you commence this process immediately.

Your Honour, I also urge you to fully activate our secret failsafe project and start field-testing the resilient strain of human, Homo chameliensis. En.Ki's latest reports show this new prototype could be capable of surviving the aftermath and repopulating Atlantis, should your own People not make it. We both know this project is woefully behind schedule; Askew and his team have so far only managed to produce one live sample – a male, I believe. As you know, their first creation did not survive, but I understand there is a third in the early stages of production, a female.

I will return to Atlantis shortly, but I must first make sure that the Builders have all the resources they need to complete the power plant. Without the three gold capstones in place, Earth will be plunged into an eternity of darkness and falling debris. The Stasis Giants must now be awakened if we are to have any hope of activating the pyramids before calamity strikes.

As you requested, I am also assembling an intergalactic mission, briefed to be discreetly on hand but to intervene on Earth only if it should prove absolutely necessary.

Could I ask that you now allow me to make arrangements for the inauguration ceremony for the New Atlantis? I humbly suggest it should take place in front of the pyramids at the start of the new Sothic Cycle to mark the beginning of the Age of Leo. Any later than that, the flood-waters will rise and it will be too late.

Tehuti

THE SPHINX CODEX

PART 1 OF LEON'S STORY

Tablet I

ETHERIA

T HE MALE 'CHILD' WAS the oddest of the three. He had the palest blue eyes, very white skin and hair the colour of monatomic gold. Under the bright lights of En.Ki's main laboratory, his skin looked almost translucent and his blue eyes stared straight ahead, completely unseeing. As the two research scientists assigned to the project, I and my supervisor, Colonel Askew, tended him like all our other genetically-engineered creations – with a mixture of pride, care and curiosity. The child's hair grew into golden, wavy locks so Askew and I started calling him Leon, because, despite his virtual blindness, he looked –

and at times behaved – like a young lion. Leon slept more than the other two, ate less often, growled more than he spoke, and grew more muscles. We knew early on he would become the strongest and tallest of the three, as well as the most determined, the most fierce. It was as if a seething, roiling anger had been bred into him, which compensated for his lack of vision; he seemed to hear and feel things more keenly because he was not seduced and sedated by the gift of sight.

Around the age of four, Leon's unusual mental and physical powers started to kick in. We would know, for instance, that a storm was brewing somewhere up in Earth's atmosphere, because Leon would start acting up. It was as if his emotional state was connected in some way to the weather; his behaviour anticipated it by a few hours – sometimes even a few days – so we always knew when external conditions in Atlantis were about to take a turn for the worse. Being so wrapped up in my work, I was never one to pay much attention to the weather but, as Leon's outbursts got more and more violent and frequent, I couldn't help noticing how many news stories there were about the weather in Atlantis becoming increasingly wild. Leon was my barometer and the only proof I needed; the speed with which his mood could escalate spoke volumes about the unusual volatility in atmospheric pressure. And it wasn't just storms, either – his mood mirrored more of Earth's unprecedented symptoms: earthquakes, volcanic eruptions and tsunamis all caused turmoil in Leon's fragile psyche, unleashing wave after wave of intense emotional paroxysms.

Regardless of the strange occurrences going on outside the lab, for me it was more fascinating to observe what was happening inside Leon's brain as he responded to our relentless schedule of experiments, sensing the imminent pain and tensing up before the electrodes even touched his forehead. At six years old, he could scale the lab's climbing wall like a baboon in less than a minute and eat a plate of fresh meat even faster. A zoologist by training, Askew harboured a plan to field-test Leon with a family of primates or even a pride of sabre-toothed cats, but I was against the idea. I was always more cautious, more sensitive to the needs of my experimental 'offspring', and made sure they were comfortable and well rested. I knew my care-giving was perceived by En.Ki as excessively paternal and that I was being closely monitored by the board of directors, who lived in fear of our royal patron shutting down the project, and wished to prevent me from becoming as emotionally attached to Leon as I was to my earlier test subject, Kam.

En.Ki were so concerned about how much I cared about Leon that they completely missed the fact that Askew was up to no good. They constantly scrutinised my actions and whereabouts but failed to notice that Askew was scheming to sell the genetic code for our prototypes, much to my disapproval. Askew maintained that he owned this fringe technology and took credit not only for the innovation of the blue eyes (which I'd painstakingly crafted onto chromosome 15 using strands of King Atlas's DNA) but also their shapeshifting or chameleonoid capabilities (a gene sequence I stitched into chromosome 2, adapted from a rare species of chameleon found on Sirius, which can change form or colour depending on its surroundings or its emotional state). But this is not about who's to blame or who takes credit. While the blue eyes were apparent from birth, both Askew and I knew the true shapeshifting abilities would most likely emerge around the time of puberty, triggered by freewheeling emotions and the onslaught of new hormones in the bodies of our creations. So, when the time came, we both took a particular interest in Leon's ability to change state.

Leon's shapeshifting powers were not, however, quite what we had been expecting. Rather than changing his physical form, he could manipulate his whereabouts in time, which I suspected was a defensive move to prevent anything intruding into his physical space. Around the age of thirteen, he began to 'step out', as Askew called it. This could happen in one of two ways: Leon either located himself slightly in the past, delaying or putting a slight drag effect on the current timeline so that he had more control over it, or – and this happened more often – propelled himself a minute or so forwards in time, so that he could effectively bypass the present moment altogether until the situation resolved into something he felt he could handle. This subtle flexing of time fascinated me, and I started to invent games to play with Leon, coaxing him to increase gradually the length of time he could project himself forwards or backwards without tiring. When I took a sample of Leon's blood after he'd shifted in time for more than a few minutes, I found that it was infused with an entirely new hormone that I named 'etheria'.

To keep track of Leon's episodes of 'stepping out' and also to counter the side effects of too much etheria (which, not unlike adrenaline, left him uncontrollably pumped up), I created a tracking device that I inserted into Leon's C1 vertebra. Although this meant I could download Leon's temporal whereabouts, I had no control over him stepping out. Not long after the device was introduced, I noticed a strange mutation in Leon's nervous system, which forced me to also install in his brain a Blocker, which I based on a piece of black-market tech my brother Jainko developed at Black Khanus' labs back on Sirius. The Blocker ensured that no entities or hive minds could infiltrate Leon's consciousness, not even Askew with his En.Ki level 9 security clearance. But it did nothing to stem Leon's production of etheria.

When the time came to field-test Leon, I worked tirelessly with the field placement team to find a suitable environment in Atlantis where Leon's unique talents would be sufficiently developed and challenged. After many long committee meetings, we eventually settled on a solution that I felt would be ideal for Leon: a secure underground installation built by the Atlantean military to store their vast reserves of orichalcum bullion and where they train new soldiers for deep-dive combat. The base was notoriously dimly lit compared to conditions on the surface but, given Leon's virtual blindness, he was hardly likely to be bothered by the lack of daylight.

I was concerned, however, that, being on a military base, he might be exposed to influences and circumstances that could trigger the kind of violent episodes we'd seen in his early childhood: he would inflict harm on himself or his surroundings when he was angry or frustrated, breaking things in the lab, or giving himself cuts and bruises. We managed the situation back then with low-level psychotic medication and he eventually grew out of it, but I had no way of knowing if the same approach would work now that he was approaching adulthood.

On the morning of Leon's sixteenth 'birthday', we hit a new problem. He must have heard us talking about his upcoming relocation to the underground base and decided to step out well before the lab assistant came to unlock Leon's enclosure. When Askew got wind of this, he accused me of letting Leon's etheria levels get out of control and went immediately to report the incident to our superiors. I then spent hours patiently trying every protocol we'd used on previous occasions: soothing music, enticing food items, new toys, stronger hallucinogens. But by now Leon could anticipate all our tricks and remained steadfastly in his timeless bubble until I reluctantly agreed to allow En.Ki's emergency sweeper team to take over. Leon had, of course, sensed this coming too, and managed to sidestep the strong electromagnetic fields they put through the lab. No one at En.Ki – not even Askew – had realised how knowing Leon had become in respect of his shapeshifting. He knew, for example, that if he dropped his guard for a moment, an arm or a leg could get stuck and become fused with the lab walls or fittings, because he'd been aware of it happening to countless other lab rats.

On this particular occasion Leon was lurking in an inter-dimensional plane roughly two minutes ahead of where I was. He must have learned how to sense minute changes in heat and air pressure or been picking up sound and electrical vibrations in the lab. The sweepers made one more pass, pulsing through the whole area with the kind of fine-grade microwaves that cooked most rodents, before packing up their gear to go. Canny as ever, Leon then waited until Askew and I were summoned to our weekly meeting with En.Ki's board of directors before he slid back into the normal timeframe and made his move.

Tablet II

CRYSTAL

L EON MUST HAVE MEMORISED every nook and cranny of the En.Ki lab, squirrelling away the information about his surroundings for years. In the early days, it was probably something he did without thinking, to alleviate the tedium of the pointless, repetitive experiments we put him through. But as he grew older and more restless, Leon must have started to regard this information as useful in case he ever needed to escape. However, since he had never been beyond the perimeter of En.Ki's research compound, he had no way of straying any further. So that's where we found him, covered with weals caused by trying to pass through the electric enclosure.

But I'm jumping ahead myself now. Let me go back to the time he broke into the crystal store a few months back and helped himself to a long piece of quartz from the chiller cabinet. When we reviewed the security camera footage afterwards, we could see him smiling and chattering away to himself about the crystal he'd stolen. He carried it back to his enclosure inside the sleeve of his robe, slid it under his sleeping mat and, according to his brainwave readouts the next morning, had the wildest dreams he'd ever experienced.

I could see crystals were like toys for Leon, so I decided to see whether they could help our experiment. Over the next few weeks I introduced him to a range of crystals used in the lab. It was fascinating to see how quickly his brain activity could align with the inherent frequency of each crystal; and then, as he grew in confidence, he began to be able to attune them to his own brainwaves so that, after just a few sessions, he only needed to come into the vicinity of a new crystal and it would become entrained by his thought-forms. He could even pull emotional vibrations out of crystals, sort of sucking them dry, and consequently taking on whatever emotion the crystal had absorbed, be it positive or negative. If a rose quartz contained a happy vibe, he would be off the charts, singing in a pure, high voice like an angel for several hours after handling it.

Askew regarded this crystal work as nothing more than a side project, and encouraged me to drop it in order to prepare Leon for his gruelling schedule on the military base. By that stage, I'd tried out various crystals with Leon – several quartzes, red jasper, black obsidian – and found there was one in particular – a milky-white selenite wand – for which he developed a particular liking, so, to keep him calm, I let him sleep with it under his pillow.

Tablet III

BABOON

WITH PREPARATIONS FOR HIS relocation complete, Leon was given a full medical by En.Ki's team of doctors and veterinarians, which Askew supervised. Once his final health checks were complete, I had to transfer Leon to his new home without him exhibiting any sort of violent outburst. He had been spouting a lot of nonsense about how he was going to be the 'best soldier ever'. I sincerely hoped so because, in order to complete my secondment to Earth, I needed this project to be a success: according to the small print in my contract with En.Ki, we had to field-test at least two prototypes – only then would I be allowed to return to my family on Sirius.

Never having known any different, I suppose Leon's relationship with me was the closest he will ever experience to having a parent. For my part, owing to my extended periods away from my actual family on Sirius, I had limited experience of parenting – and, in any case, I only have daughters. If I'm honest, Leon is the closest I've ever had to a son – which explains not only why I let him call me 'Pa', but also how guilty I felt whenever he became excessively clingy. This is exactly what happened when he realised I was about to offload him onto a hard-as-nails squadron leader by the name of Methuselah Beltane, known on the base simply as 'Meth'.

That was the precise moment Leon chose to let me know what it felt like to 'step out'. One minute we were standing beside the booth in the registration bay of the underground base, right outside the huge orichalcum security doors, and the next I was immobilised and hovering above the ground with Leon, in a fuzzy parallel zone where I could observe what was going on but could play no part in it. Leon grinned mischievously and I couldn't help marvelling at his adolescent mastery of this new-found ability.

Meth looked somewhat confused, pulled off his dark glasses, flexed his shoulder blades and, after waiting for a minute or so, strode back to his office beyond the security doors. Cool as anything, Leon then dropped us back into the timeline, and started to walk in the opposite direction.

'Where are you going, Leon?' I asked.

'Home,' he announced matter-of-factly.

'You don't even know what "home" is, kid,' I muttered sadly.

Leon looked at me nervously. If I'm absolutely honest, I thought we'd bred a human prototype that was a little more courageous and accepting of new circumstances, but maybe Leon was strong only physically, not mentally. I remember thinking to myself that the next phase of the experiment could prove challenging.

'Come on, pal, let's go find your new enclosure. I've arranged for you to share your quarters with a special baboon. You've always wanted a pet, haven't you?'

Leon smiled shyly and held my hand as we walked through the huge doors. Once they clanged shut behind us, he went a bit loopy and started jumping around, bashing his head and shrieking, 'Where's my baboon? I want to meet baboon!'

Meth was standing with his arms folded at the end of the long corridor that led to Leon's new quarters.

'I thought you told me he was an adult prototype. He acts like a complete kid. He'd better shape up soon, or I'll be shipping him straight back to En.Ki with a toe-tag in a body bag.'

I rolled my eyes at the squadron leader's false bravado. He was being lavishly compensated by En.Ki for his part in this experiment and seemed to be wallowing in the sense of power this gave him.

'So long as he gets eight hours' sleep a night and a decent quantity of rations, he'll be fine. He only acts up when he's nervous, tired or hungry, so treat him well and it won't happen again.'

Meth stared back at me, bored and humourless. There was an awkward silence.

'Well, that's it, then.'

I was about to give Leon a hug, but Meth wheeled round, grabbed him by the scruff of his neck and barked, 'This way, idiot.'

'Let go, you hurt me!' Leon kept yelling as he was frogmarched away from me.

I was suddenly very unsure about leaving Leon in an environment potentially much more hostile than our lab. As I made my way back to En.Ki to write up my report, a vivid memory of Kam stirred in my mind. I remembered handing this sweet little bundle with wide blue eyes over to my wife and saying, 'Ma, you're to take good care of this child while I'm gone, just as if it was one of our own'.

I sighed. It was beginning to dawn on me that returning home to Sirius was still a long way off.

Tablet IV

NAZAR

IN RETURN FOR TAKING on Leon as a trainee 'soldier' and allowing us weekly access to monitor him, En.Ki agreed to pay for any infrastructural requirements at Meth's underground base, which, from the schedules I'd seen, involved improvements to ventilation shafts, a new subterranean Terraformer vehicle, providing additional surveillance equipment and so on. Askew also agreed to sell illegal minerals and such like for Meth on the side. I didn't approve of this last part of the arrangement and told Askew as much, but he insisted we had no choice in the matter if we wanted Leon to be well looked after and to have privileges not normally given to new recruits. So, I was often forced to act as the go-between, carrying the illegal booty from Meth to Askew on a weekly basis, and returning the next time with pouches of black-market mono or blood products – payment Askew obtained from his shady buyers.

Despite his virtual blindness, Leon seemed to cope quite well at the base to begin with. He quickly found his way around by feeling along the walls and reading the raised lettering on the signage, so by the time I made my first visit he was confident enough to come up to the main entrance gates by himself to meet me. Or so I thought. As soon as the big doors slid back, Leon made a run for it, darting past me and the security guards, his pet baboon lolloping after him, screeching with delight. He headed for the emergency exit stairs next to the large goods lift that led back to the surface, but the guards had locked them remotely as soon as the buzzer went off, so Leon stood by the door, rattling the handle and growling fiercely.

I waited a few minutes and then approached him slowly.

'What have you called your baboon, Leon?'

'Secret,' he muttered.

'"Secret"? That's its name?'

'Not telling.'

'I see. Is she a good pet? Would she let me stroke her?' I walked a little closer, and Leon moved the animal to his opposite shoulder.

'You bring crystal, Pa?'

'Why do you want a crystal, Leon?'

'Not for me. Present for Babi.'

I had the white selenite crystal Leon was so fond of in my pocket and I handed it to him. I don't know why I took it with me that day – some instinct must have told me I might need it. But I knew we were not out of danger yet.

'Babi – is that the name of your baboon?'

'No.' Leon smirked, realising he'd been tricked into revealing his companion's name. He dropped the baboon to its feet, and it circled round him, curling its tail around his legs. I could sense that Leon was liable to step out at any moment and I needed to prevent that from happening as quickly as possible.

'Are you hungry, Leon?'

I ventured a little closer, proffering a juicy dragon fruit that I had also brought with me as a gift. Leon could smell its sweet flesh and immediately sniffed the air and held out his hand. I knew from past experience that food and drink were the quickest ways to ground him, then the chances of stepping out would be minimal.

With juice from the dragon fruit dripping down his chin and the baboon gobbling up the last mouthful, I led Leon back inside the base to his quarters. He chattered away quite happily for a while and we played a few of his favourite games but, when the time came for me to leave, Leon became very clingy and vocal. In the end they had to call the medical supervisor to put him in restraints. I could see it was necessary in order that I could leave without him trying anything on but, when they put a muzzle on him, I must admit I over-reacted. They insisted that, since he'd bitten one of the guards the day before, they were obliged to follow orders. I sighed and quietly withdrew, feeling guilty about leaving Leon again, and about not training him better.

Meth made me wait a month before I visited again. He maintained that my presence must have upset Leon and caused the outburst. To my mind, the baboon seemed more distraught than Leon but, in order to humour Meth, I reluctantly agreed. The next time I visited, Leon had been assigned a minder: a middle-aged female prisoner by the name of Nazar. Meth told me she had been caught spying on the base and was suspected of working for the Trojans. Instead of being put to death as per Atlantean penal law, Meth had decided to retain Nazar, believing she could prove useful, especially once he discovered she was a highly skilled Trojan pilot.

When I entered Leon's quarters and saw Leon and Nazar together, I could tell the bond between them was already close and I actually felt a pang of jealousy. His white-blond mane was almost touching her greying locks as he leaned towards her and listened with wide, unseeing eyes to her story, which seemed to involve an icy planet and a lost crew member. Her voice was warm and soothing. I told myself it was only natural that he would take to an older woman like that, as he'd never known any kind of maternal influence. I greeted her politely and she stared at me intently with dark eyes, as if she wanted very much to ask me a question but knew she couldn't risk it. Instead, she got up, shook my hand with a firm grip and left the room.

Once we were alone, I asked Leon a few questions. He sat holding his white crystal.

'Do you like Nazar, Leon?'

'She my friend. She Babi friend too.'

'What do you do with Nazar?'

'She tell me stories. Before I go sleep.'

'That must be nice for you.'

'She know all the planets. She been there.'

'Which planets?'

'Jupiter and Mars.'

'And the Moon?'

'Moon not a planet, Pa.'

'No, of course it isn't.'

'She fly spaceships. She want to 'scape, like me.'

'But you're not going to do anything you shouldn't, are you, Leon?'

'Not today.' Leon picked up his pillow and threw it at me.

'Nice aim. How are you liking military training?'

'Leon kill big snake. Nazar show me.'

Tablet V

THIRD EYE

I T WAS ASKEW, NOT me, who was instructed by En.Ki to make the next visit. I was anxious about Leon's developing relationship with Nazar – not from an emotional attachment point of view, but because I felt she might teach him things he should not know. If she really was a spy, for instance, she might lead him astray, and I also didn't want Leon teaching Nazar a thing or two, like how to step out. I also knew from experience that En.Ki's patron, King Atlas, was paranoid about this experimental technology falling into the wrong hands.

To ensure we obtained objective scientific data from

our genetic prototype, we had not told Meth about Leon's shapeshifting capabilities, but to do this we needed to monitor Leon's progress more closely than our limited access to him allowed, so I needed Askew to find a way to fit Leon with a Third Eye device on this next visit. It was an invention I'd been working on that would not only stimulate Leon's optic nerve but also, more importantly, enable us to witness all his interactions, functioning like a surveillance camera. Over time, the device would cause his brain to interpret what the device was 'seeing' so he would start to see more and more.

Leon was reluctant to let Askew insert the optical device into the area between his eyebrows. He wriggled and protested until Askew had to use a sedative jab. Once it was in place, however, I could activate it and adjust the settings remotely from the lab. It was an awe-inspiring moment when the slightly blurry retinal image appeared on my screen, giving me instant access to Leon's point of view. While the sedative wore off, all I was getting was a view of the wall beside Leon's bunk, but after he came around and in the days afterwards, it captured all his interactions with staff on the base, every meal he ate and every time he looked at Nazar.

I got to know her face and all its expressions a little too well. She looked at Leon the same way Ma looks at my kids back home – with tenderness and admiration. Askew wanted to write in the report that Nazar had 'enhanced Leon's quality of life *immeasurably*', but I deleted that last word. It was too soon to say how much she had affected his sense of well-being. Thankfully, Nazar had not yet realised Leon had a Third Eye fitted – his face is always a bit grimy, and the device is no bigger than a small pimple. He scratched at it for the first couple of days, but then got used to it and left it alone.

Now that Leon was behaving better, Nazar started to take him further afield. On their first trip outside the base, she took him through the tunnel system that runs around the outer ring of Atlantis and then out along the main military highway that runs beneath the canal leading all the way to the ocean. They emerged in a small cove surrounded by tall cliffs which I'd never seen before and, for the first time in his life, Leon encountered sea air and the feel of a sea breeze on his face, and heard the sound of the huge white breakers surging in one after another. He started roaring back at the waves, like the lion that he is. The sounds he was making scared Babi, who jumped down into the swirling water and had to be rescued from being sucked under the waves by Nazar, who was almost engulfed by the sea water. At first Leon found it very funny that they were all getting wet, but when he could hear his baboon struggling for breath and felt Nazar grip his arm and drag him out of the surf he started to panic. I could tell he was trying to step out, but the saltwater must have prevented it somehow, and he just seemed to phase in and out for a few seconds, almost as if he was passing out.

Nazar finally managed to gain control of the situation and steered Leon and Babi further along the beach and away from the waves. She produced a dragon fruit from her bag to calm him down. Once he appeared stable, she wandered off to the next cove. Leon waited patiently for her to come back. She returned as the Sun was beginning to set. I could see it reflected in her eyes as Leon turned towards her, bands of pink and orange clouds forming in the western sky as the Sun dropped lower and lower. When Leon turned towards the horizon himself and the Sun set completely, I noticed my star, Sirius, in the sky, a bright pinprick of light descending slowly out of sight. I confess it brought a tear to my eye, thinking of Ma and the kids back home. But I digress: this is about Leon.

The following day, Nazar took Leon into the warren of underground tunnels deep under Atlantis. They went so deep that my Third Eye lost track of them altogether and the screen in the lab went black for several anxious hours. It only flickered back on when they entered a cave full of crystal beds. The rocks had picked up the frequency of my device and were transmitting Leon's point of view with a stronger signal and a wider field of vision than usual. I could see giant polygonal rods of quartz fanning out from the cave floor like pointing fingers, refracting the light from Nazar's lantern into beautiful patterns. Leon could sense the energy coming off them and was reaching out to touch the crystals, which were twice his height and must have been buzzing like crazy. Nazar handed him one that had been prised free, a rod of quartz wider than his palms and ten times as long. He giggled because he could obviously feel it rippling against his skin, just like the time he broke into the crystal cabinet at the lab. Getting a little over-excited, Leon gripped the crystal at one end and wielded it like a sword, pressing the tip into Nazar's chest. For a fleeting moment she looked afraid, but then she laughed and reached out to take the crystal away from him. However, Leon was not going to let go of his new treasure so easily. As he ripped it out of her hands, she stumbled backwards and seemed surprised at Leon's instantaneous display of strength and purpose.

Suddenly, Leon's temper flared up and I realised he was in the process of stepping out. It only lasted a few seconds – just enough of a window for him to drop back to the moment before Nazar handed him the crystal, so he could play the event a different way. As Leon stepped back into the timeline, I watched as Nazar approached him again with the large quartz, and this time, instead of pointing it towards her, Leon snatched it away and ran off down the tunnel, singing tunefully at the top of his voice. But as soon as he was out of range of the crystal bed, I lost the connection; I could neither see nor hear them and the screen went dark again.

Tablet VI

METHUSELAH

AFTER THE EPISODE AT the crystal cave, Meth must have decided that Nazar could not be trusted to be Leon's minder, and she was moved to another part of the base. Leon was distraught about her being sent away and kept asking for her. We heard through the grapevine that he lost his temper and stepped out so many times that Meth finally realised the boy had some unusual powers, and took it upon himself to become Leon's minder until they found someone else to take on this role.

There is something menacing about Meth that I could not work out at first. It was not until I saw him through

Leon's Third Eye that I realised what it was: he's not human. He does a pretty good job of disguising it, but the fact is he's a reptilian. The eyes give it away: their vertical yellow slits, with double nictitating eyelids. Then there's the slightly protruding shoulder blades, which are probably some kind of wings that he tries to disguise under his clothes. His skin is perfectly mapped to a human colour but has a certain sheen in some lighting conditions that gives it away: he's cold-blooded, for sure. The Atlantean Royal Guard made a point of recruiting reptilian mercenaries to fight for them during the Lemurian War, but I was not aware previously that they had retained any of these hateful creatures.

Leon didn't seem to like Meth either. Right from the start, Meth treated Leon more like a new prisoner than a paying guest, but later he seemed to make an effort to appear friendly and pleasant. I noticed that, no matter how well Meth treated him, Leon paced like a caged animal whenever he was around. In a renewed bid to get control of his new recruit, Meth proposed one-to-one combat lessons. Leon didn't exactly warm to this idea, but he didn't refuse either. The next day, Meth showed up at his quarters and took Leon to the combat hall, with its soft matted floor, for his first proper lesson in swordsmanship.

I wasn't paying attention at first, being caught up in my work on a new prototype in my lab, so the first I heard of it was the clashing of metal on metal and Leon's voice suddenly rising to a demented shriek. I rushed over to the screen and saw Meth's face flashing with dark excitement, as he lunged towards Leon with his black sword held aloft and brought it swinging round in a reckless sideswipe. Leon stepped quickly out of the way and placed himself quite sensibly a few seconds into the future, leaving Meth standing in the centre of the matted area staring all around him and yelling madly in a state of utter confusion. Leon chuckled with delight at the effectiveness of his defensive manoeuvre and slid slyly back into the timeline, approaching Meth from behind and pressing his sword between Meth's bulging shoulder-blades. Dropping his own sword, Meth wheeled around, his face now green with anger, grabbed Leon by the hair and threw him to the floor. At that point Babi hopped into the fray, shrieking in an agitated manner and climbing onto Leon's back to try to protect him. Letting out a deafening roar, Leon brushed the animal aside, lurched forwards and ripped into Meth's clothes, clawing at his reptilian skin. In desperation, Meth signalled to the security guards, who pulled Leon aside, cuffed him and escorted him back to his enclosure. As Leon turned back, Meth picked up his sword and slid the blade back into its ornate sheath.

What effect this incident had on Meth I may never know, but it left Leon in a severe state of shock. Even the baboon seemed incapable of getting his attention. Crying and shivering, he curled up in a blanket on his bunk and slept for the whole of the next day. I began to wonder if he'd been given a sedative in his meal, but on reflection it's more likely that Leon's behaviour was the result of his genetic programming responding robustly to Meth's violent nature. The 'Pa' in me felt ridiculously protective of Leon, his vulnerable situation and his unnecessary emotional suffering. The scientist in me knew that this was all part of Leon's rite of passage, a necessary stage he had to go through if we were to field-test him properly as a genetically modified hybrid. Only then would we find out if Atlas's new resilient human was a success. If Leon could prove himself to be an effective improvement on the basic human genome, En.Ki would sign off the project. Only then would my work be done, and I could leave Atlantis for good and return home to Sirius.

Desperate to make a success of Leon's placement, I sent a message to the base stating that, under the terms of En.Ki's research contract, Leon was now due to undergo a fitness test to see how much his strength and endurance had improved in the four months he'd been there. I knew they would have to consent to this, but I wasn't sure how Meth would react. Reverting to his gruff style of treatment, Meth went to fetch Leon the following morning, dragging the blanket away, kicking the baboon aside and bellowing at Leon to get up. Leon roared back and bared his teeth, but Meth had his guards put the restraints on him again. Then I saw Meth lean towards Leon's face and apply something to his forehead. My screen went dark and I realised he'd rumbled our surveillance device.

Tablet VII

URDINAK

WE WERE REFUSED ACCESS to Leon for more than a month. I believe they were torturing him. Then, out of the blue, Meth summoned Askew and told him that Leon was being treated for self-inflicted wounds at the base's medical facility. Askew asked to see Leon but was told it was not possible at that time. Given Leon's propensity for self-harm, I urged Askew to prescribe him some stronger sedatives. Askew, however, was too focused on keeping on Meth's good side, too attached to his little drug-related side deals, to press the issue.

In desperation, I had to come up with another way to

see Leon, one that Meth would not be able to resist. So, I offered to give him an exclusive preview of my new human prototype, *Homo chameliensis 3.0*. When I told him this new 'model' was black and female, he jumped at the chance. To make up for the omission of any melanin on chromosome 11 when we produced Leon, which led to his albino complexion and virtual blindness, we inadvertently gave our next prototype an excess of melanin when we were modifying the gene sequence, which to my delight meant our newest prototype's skin turned out to be a deep ebony hue, which contrasts beautifully with her bright blue eyes, her dazzling smile and her perfectly straight, white teeth. Even though I say so myself, she is a looker.

The mistake with the melanin turned out to be what distinguishes her more than anything else from our other attempts at shapeshifting humanoids, so Askew and I nicknamed her 'Mel'. We'd improved on the other two in many respects, especially since we managed to skip past the juvenile stage with Mel and all the issues this throws up in terms of childhood memories, parental programming and other external influencing of the basic personality type. Instead, Mel emerged fully fledged as a blossoming girl of sixteen or thereabouts. Like Leon, she also has chameleonoid functionality, which gives her a similarly uncanny relationship to time. In Mel's case, rather than being able to 'step out', it has manifested as a form of clairvoyance: she can see into the future.

But I am jumping ahead again. The point of this report is to account for what happened to Leon. So, I will restrict myself to describing what happened when I took Mel to the underground base – or more specifically, what *should* have happened. I am still cursing my poor timing. My only excuse is that I was so keen to show Mel off to a group of visiting scientists that I postponed my trip to the military base by an extra day. If only I had gone twenty-four hours earlier, things might have turned out differently.

It pains me to recall Meth's evident pleasure at finally meeting my beauty, Mel, who cringed – and I mean literally shrank away – when she was introduced to him. Her powerfully attractive aura distracted him and that was when he let slip that Leon had escaped from the base and was still missing.

'He'll be found soon enough. He's just groping around in a tunnel somewhere, no doubt,' Meth muttered in a bored monotone, as if the whole issue was not his problem.

'I wouldn't be so sure,' I replied irritably. 'Did he leave anything behind?'

'We searched his quarters, of course. The baboon and his box of belongings appear to be missing, but we see no reason to be alarmed. At least, not yet…' He broke off, enchanted by Mel's wonder as she looked around Meth's meeting chamber at all the ancient Atlantean artefacts lining the walls. She paused in front of a particularly imposing orichalcum sculpture of a huge, powerfully built man holding a globe aloft.

Turning to me, she asked in her naive, childlike voice, 'Pa, who is this?'

Meth let out a volley of laughter and strode across the room. He stood a little too close to her and, placing his hand on her waist, whispered into her ear, 'That, my dear, is Atlas, the King of Atlantis. He's your sp...'

I steered Mel out from Meth's clutches and dangled a new distraction for Meth to grab hold of.

'She also has unusual skills like Leon, you know. Mel, why don't you tell Meth something about his future?'

'She can do that?' Meth asked breathily.

I watched Mel's face as she pondered this invitation to show off her clairvoyance. Although I had managed to hide my sense of achievement with Leon, I found it more difficult to contain my pride where Mel was concerned. Everyone who came to the lab to see my work was entranced by her gentle manner, her soft voice, her smile and her exquisite blue eyes. Several visitors commented that she seemed 'special' and 'like royalty', implying that she had blue blood as well. It is true: Mel is something of a princess.

But again, I digress. I am confident that Leon's disappearance is not an extended period of stepping out, because he would not have taken his belongings and his baboon with him – shapeshifting in time has always been a reflex, a defence mechanism, not a premeditated act. I believe he has somehow found a way off the base, and I will simply have to remain vigilant and hope that he comes back online or within range of some crystals. I have tried everything imaginable to recover access to his Third Eye, which Meth took offline, but to no avail.

The other problem is that Mel is taking up quite a lot of my research time now. What with Askew spending half his time preparing for his new secondment – working at the Lunar Quarantine Facility as En.Ki's chief vet – I don't have the resources at my disposal to search for Leon. So, when I received a letter from the Royal Palace requesting that Mel and I paid a visit, I jumped at the chance.

Field-testing Mel within the royal household would be a perfect contrast to Leon's placement in a military setting. We would get to observe how our genetically modified human adapts to the social pressures of having to conform to royal protocols, learning to serve and represent the sovereign. We would find out what behaviours emerge when a GM human is subjected to all the attentions and expectations that come with a high-profile role. I have to admit I am intrigued to see how 'Princess Mel' would fare under such circumstances and also how she would be received by her surrogate family.

Now that the Queen's youngest daughter is married and no longer living at the palace, a beautiful surrogate 'daughter' could be just what she needs. I feel sure this is the perfect solution for Mel. So, I have arranged for the Queen to have the pleasure of Mel's company for an afternoon and for Mel to gain the royal seal of approval. Then I will be able to concentrate on recovering our other asset, Leon Urdinak.*

---

*   *I gave this surname to our three assets for practical purposes, as it did not seem appropriate to use the species denominator 'Homo chameliensis' during field-testing. 'Urdinak' means 'blue' in Atlantean, which seemed quite apt given their blue eyes.*

Tablet VIII

MINTAKA

A ND THEN THE TROUBLE started. On the same morning that I was due to take Mel to meet the Queen and her entourage, Meth had the audacity to make Askew an outrageous deal: if he finds Leon and returns him to us, we let him have Mel. Without even consulting me, Askew has agreed. I pointed out that, if the Queen decides she wants Mel to stay at the palace indefinitely, we won't be able to stick to our half of the bargain, but Askew always thinks there will be a work-around. He just said dismissively, 'If it comes to it, we can just make another one with dark skin, Jainko.'

So, it was with a heavy heart that I escorted the beautiful girl to the Royal Palace. Mel was chattering happily the whole time she was being prepared for this occasion. I'd hired a lady's maid, a young Dogon woman called Saha'Ra who was an ex-employee of the palace. I needed someone who knew how to groom and dress Mel, who could arrange her somewhat unruly hair and teach her some basic manners. Saha'Ra took Mel around the whole En.Ki compound, let her have lunch in the staff mess a few times, that sort of thing, to get her used to being around people, and to get her to practise her small talk with strangers.

Since Mel has no pre-pubescent memories, she is a clean slate, so to speak. Some scientists would describe her as a 'walk-in', because her consciousness arrived after the 'birth' of her body, but since she has been synthetically designed, I am not sure I would go as far as to say she even has a consciousness in the normal sense of the word. If there is such a thing controlling her mind, it's fully synthetic. What's more, her mind has proved eminently trainable: you only have to show Mel something once and she gets it. She's an excellent mimic and, unlike Leon, speaks Atlantean fluently with grace and inventiveness. We also programmed her to be able to play the kamelan, a delightful orchestral instrument used in Atlantean court music, and installed various other modules enabling her to understand a range of spoken languages, including Saha'Ra's native Dogon tongue and my own Sirian dialect.

At last it was time for Mel to take my arm and leave En.Ki's labs. We walked down the main steps and into a waiting carriage. There was a storm brewing, but Mel was all smiles. She looked particularly stunning that day, wearing a flowing blue silk dress that Saha'Ra had sewn for her from the same fabric I had wrapped Kam in as a baby. Mel had chosen a finely-wrought orichalcum necklace set with cobalt crystals to wear around her neck. Just before entering the carriage, she picked up her skirts as she'd been taught, and Saha'Ra waited behind her as Mel turned into the wind to face her imaginary crowd, smiled and waved her elegantly-gloved hand, her whole being radiant in that moment. I felt my heart swell with pride as she stepped into the carriage, every bit a princess.

'Come, Pa – let's go now, I'm ready,' Mel chirped, patting the seat opposite her.

I smiled and waited for Saha'Ra to enter the carriage before climbing in myself and closing the door. On the short journey to the palace I was going to have to address the issue of what Mel should call me from now on; the nickname 'Pa' no longer seemed appropriate.

En.Ki's labs are located in the third and outer ring of the concentrically designed city of Atlantis and the Royal Palace lies at its heart; I felt like an arrow slowly targeting a bull's eye as we made our way there. I knew I was about to shatter Mel's world, delivering shockwaves of truth at the very moment we reached our destination in the dead centre. How do you explain to someone you made that you're not really her father? How do you explain to someone who has no experience growing up, a set of facts that would make any normal child grow up rather too quickly? But then it struck me that everything in Mel's life so far had been abrupt and without precedence, so she might cope just fine.

As the wind buffeted the carriage outside, I watched Mel laughing and chattering merrily with Saha'Ra, asking her about the things we were passing en route to the palace. Saha'Ra was explaining patiently how the buildings were all made of black lava, red tufa and white pumice stone, how the roads, houses and canals curved round in a circle, and how the city looked like a giant eye from above, 'but only the gods can see that'.

Suddenly, I heard Saha'Ra say, 'Look, Miss Mel, that's where I live. And just over there, can you see that little park? There's my daughter Mintaka playing with her friends.'

For some reason, it had never occurred to me that the maid would have a child of her own. I wondered for a moment who her child's Pa was. Before I had time to stop her, Mel had commanded the driver to stop the carriage so that she could get out and meet Saha'Ra's daughter. She crossed the wide, tree-lined road with Saha'Ra and walked towards the little public garden. Mintaka was with some friends and their mothers, playing under a clump of banyan trees. Mel looked enthralled as she approached the group, and I realised that she'd never actually seen a child before, let alone been one. Saha'Ra called out to her daughter, who ran into her arms, delighted to see her, and then looked very shy when her mother introduced her to 'Miss Mel'.

I was particularly impressed to see that Mel instinctively crouched down to talk to Mintaka at her eye level. I guessed she was similar in age to my daughter, Laika. She was a pretty little thing with dark hair that fell to her waist but a somewhat sickly demeanour. The other mothers regarded Mel and me warily, and I wondered what Saha'Ra must have told them about her new employer. En.Ki doesn't have the best reputation among the people of Atlantis, who are suspicious of our genetic experiments. I stood back and watched the whole event play out; Mel, gracious and regal in her blue dress, surrounded by the Atlantean women. She was so engrossed in the experience that it was difficult to drag her away, but I pointed out that we couldn't keep the Queen waiting, and eventually they bade her farewell and we returned to the carriage.

'Your child is so beautiful,' Mel said to Saha'Ra, 'but is something wrong with her health?'

My heart stopped. I prayed that Mel had developed enough sensitivity not to predict any outcome where Mintaka was concerned, at least not out loud to the child's mother. I could tell from the look on her face that Mel was seeing some future moment. Saha'Ra must have sensed something too, because she took her time replying.

'Mintaka is not well,' she ventured slowly. 'She has a rare blood condition, which is expensive to treat.' Saha'Ra bit her lip and looked at me slightly guiltily. 'That's why I took this job, to pay for her medicine.'

'What is the medicine she needs to take?' Mel asked, her blue eyes wide with concern and compassion. 'We have lots of medical supplies in the lab, don't we, Pa?' She turned to me with a questioning look, wanting my support.

'That's very kind, Miss Mel, but we manage quite well. Thanks to my income from En.Ki, Mintaka now takes a gram of monatomic gold powder three times a day and her last blood tests show that her condition is now under control.'

Saha'Ra smiled sweetly, but I could see she was embarrassed.

Mel heaved a sigh of relief, and then turned to ask me, 'Pa, are we nearly there?'

I looked out of the carriage window and, as the storm clouds parted, I could see the gates to the royal compound looming into view. I took Mel's hands in mine and stared for a long time into her blue eyes, unable to find the words I wanted to speak.

'I'm afraid we are, my dear.'

'Why are you afraid, Pa?'

Mel's innocent question set off a sharp pain in my chest. There were so many things I was afraid of floating through my mind. I was afraid of losing Mel. Of telling her I am not her Pa. Never finding Leon. Never seeing my family on Sirius again. Losing everything that has ever mattered to me. Being captured and tortured again. Being found out for smuggling Kam, our first prototype, back to Sirius.

Tablet IX

DOGON

WITH MEL SAFELY ENSCONCED in the Royal Palace, I could now turn my attention to locating Leon. Driven by the hope of gaining Mel in exchange, Meth had pulled out all the stops and assigned all his resources to the task of recovering our male asset. I was desperate that he should not succeed under any circumstances, as I was not prepared to give up Mel that easily. But my own resources were much more limited: our lab technicians had been dismissed now that Askew was about to be transferred to his new post and there was only the final write-up to do, which, as you can see, has been assigned to me.

Every day, I arrive at the lab early and review Leon's Third Eye footage, but it's just hours and hours of blank feed. He is either too deep underground now for the device to relay a signal, or whatever Meth attached to his forehead is still obscuring the tiny lens. All I know is that Leon is still alive, still has a heartbeat – which is something, I suppose. Looking at these readings, by my estimation, the levels of etheria in his system fall within the range defined as 'normal', which is to say he is functioning without needing to step out, from which I can surmise that he is not suffering from undue stress – otherwise, this would have gone into overdrive.

That was all the data I had to put in my report, until yesterday, when I got word from the underground base that it had come to their attention that Leon had taken his white crystal, Meth's sword and a small quantity of orichalcum bullion. I felt strangely proud when I heard this, because it meant Leon's disappearance was definitely premeditated and that he had enough common sense to equip himself with a weapon and the means to trade or bribe. I also knew that stepping out would give Leon the upper hand with any adversary he encountered, since he is not likely to run into any other GM humans on his travels who can shapeshift in time like he can.

What concerns me, however, is how easy it would be for him to get disorientated and distressed in the extensive network of underground tunnels, caves and strongholds, which reach far beyond the mountains to the north of Atlantis, further east than Libia and possibly as far as Khem. To my dismay, I have begun to realise that Leon could now be anywhere in this vast labyrinth and finding his way out again, even if he wanted to, would be more a matter of luck than of skill.

Today, acting on a hunch and in breach of my security clearance, I managed to gain access to the classified section of En.Ki's datafiles. I discovered the real reason Meth's reptilian squadron is stationed at the base: it is not to guard the precious high-grade orichalcum bullion, but to protect the main entrance to this underground network and continue its excavation. The base is nicknamed 'Agartha Outpost' and, as far as I can tell, it's one of the most ambitious and most secret engineering projects ever undertaken. They only employ contractors who are experienced in dangerous subterranean work, tough individuals such as reptilians and octopods, who are accustomed to radioactive environments and volatile mineral extraction. It was shocking to discover there is another world – an inner Earth, if you will – right beneath our feet, deep inside the bowels of this planet, where life forms of various kinds have been able to flourish. I am even more shocked that even someone like me – a scientist working on a black ops project – knew absolutely nothing about it.

It appears this hollow world has provided a safe haven for eons and has been used at times when life on the surface became untenable. I can only surmise that, if Atlas is putting so much effort into this work and doing it so secretively, something is up. Being a scientist who's always absorbed in my lab work, I admit I am not the best at keeping up with what's going on in the wider world. I know the weather has been getting steadily worse, and I often hear Colonel Askew talking with Saha'Ra about how the seasons are all a little messed up and how a string of new volcanoes is erupting under the ocean west of Atlantis. There is obviously something strange going on, judging by all this effort to expand and guard Meth's underground complex; it must mean the military think it's going to be needed again. If conditions in Atlantis are really going to get worse, as people say, perhaps this is where we will be forced to take cover, to 'weather it out'.

Whatever the reason for this subterranean investment, I am more concerned about Leon getting freaked and stepping out if he is down there. What if he encounters other species? I'd always thought that his ability to step out would keep him safer, but what if it makes him more vulnerable? As I lay awake in my dorm this morning, unable to sleep, I mulled over the situation again and again. With Mel safe and sound living under the watchful eye of the royal family, and Askew about to take up another post, finding Leon is now my full-time responsibility.

But I don't have much time: En.Ki are expecting me to file my final report by the end of Misra, and I cannot submit the report without the asset. So, I have two options: I can either go looking for Leon myself down in Agartha, which is risky and has a low likelihood of success; or I can take the coward's route and return home to Sirius now, leaving Leon at large, the project unfinished and my already tarnished reputation completely in ruins.

Uncertain which course of action to take, I am going to seek the advice of the Dogon tribe. It will not be the first time I have sought their help: to avoid Kam being subjected to En.Ki's abusive regime of testing, I asked the Dogon to take care of the baby for me until my next period of leave when I could take Kam back to Sirius. The Dogon people are totally reliable and very discreet and they hold us Sirians in high regard, because my ancestors, the first Nommo, came to Earth from Sirius eons ago. The Dogon believe that the Nommo arrived in a magnificent spaceship and brought eight kinds of grain. They taught the Dogon how to farm, how to read the stars and how to speak our language. How shameful, then, that I – a descendent of the first Nommo – should have to beg the Dogon for help. What an embarrassment I am to the Jainko family, yet again proving that I am incapable of finishing a task without getting myself into trouble.

The Dogon village is a day's ride into the mountains to the north of Atlantis. Tomorrow before dawn I will bury my shame, put on my Sirian robes, anoint my forehead with the white markings of my ancestral line and set out with Askew and two camels via the north gate of the city, in the hope of reaching the Dogon village by nightfall.

THE

DOGON

SCROLLS

(PART 1 OF MEL'S STORY)

Scroll I

OF ATLANTIS

L ET ME TELL YOU what I know about Atlantis. Our beautiful city is laid out in a series of rings, with the royal compound, where I now live, right at the centre. The first ring out from the centre is where the townsfolk live, their red-roofed houses all facing inwards towards the Royal Palace and the Temple precinct, and the second ring is where the army and navy are based, with their ships, horses and elephants. The ring of water which surrounds the second ring connects to a long straight canal that leads south all the way to the ocean. To the north is nothing but mountains, where the Dogon people live, and there are several rivers that flow down the mountainsides towards Atlantis, bringing fresh water. There are also wells that bring up sea-water and fresh water from deep below the city – so my new father, King Atlas, tells me.

The palace consists of a lot of very grand buildings behind a high circular wall. The grounds are so big I still have not explored them all. They rise up to a mound in the centre, where the Temple of Enesidaone, god of storms and earthquakes, stands. It is forbidden to enter the Temple except on Holy Days, such as the Feast of Enesidaone, which has just taken place. Everyone, including me, had to lay offerings to the founder of Atlantis. Inside, the walls are covered in gold and the roof is held up with long, curved elephant tusks, their tips forming a hole in the middle of the roof. Light shines down on the statue below, which is of Enesidaone, riding the ocean waves in his chariot with six horses pulling it and hundreds of dolphins swimming all around him. Everywhere you look there are altars and offerings of exotic fruits, and candles with big fat flames that make everything glitter and dance. Even the outside walls are covered with silver, and on the roof are solid gold pinnacles.

Dotted around the palace grounds are lots of other smaller temples dedicated to weird and wonderful gods of the sky and sea. In front of each temple is a courtyard with a crystal fountain in the middle. When I first arrived, I thought all the fountains looked the same, until I noticed that each of the carved dolphins, dogs and elephants was different. Some of the courtyards lead into bathhouses. I've never been inside the ones for the menfolk, but the women's are very beautiful, covered in blue enamel tiles and fed from hot-water springs deep below the city. Some are saltwater, some are fresh; you can go in either, depending on which you prefer.

The royal compound also has an arboretum, which Saha'Ra says contains one of every fruit tree found in the world, such as apple, pomegranate, pear, fig and olive. The trees have been brought here by kings, queens, priests and foreign visitors as gifts for the King and Queen. Many of them have strange leaves and knobbly bark and are hundreds of years old. Some even date back to Lemurian times. Sometimes I like to play a game where I ask Saha'Ra to blindfold Mintaka and me, and then lead us to a tree so we can try to guess its name by just touching its trunk. My favourite is the baobab tree, which has a fat, lumpy trunk.

When the wind blows from the south, I can sometimes hear the hubbub down at the harbour, one ring away from the palace. It sounds so exciting – all sorts of wonderful things arriving from overseas and the foreign voices of lots of people milling around, buying and selling. I would love to watch the Atlantean merchants hauling the cases ashore and breaking open their lids to inspect the contents. I imagine them to be full of snakes or swords or silks, or colourful birds with long tail feathers. When the wind is blowing from the north, you can almost taste the snow from the mountain peaks, or feel snowflakes brush against your skin, and imagine it settling on the roofs of the mud-houses which the Dogon people have built high into the cliffs because for some reason they are expecting a massive flood.

Down in Atlantis we never get snow (and as far as I know it never floods, either), but we do have two harvests a year – one at the spring equinox and one at the autumn equinox, the two days of the year when day and night last exactly as long as each other. On those days, offerings are brought into the Temple, and laid before the altar. They sacrifice lambs and bulls sometimes too, but I've told Saha'Ra I never want to be involved in that kind of ceremony because I couldn't bear to see the animals die or watch their blood run out across the marble floor. The royal bulls are allowed to wander around inside the Temple walls, which is quite scary sometimes, because they have sharp horns and a way of not noticing what they are stepping on. They sacrifice one of them every fifth or sixth year when the royal family all gets together. It's called the Purification, but it's the least pure, most heartless thing I've ever heard of. First, they sit up all night discussing new laws and deciding which old ones to get rid of, and then, at sunrise, the priests bring a bull and they perform their horrid deed as the first rays hit the Omphalos, which is a tall tapering crystal in front of Enesidaone's temple. It's much crueller than anything Pa or Askew ever did to me in En.Ki's lab, and it gives me nightmares just thinking about it.

I seem to have a lot of strange nightmares these days. People are either fighting or dying all around me, or the trees are all on fire and the whole of Atlantis is burning down. The nightmare I had a few nights ago was the worst one yet: I dreamed that some figures in hooded robes dragged me into a circular chamber in an underground temple and were about to sacrifice me. I was wearing a red dress and they were tying ropes round my wrists and ankles. A young white girl with blue eyes was trying to stop them, but then the ground beneath us started shaking and water started to flood the temple. There were giants coming towards me and a boy who also had blue eyes, and he was roaring and gasping for air as the water rose higher. We were all about to die. Then I woke up. That's the sort of dream I mean. It doesn't make any sense, but it still gives me chills.

Last night I dreamed I was flying high over the city in a golden prism and, as I looked down, I saw the ocean creeping inland towards Atlantis, huge dirty grey waves flowing across the plains, covering them with mud and ash. Ships were stuck, unable to reach the harbour in Atlantis because the canal from the sea was full of thick mud. I was carried higher and higher in the prism, so high that I could see the curvature of the Earth. Up there, Atlantis looked like a giant eye – just like Saha'Ra told me – but it was crying a sea of tears. As far as I could see in every direction, all the lovely green plains and orchards surrounding Atlantis, all the farms and valleys, were covered in the same thick, brown mud.

This morning I told Saha'Ra about my dream and she looked at me strangely.

'That's very odd you should have a dream like that, Miss Mel. Only yesterday I heard that the royal mapmaker has been asked to draw new charts for the whole of Atlantis, because the coastline keeps shrinking.'

*

Today was the midsummer solstice, which means it is also race day. Saha'Ra, Mintaka and I were allowed to watch the famous Atlantean horse race, the Orichalcum Cup, from high up in a hot air balloon tethered to the palace gates. It's called that because the cup you win is made of orichalcum, a special kind of copper that Atlantis is famous for. While we were floating above the city like a giant bird of prey, fifty horses lined up to start the race on the racetrack that runs around the outer ring of Atlantis, in between the military barracks. On race days, they dress the road with sand and lay out field markers ready for the stampede. The horse race is once round the outer ring, which takes about an hour with a good horse and a nice tail-wind.

While Saha'Ra and Mintaka peered down at the galloping horses and the plumes of dust they created, trying to make out which rider was winning, I spent the time gazing down at all the glistening red and black rooftops of Atlantis, thinking about the journey across the city with Pa when he brought me here from En.Ki's labs a few months ago, and remembering how excited and happy I had felt that day.

I miss Pa more than I could ever explain to anyone.

I stared down at the families gathered around the edge of the racetrack to watch and felt full of envy. They'd brought baskets laden with food and were laughing and eating. I could see mothers and fathers, sons and daughters, brothers and sisters, so many joyous little gatherings, and I longed to be down there on the ground, spreading out a blanket with Pa, or playing with siblings of my own, just like all the ordinary people of Atlantis.

About halfway through the race, a freak storm suddenly blew up and the officials had to cancel it. It was very scary being up in the balloon, I can tell you. The wind stirred up a thick cloud of sand and dust that blew in our faces, and then a freak wave came rushing up the canal from the ocean and swept around the circular channels, making the water slosh around and flood all the neighbouring streets. The people sitting on the ground eating their picnics had to abandon everything and run away. I was panicking that the royal staff had forgotten we were up in the balloon, and when someone finally remembered and tried to bring us back down, Mintaka and I got really scared because the wind made the basket jerk around so badly I thought we were going to fall out. Once they got control of the ropes, they were stretched so tightly I thought they would snap and we'd be blown away.

In the end it took twenty soldiers and two full-grown elephants to finally tug us back to the ground, and that wasn't even the worst part: we landed in the middle of a barricaded street where fighting had broken out and the townsfolk were completely out of control! We were surrounded by men with angry faces, their eyes wide and their voices screaming as they charged at each other. The head priest eventually came to shepherd us back to the royal compound in the midst of all the mayhem. Even now, I can still hear the din of all the people shouting at the top of their lungs things like 'I'm not leaving!', 'Atlantis is my home!', 'I was born here, and I will die here!' and 'Let them try to take me!'

We heard afterwards that, in all the frenzy that afternoon, one of the horses had thrown off its rider and bolted right through the middle of the crowds! It ran all the way to the North Gate, near where Saha'Ra and Mintaka's family lives, and sped away. I have to admit I felt a pang of envy towards that horse, free at last as it headed into the mountains where the Dogon live.

Scroll II

OF GRAVITY

RECENTLY, I HAVE STARTED to lose contact with my own body. At first it only happened just as I was falling asleep. I would get the sense that I was much too light and that I was lifting out of my body and rising slowly up towards the crystal roof above my bed and then passing right through it, as if I was being drawn up by the stars. It felt a bit like going up in the hot air balloon, but this time there was no basket, just me. If I concentrated hard enough and thought very heavy thoughts, I could will myself back down. But some nights I rise up so high into the inky blackness, I can't get back down. It's terrifying.

I told Saha'Ra I was feeling cold at night and needed a heavier quilt for my bed. She ordered the palace seamstress to make me a thicker bedcover in the traditional Atlantean way out of thousands of tiny triangles of red, black and white cloth. She said it would be stuffed with feathers, but I told her I needed something heavier, so instead Saha'Ra asked the seamstress to pack it with wool and horsehair. The first night I lay under the quilt, I felt sure my nights of drifting out of my body were over, but it got worse.

In the end I told Saha'Ra about my battles with gravity. She offered to stay in my room and watch what happened to me during the night. She made up a second bed for herself right next to mine and covered it with my old quilt. After we'd talked and talked long into the night, Saha'Ra said I should try to sleep, otherwise she might fall asleep before me. In the morning she informed me wearily that my body had stayed put under the heavy quilt all night, and she refused to believe me when I told her that, on the contrary, I'd spent the whole night hovering around over the city, moving between the clouds, as if I was some kind of angel who'd been given the job of watching over the people of Atlantis while they slept. She looked very concerned and said she would speak to the Queen about it. I begged her not to, but she said the Queen had a soothsayer who might know what to do. When I asked her what a soothsayer was, Saha'Ra replied 'someone who can see into the future'.

The next day, Saha'Ra gave me a hand-sewn doll made from black velvet. It was embroidered with big blue eyes and wore a red dress. I said I was too old for toys and gave it back to her, but she insisted it was not a toy and that it would stop my night-time drifting.

'And anyway, you cannot refuse something from the Queen. It would be rude,' Saha'Ra chided.

'So, if it isn't a toy, what is it?' I asked.

'It represents you. That's why it has blue eyes.'

'What am I supposed to do with it?'

'You must wrap it tightly in a piece of cloth and lie it in a box with a close-fitting lid before you go to bed.'

'Then what?'

'Then the spirits will do the rest. Those were the soothsayer's instructions.'

Reluctantly I took the doll, even though there was something sinister about the red dress and the staring blue eyes. That evening, I found a box in the linen room and lined it with scraps of silk, then laid the doll inside and closed the lid. I carried it up to my bedchamber and pushed it into the shadows under the bed. When I lay under my quilt that night, I felt as though there were strong silken threads connecting my body to the doll in the box, weighing me down, and I began to think it might work. When I turned on my side, I could feel the strands digging into my skin where they were attached around my wrists and ankles. It was starting to get a bit painful, so I sat up – that's when I realised there was something around my chest and neck, too, tied so tightly that I could hardly breathe. I tossed from side to side, wriggling and gasping for air, but could not get free. In the end, exhausted from the effort, I must have dropped off.

I dreamt I was wearing a bright red dress, just like the doll, and was plummeting through space, falling into an immense void, my limbs flailing around, my embroidered blue eyes starting to fall off my face. Then I felt myself being caught in someone's arms but, when I looked to see who it was, it was that strange man called Meth, to whom Pa had introduced me at the military base. He was pressing down on me and breathing heavily in my face. I was screaming at him to get off me, and the last thing I remember was his angry yellow eyes.

I awoke to find I was sweating all over, curled up in a ball under my bed next to the box with the doll. The box was empty. I searched under the bed for the doll and, when I found it, the eyes were gone and there was a gash on one arm where the stuffing was coming out. Too afraid to go back to sleep, I woke Saha'Ra and asked her to play chess with me. It was Pa who taught me how to play, and I was quick to learn how to checkmate the king. I was just about to make my move, when I accidentally knocked my own king over. As I stood the ebony piece back up, I noticed the expression on my queen's face change, as if she had been frightened by what had just happened. Then I noticed something strange happening to the knight on the square next to her; instead of having a horse's head, it was growing a long trunk and turning into an elephant. I shrieked and jumped away, sending all the chess pieces flying. Saha'Ra looked at me with a mixture of shock and confusion.

'Miss Mel, what on earth is the matter?'

I burst into tears and ran out of the chamber into the courtyard. When I returned, Saha'Ra was on her hands and knees gathering up all the chess pieces. The chess set is now ruined. There are two missing pieces – the black king and queen.

Scroll III

OF ELEPHANTS

WHEN I ARRIVED IN the royal household, they weren't sure what to do about continuing my education. Pa had taught me everything I knew up until that point. Then Saha'Ra had an idea: I could go to school with her daughter, Mintaka. Even though I am six years older than her, she knows more than me about a lot of things and has read a great deal. I love her dearly, so I immediately fell for this plan and begged the Queen to arrange it.

At school, the Atlantean priests mainly teach us music, mathematics and religious education. Mintaka and I love listening to them reading aloud from the

Emerald Tablets every morning. Much to the King's delight, I can now recite every single one by heart. Next month, at the Royal Banquet, he wants me to stand up in front of all the guests and recite all thirteen tablets right after dinner before the dancing begins. Just thinking about it makes me nervous.

Last night I was worrying about it so much I had a dream that I was surrounded by people in an underground chamber. Except they weren't ordinary Atlantean folk – they were giants. I was reciting the Emerald Tablets, and running in circles around my ankles was a baboon with a long tail who seemed to be my companion. I knew I had to be somewhere else, but the giants would not let me past. I could hear Saha'Ra's voice calling me: 'Miss Mel, it's time, we have to go, we have to go now!' I felt Mintaka – or was it the baboon? – get hold of my hand and pull me. Suddenly, we were in the palace gardens and I had a black crystal in my hand and I knew I had to leave immediately.

'What is the matter?' Saha'Ra asked me when she came to wake me this morning and saw a strange expression on my face.

'I am afraid.'

'What are you afraid of, Miss Mel?'

'I don't know. Pa never told me.'

*

At present we are learning to play the kamelan. It's a set of musical instruments made of wood, crystal, orichalcum and animal hide. The Queen wants us to give a musical performance at the start of the Royal Banquet. I find playing the kamelan very soothing. Each morning before we arrive for lessons, the priests set up the instruments on a circular platform in the centre of our school courtyard, with all the gongs, bowls and tambours laid out in concentric circles on white linen cloths, so it looks a bit like a model of Atlantis from above, and then we each sit in front of our instruments facing inwards, waiting for the signal to begin. When the Sun hits the crystal in the middle of the courtyard, you can feel a vibration running right through you, and the rose-gold gongs start to hum as if they are playing themselves. The priests are the only people who know how to make gongs – they learned how to do it from the Lemurians. We've been learning about the Lemurian civilisation in class, and about how the Atlanteans defeated them in the last Age.

When I'm playing the kamelan I am not 'Miss Mel'. I am not pretending to be a princess. I do not belong to Pa or Atlas or anyone; I am just a musician. I sit quietly and play my part, listening intently for the right place to make my musical offering to the gods. Playing the kamelan requires a lot of concentration, and the music feels as if you're drawing giant invisible circles in space. Each circle lasts as long as your breath. I can't explain it, really, but when it works, it feels like the air is singing all around me, and my heart starts beating faster and suddenly it's as if everything is about to lift off the ground. But it's not all about making sound; an important part of playing the kamelan is when there is silence. Sometimes the silence lasts so long after a gong has sounded that everyone thinks the ceremony has ended, but we keep our faith and wait for the light to burst through.

*

Have I told you that Atlantis is famous not only for its copper but also for its elephants? Last week we went on a school trip to see them. It is one of the few times since I arrived here that I have left the royal compound. We had to walk in a long line behind the priests, across the bridges and all the way to the outermost ring of the city, where the elephant house is located. The reason for our visit was that one of the elephants, Elisha, had just given birth.

The day of the trip was supposed to be a hot, sunny day, but suddenly, before we had even reached the outer ring of the city, the blue skies clouded over and, without any warning, hailstones the size of apples plummeted from the sky. It was quite painful when they landed on your head, even worse than some of Pa's tests. The priests didn't know what to do and tried to make us turn back, but I protested that we were almost there and would get just as wet if we walked back. So, we sheltered in the house of a kind Atlantean lady until the hail stopped, and then carried on to the elephant house.

Ever since Pa showed me a picture of one, I have been obsessed with elephants. So, as you can probably imagine, it was the most thrilling experience to get up close to this tiny helpless creature lying in the hay beneath his mother's towering body, and to see him stagger to his feet and clamber through her legs towards me. As I dropped to my knees, he reached out his little trunk to sniff me. His skin was soft and hairy, and he made a funny bleating noise before flopping into my lap. Elisha started swinging her trunk nervously but, when she heard the noises her son was making, she relaxed and realised he had just made a new friend.

Later I discovered that I was more than this baby elephant's new friend – I was his new owner! As a present to welcome me into the royal family, the King and Queen have arranged for the elephant keeper to bring the baby to the palace once he is old enough to leave his mother. I can hardly believe it! It's the best present ever. I will have to be patient, because it will be six months before he is ready to come to live with us in the royal compound. I've been thinking hard about what to call him, and then today a name popped into my head: Elijah. I think that's what his mother would have called him. It has a kind of majestic sound to it, don't you think? King Atlas has agreed to build an elephant house for him in the gardens, and I've already made a sign to hang on the door. It says in large letters 'Elijah lives here'. When he arrives, every morning after eating my breakfast of simmered millet and sliced dragon fruit, I will wander down to the elephant house and check that the servants have cleaned out Elijah's bed and put down fresh hay. I can't wait to tell Pa: he's coming to visit next week, to see how I've settled into my new life.

Scroll IV

PA'S VISIT

I HAVE BEEN ALLOWED to miss school today because Pa is coming to do some tests and ask me questions. It's been so long since his last visit that I can hardly remember what he looks like. Come to think of it, I can hardly remember much about my life before I came to the Royal Palace, either. It's as if I hardly existed before I came here, but I must have, because I am sixteen years old, and anyone who's been alive that many years should have lots of memories. So why can't I remember anything?

I've decided to try and pay more attention to the little details from now on, in the hope that maybe my memories of what it was like to be a child growing up will come back to me. Mintaka is always talking about things she remembers from when she was little. Who was I, and where was I living when I was younger? I will ask Pa later. I hope that, after I've done the tests, he will have time to answer my questions.

*

Saha'Ra helped me get ready. I put on the blue dress I wore the day I came here, even though it's a bit tight now – I must have been eating too well since I arrived. Palace food is always lovely and fresh and tasty. I have a vague recollection of eating mostly tasteless mushy stuff out of a tin tray at En.Ki, that the technicians heated up in a little oven in the corner of the lab. But that's not the sort of memory I want to have – it's neither special nor important, nor interesting. I want to remember the first time I saw a rainbow, or the way my mother smiled at me, or what it felt like to walk barefoot along the seashore.

I stared into the mirror while Saha'Ra piled my black hair up into a proper Atlantean style. My blue eyes looked misty and sad today, even though I was excited to see Pa. Sometimes it's like my eyes don't really belong to me; they are just two luminous jewels that people like to stare at, but they don't see me at all, just the colour of my irises. Perhaps an iris flower feels the same way: when we see its beautiful blue petals, in fact we're just marvelling at the beauty of its surface, while the flower's true nature is overlooked completely.

*

Pa was late. He didn't come straight to see me like he said he would, but had a private meeting first with King Atlas. I get the feeling Pa is in some kind of trouble or has lost something. He looks distracted and only smiles with his mouth, not his eyes. Today I was trying hard to see past his appearance to what his true nature is, but all I can tell you is that his eyes are brown and that his skin is like walnut shell and he has a Sirian tattoo on his forehead. He walks with his feet turned out slightly, and often tips his head on one side when he's listening to someone. His teeth are a bit uneven and one or two are missing so that, when he takes a breath, sometimes you can hear the air whistling past his lips and through the gaps. There are other kinds of gaps, too – times when he only seems to be telling me half the story.

Pa said that, if I was really good, he would give me a present, but that I needed to do some tests before I could have it. I tried my best to concentrate for the tests and not complain about having bits of my hair shaved off so that Pa could fit the helmet over my head. He said he wanted to help me stay more connected with him, but he seemed more distant than ever after it was done. He asked me a lot of questions about my feelings, my thoughts and, my appetite, and then he measured me and scanned me from all angles, like I was a science experiment.

At last he took the helmet off. My head felt painful and I rubbed my temples for a while to make the pain go away.

'Can I have my present now?' I asked.

'Of course, how could I forget?'

Pa smiled then, and it nearly filled his face. He reached into his pocket and gave me a box. I opened it and saw that inside was a black crystal, shaped like a large teardrop. Weirdly, it was just like the one in the dream I'd had about the baboon and the giants.

'Thank you, Pa. I had a dream about a crystal just like this. What is it?'

'It's obsidian. It erupted from a volcano far from here called Mount Toba, which nearly destroyed everything on Earth thousands of years ago. I want you to have it, because I think it will help connect you with the Earth and give you strength, courage and hope in the face of adversity. With this crystal, you will always know how to find your way home, Mel. Keep it with you, and you will always be safe.'

Pa was shaking as he said this. He suddenly took hold of my hands and told me that, no matter what happened from now on, I just needed to be brave and everything would be alright. But the tone of desperation in his voice told me otherwise. I wanted to tell him about the doll with the blue eyes and the other strange dreams I'd been having about floods and Atlantis getting destroyed, but I knew it would only make him sadder and more distant. I looked down at the crystal in my hands; it didn't seem to make me feel safe right then.

'Oh Pa, I almost forgot,' I said, changing the subject. 'The Queen gave me a present, too. It's an elephant – a real one. He's called Elijah. He's so adorable. Would you like to visit him with me?'

'That would be nice, my dear, but I have to get back to the lab; I have an important report to finish.'

'Surely you can stay and have something to eat with Saha'Ra and me?'

At a loss for words, he shrugged as if everything was out of his hands now.

'Is everything OK, Pa? Are you sleeping properly?'

'Yes, of course, Mel – so sweet of you to ask.' He beamed at me for a moment, then his expression shifted. 'But I may have to go away for a while.'

'Where? Why? What's happened, Pa?'

'I can't tell you, I'm afraid.'

'Why do you always say that you are afraid?'

'One day you will understand.'

Perhaps I already do.

Scroll V

THE LAST BANQUET

L IVING AT THE LUXURIOUS royal compound in the centre of this wondrous city has recently started to seem like a life sentence. There are times when being sent away from Pa to live life as an Atlantean princess seems so unfair, so unbearable, even though most people would give anything to play this role. But that's it: I've realised it's just a role. I am not helping anyone or anything. Except perhaps Pa, because he was so pleased and honoured when Atlas agreed to let me live here. I know that the

Queen enjoys my company, and that it makes the palace gardeners happy when I admire their work, and that Mintaka is very attached to me. But I also know I have a bigger purpose to fulfil in my life than this.

As well as the black crystal, Pa gave me a letter when he left early. In the letter he apologised to me that he would not be coming to the banquet and stressed how important it is that I accept my new life with an open heart and how I need to understand that my behaviour, my choices, my words must always be in accordance with royal protocol. But today is one of those days when I am full of anger and frustration and feel totally abandoned by him. Why did he leave me here? Why does everyone I meet stare at my blue eyes? And what does it mean in the letter when Pa says, 'One day you will understand why all three of you mean so much to me'? Who are the other two people? Does he mean Saha'Ra and Mintaka?

Today, more than ever, I must follow royal protocol, because Saha'Ra has arrived to get me ready for the Royal Banquet. Later there will be over a hundred guests arriving, including all King Atlas's siblings from neighbouring kingdoms, to gather in the Great Hall this evening for a glittering dinner. I am no longer worried I will forget the sacred words I am to recite or that I will make mistakes in the kamelan music I am to play. But I am nervous about greeting all the guests. Saha'Ra says I am just a bit shy, and that it's only small talk. She suggested that, if I smile sweetly and pay each person a compliment, it's easy to have a conversation with them. I don't mind having to talk to Pa's colleague Colonel Askew, next to whom I have been seated at the banquet, because he is quite easy to talk to, but I won't know how to compliment someone like Meth. He is the least nice person I've ever met. He's – how can I say it – *creepy*. And he's going to be here this evening, in the palace.

*

When the King and Queen summoned me to their chambers before the guests arrived, I thought it was to receive some kind of royal briefing. I knelt before them on that silk carpet in a room full of vases of lilies and felt as if I was going to faint. It was a warm evening and the scent from the lilies was quite strong, but it was the tense atmosphere that got to me most. I waited a long time before they spoke. The Queen's brow was knotted in a permanent frown and Atlas was pacing up and down behind her. I thought at first they were angry at something I had done, but when they started to explain that Atlantis was in danger, that the Royal Palace was at risk, all those dreams I'd been having started to flood back to me, and I hardly heard what they were saying because their words were drowned out by the voices in my head.

'Of course, you must not speak about any of this, especially the possibility of a coup, to anyone during the banquet – is that understood, my dear?' Atlas concluded, holding me by the elbow and steering me back towards the big silver double doors. 'This may well be the last state banquet we ever hold here. The preparations for Atlantis to be evacuated are already underway, and tomorrow the

Queen and I are leaving to visit the place we have chosen to be the site for the New Atlantis. It is far to the east from here, and you are to remain here with Saha'Ra and the rest of the royal household until we return for you. Do you understand?'

'Yes, yes,' I stammered. 'But why is this happening?' I could feel a lump forming in my throat and a sense of panic starting to grip me. 'And if we have to evacuate, what will happen to Elijah?'

Atlas took a deep breath and led me towards a strange floating set of orbs in the centre of the chamber that he told me was an orrery – a model of our sun and all the planets that encircle it. Gently nudging the blue sphere that rotated slowly around a bright central orb of light, he sighed and collected his thoughts.

'It is not the first time our planet – this blue one here – has got out of kilter. Nor is it the first time for our solar system. I am afraid to tell you, but we are entering a period of profound change. Earth's fragile energy field has become very unstable and is in danger of being completely destroyed. I have tried my best to find a way to save Atlantis, I have even sought assistance from – shall we say – resources that lie outside my fields of expertise and beyond my jurisdiction. Since I can do nothing to prevent the calamity that is about to occur, I can only try to move my people out of harm's way and pray we will all survive to rebuild our great Atlantean culture in a new land far from here.'

On hearing this, I burst into tears. I was trying my best to stifle the sobs and Atlas's calm, serious expression only made things worse. It struck me that he'd used the same phrase that Pa was always saying: 'I am afraid'. The Queen had been silent all this time, but she shifted in her velvet seat and, dabbing away a tear, looked at me imploringly.

'My dear Princess Mel, I know this is difficult for you – for all of us. We just have to pray that God will protect us and keep us safe.'

I thought about the crystal Pa had given me and whether anything could keep us safe from a catastrophe such as this. The Queen let out a small sob of her own, then recovered her poise and continued speaking.

'My soothsayer tells me that you will have an important part to play in this difficult transition, Princess Mel. The three of you represent a unique genetic solution to this planetary reset and the potential for us to …'

'I think she has heard enough for now, my dear,' Atlas interrupted, signalling that my audience with the royal couple was over.

I curtsied and withdrew without turning my back, just as Saha'Ra had taught me. But I would have preferred to turn away, because I could see tears were rolling down the Queen's cheeks now as Atlas heaved on his royal cloak and, helping her up from her seat, led her away.

Whatever else lay ahead, the banquet was the next challenge to be overcome. As I walked back to my own chambers, I realised that behind Atlas's words lurked another story, one that I was in the process of being written into. What was this role the Queen's soothsayer thought I was to play? What did the Queen mean by 'the three of you' – the same phrase Pa wrote in his letter?

I was so lost in thought that I wasn't really looking where I was going. As I turned the next corner, who should I run into but Meth.

'Not so fast, my beauty,' he murmured, hooking a finger under my chin to force me to look up at him. His yellow slit-like eyes locked onto my hard, blue gaze. I tilted my jaw sideways and mumbled something about needing to get ready.

'Will you be gracing us with your presence this evening, Princess Mel?'

His hand dangled near my shoulder, brushing my skin and making it crawl.

'I will, Sir, yes.'

'And may I claim the first dance with you later?'

He said it in such a way that it was not a question, but something he'd already decided would happen.

'You… may. Now may I go, please?'

'Tonight, we dance, and then I will come for you.'

He chuckled and then stood out of my way with a strange flourish that made his shoulder-blades flex beneath his jacket.

*

The after-effects of the banquet rang through my head like a bell for hours. I had managed to avoid having to dance with anyone; all the rich food and drink had made me feel nauseous and I left before the dancing had even started. The hall amplified the chatter of all the voices, the clinking of plates and goblets, the applause and the musical interludes, so much so there were several points during the evening when I felt myself slip out of my body and hover somewhere above it all, staring down at the exquisite food, the long tables and the tall candles, while a tangled mess of feelings stewed inside me. No one noticed, not even Colonel Askew, even though he was sitting right next to me all evening. He kept sniffing a substance that he had in his pocket and seemed very preoccupied, as if his mind was somewhere else.

It seemed to me that everyone – including Colonel Askew – knew about the impending disaster. They were all aware of what Atlas had told me, but it was as if they were all bound by oath to avoid mentioning it. Perhaps all civilisations end this way, with the people who have reached the top, the most wealthy and privileged, pretending nothing bad is happening while they squeeze every last drop out of their sumptuous way of life. Was this banquet to congratulate themselves for all that Atlantis had achieved, to celebrate their triumphs, their wealth, all the while pretending not to notice the warning signs of the imminent collapse of which King Atlas had spoken? Was everyone here trying to ignore the moment when it all comes crashing down? And where exactly are these thoughts of mine coming from? Were they put into me? Did Pa do this? They feel like they don't belong to me, and they only half make sense.

'Ladies and gentlemen,' King Atlas boomed, standing up from his half-eaten feast. 'I present to you my most recent and successful project: Princess Mel!'

He turned to me and indicated that I should begin. As I stood in the spotlight and recited all thirteen of the Emerald Tablets, the words flowed from my mouth as if they came from another place, a simpler time, and I was just the voice that had been chosen to speak them. The whole banqueting hall fell silent, and all eyes turned to me – a hundred pairs of eyes, not a blue one or a dry one among them. I kept going, the beautiful sacred rhythm of the words carrying me and everyone in the room to the very end, even if their meaning was too obscure for me to understand.

> 'Races shall rise and races shall fall.
> Forgotten shalt thou be of the children of men.
> Yet thou shalt have moved
> To a star-space beyond this
> Leaving behind this place where thou hast dwelt.'

I finished with the lines about conquering death at the end of the thirteenth tablet, sensing for the first time that a great sense of foreboding was embedded in the words, as though they were only written to be uttered at this very moment in time, and only had meaning for the people who sat rapt before me.

And then there was silence. Saha'Ra had told me that the guests would clap and cheer afterwards, but no one did. I waited, rooted to the spot, unsure what the royal protocol was at such a moment, until finally Atlas stood up and lifted his arms above his head in a gesture that looked as if he wanted to gather me up along with everyone there, and lift us all high above him in a gesture of salvation.

Now there were tears rolling down his cheeks as well as the Queen's.

'Brava!' he bellowed, and his giant voice reverberated around the hall. 'Brava!'

I bowed my head, picked up my skirts and ran.

Scroll VI

THE
ASSASSINATION

B ACK IN MY CHAMBER, I stared into the mirror. I could now see what Meth had seen earlier when he accosted me: a pampered, naive young woman with not one black hair out of place, not one furrow between my dark brows, not a hint of worldliness in my blue eyes. But I could also see something else: behind my eyes lurked an awareness that everything was about to change. Very soon my intuitions would be heard, my voice would count, my instincts would be followed, not just by the Royal Palace, but by all the people of Atlantis.

I fell into an uneasy slumber and woke in the middle of the night with a sharp pain in my chest. I sat up in bed, doubled over and sweating profusely. Saha'Ra must have heard me groaning and sobbing, because she and Mintaka ran into my chamber to see what was the matter. In my mind's eye, I could see faces writhing with pain. Faces I loved.

'What is it, Miss Mel? Are you ill?'

'It's the King and Queen – they're in danger. We have to do something!' I gasped, hardly able to see straight due to the stabbing sensation in my heart. I saw them clinging to each other in their bed, shock and horror on their faces, the life force ebbing out of them. And I saw *his* face, clear as day, leering over them – Meth. He withdrew his sword, sheathed the blade, licked the blood off his thumb, then turned and walked away.

I don't know how, but I could feel Meth moving through the palace. He had murdered them and now he was coming for me.

'Quickly, Saha'Ra – we have to leave!'

Saha'Ra stared at me blankly, Mintaka clinging to her nightgown. Neither of them moved while I dressed and slipped out of my chamber, my heart in my mouth.

*

I will spare you the details of the next few hours. It was not easy to come upon a scene of a bloody massacre, to find the people you love and respect savagely murdered. It made me so angry to think that no one at the banquet really cared, and that no one – not even Askew – had tried to stop Meth in his tracks. I was disgusted when I saw the Colonel fast asleep in a corner of the banqueting hall, like so many of the other guests who littered the hallways, half-clothed, open-mouthed, snoring or delirious. If Pa had been there, he would have stopped this from happening, I'm sure of it. He would have raised the alarm and got the King and Queen to a place of safety. He would have told the guards to lock the gates until the murderer was found. I was crying tears of anger and despair, but I knew inside that it was too late to think what might have happened. If only I'd seen it coming sooner! What's the use of being able to see into the future, but not far enough to have time to prevent a tragedy from taking place? The only thing I could do was run back to my chamber and make sure Saha'Ra, Mintaka and I didn't suffer the same fate.

*

Before the priests had even discovered the pools of blood on the silken bedsheets and heard the anguished cries of the servants, before they had placed the bodies in the Temple and sounded the royal death knell, Saha'Ra, Mintaka and I were gone.

We packed a few days' worth of clothes and food into one of the gardeners' handcarts, as well as a mattress for Mintaka and blankets for all three of us. I also remembered to take the black crystal that Pa had given me. Saha'Ra had never seen me act with such purpose before but, given the accuracy of my premonitions, neither she nor Mintaka once questioned me. I told her we needed to leave the palace by the gardeners' entrance to the rear of the wilderness area, dressed as stable boys to avoid detection. Once we were ready, I pulled up my hood and pushed the handcart into the wind and out through the gate, my heart racing faster than my legs could carry me.

'Where are we going?' whispered Mintaka after we crossed the first canal.

'To get Elijah and his mother,' I replied.

'Then what?' asked Saha'Ra, her voice unsteady. It was starting to rain heavily.

'We leave Atlantis, go to the Dogon Village and seek help from your people.'

I hadn't even realised this was my plan until that moment. Saha'Ra just nodded, and the three of us pressed on, both time and the weather against us. It was market day in the city and, even though it was hours before dawn, the streets were already full of sellers shouting their wares and prices, buyers haggling for ripe mangoes and bags of millet. We slipped among them, our handcart looking very similar to the ones used by the stallholders, and the blankets covering our belongings might just as easily have been covering a heap of yams and sweet potatoes. When we crossed over to the outer ring, I saw that the canal had overflowed onto the bridge. We had no choice but to wade through the muddy water, our belongings mostly dry but our shoes ruined.

The journey to the elephant house was a lot further

than I remembered from the day we'd walked there with the priests on our school outing, partly because this time we had to pick our way carefully through the flooded streets and partly because the city felt different. I wanted to warn everyone about what had just happened at the palace and tell them that their city was not safe anymore but, judging by the number of people who seemed to be packing up or were already on the move just like us, it seemed they already knew. When we got to the barracks on the outer ring, there were horses just wandering around in the rain, their stable doors standing open and the barracks empty. It seemed that the soldiers had all fled, and I knew instinctively that they were out looking for either Meth or me.

'This way! It's very close now – can you smell the hay?' I whispered to Mintaka.

Elijah trumpeted when he heard us, but his mother looked dejected. They had not been cleaned out in days and had no water to drink. I found a tap and filled up their tank. Elisha drank for a long time and urged her son to do the same. While Mintaka was petting Elijah and telling Saha'Ra about what had happened the previous time we had visited, it occurred to me that I had no idea how to mount or ride an elephant.

I looked around for inspiration and finally dragged a table alongside Elisha and threw a piece of rope over her back. Then I walked round and tied it to her right flank. Standing on the table, I pulled my way up the rope until I was sitting astride her neck, just behind her ears. She shuffled around a bit, unused to the feeling of someone sitting on her.

I slid back down and helped Mintaka up. Then I tied the handcart to Elijah, so he could pull it along behind him, while the three of us rode on his mother.

'Why are we taking the elephants?' asked Mintaka as she climbed up onto Elisha's back.

'Because we need to get away from Atlantis.'

'But why?'

'Because our lives are in danger, Min.'

Scroll VII

THE EXODUS

WITH THE TWO ELEPHANTS fed and watered, we set off, somewhat slowly and waywardly, since Elijah seemed incapable of walking in a straight line and kept zigzagging across the street, the handcart swinging out wide behind him, until eventually I got down from his mother and showed him how to hold her tail and walk along behind her. We stayed on the outer ring of Atlantis and followed the curve of the racetrack, because I was nervous about going anywhere near the Royal Palace in case Meth's soldiers were looking for us there. Finally, we found ourselves at the North Bridge, the one where the horse had bolted on race day, and it occurred to me that here I was, escaping into the mountains, just as I had envied the horse doing that fateful day.

The guard in the gatehouse on the far side of the bridge left his post and came out into the rain to stop us. He was armed, but friendly enough. I pretended to be asleep so he would not see my blue eyes, and Saha'Ra told him her daughter and sister were sick and she was taking us to see a Medicine Man in the Dogon village north of the city. He poked around under the blanket and when he could see all we had were clothes, blankets and some food, he let us pass.

Not long after we'd left the outer perimeter of the city and begun to make our way to higher ground, the elephants became strangely restless and suddenly a huge shuddering movement swept through the ground beneath our feet, as if the bedrock was trying to roll like an ocean wave. A long crack opened up right across our path, and Elisha reared up abruptly as she tried to avoid falling into it. The sky was not yet light and unfortunately Elijah didn't see it in time; he lurched headlong into the crack and lay on this side, whimpering. It took all of us to haul him back out.

'What was that?' asked Mintaka, just as stunned as Elijah.

'I think it was an earthquake,' her mother replied, her voice strained and high-pitched. 'People have been saying it was coming.'

'But why? We never have earthquakes in Atlantis.'

Just as she said this, I heard a strange 'whooshing' sound in the distance and, as we turned to peer down at the city, a huge wave swept up the canal and washed over the whole city in a matter of seconds, covering it with water. The neat circular outline of Atlantis was no longer visible and even when the wave receded, all I could make out was water everywhere.

'Was that Enesidaone coming in his chariot to see what just happened?'

'No, Min, I think that was a tsunami caused by the earthquake,' I said quietly, knowing this was not something the priests had taught us and wondering how it was I knew. It was as if, instead of memories, I had flashes of insight about things I'd never even experienced.

We continued in silence, picking our way between the rocks and glancing now and then back at the city as the rumblings continued. The ground shook from time to time, rocking the handcart from side to side, and the elephants were clearly determined to get away from the tremors as quickly as possible; Elisha stepped up her pace.

As the city receded into the distance, I knew I would never return, and that this journey, this ordeal, was far from over. If we survived, our memories of this fateful night would come back to haunt us. Perhaps it was better not to have memories, after all.

We walked and walked, ever more slowly, up the steep valley that led into the Atlas Mountains. Long after sunset, with a fierce wind now at our backs, we arrived in a remote mountain village, hungry, tired and with hearts much heavier than the load the elephants were carrying. The Dogon people seemed to be expecting us, and I was brought before their Chief, a tall, elderly man wearing a long, frayed cape and a strange necklace, standing in front of a low building with a thickly-thatched roof.

The Dogon Chief spoke slowly and deliberately in Atlantean with a strong Dogon accent.

'Your instincts have served you well, Princess Urdinak. Atlantis is indeed in grave danger. You must not go back. My people will go down into the city and make sure the King and his Queen receive a proper Atlantean burial. The future of Atlantean civilisation is now in your hands. It is up to the three of you.'

'The three of us?'

'This was foretold. The ones with eyes like the sky must lead the way.'

I gave Saha'Ra a puzzled look.

'I think he means you, Miss Mel.'

'Me?'

I looked at the wizened face of the Dogon Chief. He nodded.

'Yes, it is time.'

From: camille.warden@ucl.ac.uk
To: ian.clyffe@queensland.edu.au
Date: 2/2/22 08:03
Subject: 'Operation Chameleon'

Dear Professor Clyffe,

I realise I am writing to you out of the blue, but I find myself in a difficult situation and I have no one to turn to who I can trust.

I am an archaeologist at the University of London working on the translation of two ancient documents, which have caused quite a stir: The Sphinx Codex and The Dogon Scrolls. This is hardly surprising, since carbon-dating has proved that they are more than 12,000 years old and, despite being written by different authors and excavated at two different sites, they use the same ancient language and both allude to a place long thought to have been made up by Plato: Atlantis.

I know from your work that you are someone willing to consider theories about climate change and intense geological events that lie outside the mainstream accepted narrative and, as I am no expert in this area myself, I would very much welcome your thoughts, because these documents contain indications of an earlier period of intense climate change. In my opinion, based on what we know so far, they offer clear evidence for your 'cosmic intervention' theory.

Attached is a translated note from Tehuti to King Atlas, thought to be the ruler of Atlantis at the time it sank, after which you will find a translation of the first portion of The Sphinx Codex, which starts with a report about the creation of a new human prototype with blue eyes named Leon. These texts were inscribed onto clay tablets and found beneath the Sphinx in Egypt in what is believed to be the Hall of Records. I have also attached a translation of the first ten of The Dogon Scrolls, a strange chronicle by an Atlantean princess written in the same pre-cuneiform script, recently unearthed in a remote region of Mali.

Both documents challenge us to accept not only that Atlantis was real, but also, despite their advanced technology, that the ancient Atlanteans knew their end was near but could do nothing to prevent it. All they could do was evacuate their people and safeguard their knowledge and their treasures before disaster struck. It is my belief that both the tablets and the scrolls were deliberately placed somewhere they would not be destroyed, however extreme Earth's upheaval became, in order for future generations to learn what happened. That's why I felt it was my duty to draw them to the attention of someone who, like me, is searching for the truth.

In writing to you, I am going against the confidentiality agreement I signed with our research funders and against my own better judgement; but, given the nature of these revelations, I felt it was imperative that I let someone outside the archaeological community know. I therefore ask that you treat my letter as completely private and confidential. I look forward to your response.

Kind regards,
Dr Camille Warden

From: ian.clyffe@queensland.edu.au
To: camille.warden@ucl.ac.uk
Date: 8/2/22 21:43
Subject: RE: 'Operation Chameleon'

Dear Dr Warden,

Heaven knows how you came to write to me in this way but, having reviewed the documents that you sent to me, I am at a loss as to what to say. I think you have been taken in by an elaborate and compelling hoax, and that these translations are the product of a cleverly faked and staged publicity stunt of the kind that has become all too common these days.

That said, whoever has taken the trouble to write them went to great lengths to capture the sense of another age and they evoke a turbulent set of circumstances very convincingly.

Before I completely discount the veracity of your finds, perhaps you would be so kind as to send me some more, and include this time perhaps a couple of photographs of the originals, so that I can see for myself and make up my own mind?

It is indeed fascinating to think that a previous civilization on Earth might have known more than we do about genetic modification and such like, but the idea that we have been collaborating with extra-terrestrials is really stretching the imagination too far. There is no evidence that this has taken place, and the existence of a hollow Earth, Atlantis and advanced ancient technology are simply fanciful ideas about which there have been far too many cheap television documentaries.

I am being a tad churlish, I know; I was, in fact, rather touched and intrigued to receive your attachments, and I see from the Internet that you are a respected and admired researcher in your field, so forgive me if I seem unduly negative. I do not mean to disappoint you; I just feel this is insufficient evidence to support such a radical rethinking of human history and planetary dynamics.

Yours truly,
Professor Ian Clyffe

From: camille.warden@ucl.ac.uk
To: ian.clyffe@queensland.edu.au
Date: 14/2/22 14:25
Subject: RE: 'Operation Chameleon'

Dear Professor Clyffe,

I appreciate that, despite your reservations, you at least took the trouble to reply to my email. At the risk of being taken for a fool, I have something else which I can now reveal to you: there is a third and even more provocative artefact that, to my mind, clearly corroborates the content of the other two.

This third artefact has just been painstakingly deciphered by one of our bright young interns and is probably the first example of digitally encrypted information known to man. Originally thought to be a pre-Pharaonic necklace made from pieces of Libyan Desert glass, it is in fact a series of data disks arranged into a chronological sequence onto which was encoded the field log of the first genetically modified human, Kam.

Knowing the misgivings you expressed in your email, I am aware that what I have just described makes 'Operation Chameleon' sound even more far-fetched, but I can assure you that this is not any sort of hoax, and I have only the most sincere, dedicated and scholarly aspirations: to find the truth about our origins and our ancient past.

You will see, if you can spare the time to look over the sequence I attach from what we are calling The Sirian Disks, that Kam's unique perspective on the events already described in The Sphinx Codex and The Dogon Scrolls talks about the same climate catastrophe but from an entirely different viewpoint. Interestingly, several of the individuals she mentions also feature in the other two documents, proving that the lives of Leon, Mel and Kam were undeniably intertwined.

If nothing else, once our translations are complete, this will make a fascinating science-fiction movie. But I very much hope that you will reconsider your views regarding its factual veracity and look into it further. Could I possibly entice you to come to London, so that I can show you all that we have amassed at first hand? My research budget could even cover your airfare, if you would allow this.

Yours sincerely,
Camille Warden

THE SIRIAN DISKS

(PART 1 OF KAM'S STORY)

Disk I

THE MESSAGE

Recruits wanted for undercover rescue operation to Earth, a planet in a solar system near the Virgo Cluster currently experiencing the effects of severe climate change and geological disruption.

Only adult hominids with shapeshifting capabilities need apply.

Full training will be provided.

This is an En.Ki-sponsored All Risks Mission.

Salary to be paid in monatomic gold.

No leave granted until termination of contract.

Starts 1st day of Paoni.

Disk II

THE TEST

IT'S THE THIRD MORNING running I've woken with the same message lodged in my ceph. Now that this kind of download is getting past my Blocker, I know for sure it's no longer working properly. I ought to ask the Phys to take a look, but that costs over 10g of mono these days and Ma could never afford it. Anyway, the Phys would know straightaway that my Blocker is a Black Khanus one, which is totally illegal anywhere on Nyan Tolo, quite apart from the fact that it was tampered with by Pa.

I get out of my kot and peer out of my dorm to the West.

As the first rays of our three beautiful suns start to track across the floor, I manage to remember and write down the exact wording. I don't know if it's the effort of transcribing the message or its spine-tingling content, but I can't help thinking that since I received it – not once, not twice, but *three times* – the message is actually intended for me, Kam Urdinak!

A field position working for Pa's employer, En.ki, eons away from here is exactly the sort of gig I've been waiting for! I'd get to leave my home planet for a bit, dodge my last cycle of Ed, and get paid a deadweight in white powder for it – so much that I'd be able to buy my klan out of Relegation. It's pretty near perfect! Apart from the 'All Risks Mission' part. ARMs never go according to plan, that's what Pa always said. But I'd do anything to find him and bring him home to Ma. That would make me happier than all the mono in the galaxy.

I'll have a job convincing Zep and Aum to come too. As an advanced AI bot, Zep is bound to question my logic, but I have to take Aum – he is my pet, after all. I've already found some nerdy data that will appeal to Zep: Earth is 8.611 light years away and has an atmospheric similarity index of 83% compared to ours, which means there's enough oxygen there to breathe and it's about the same temperature as it is here on my home planet, Nyan Tolo. As for Aum, let's hope the idea of a small furry creature with long ears, nocturnal habits and incredible healing skills is just what they're looking for!

On the shapeshifting score, I'm definitely eligible – they told me when I took my last medical that I was chameleonoid. That's how I got hooked up with Zep –

he was an En.Ki bot doing data analysis at the clinic and they assigned him to me. So, there's just the issue of how I'd pass for an adult hominid. My illegal Blocker was reconditioned by Black Khanus from an elderly Sirian hominid, so their trace will still be on it, which should help with the age profiling. Anyway, once they find out I can basically mimic any skin colour or biped species up to a point, they're hardly going to care how old I am. Plus, with Zep being telepathically aligned to me, we'll seem like a very attractive option, especially as En.Ki is one of the mission sponsors.

Given the planetary time differences – like how a year is 122 days on Nyan Tolo but 360 days on Earth – what even *is* an 'adult'? So, to my mind, there's no harm in applying, even if I do have to lie about my age – it's my birthday next week, so by the end of the month of Koiak I'll be 49 in any case – one Sirian year away from achieving official adult status.

*

Zep is up for it 'in theory'. He's concerned that En.Ki might not allow him to go because they've now hired him out as a data analyst on a government livestock project, but he agreed he'd much rather be doing a top-secret mission instead. With Aum it's more complicated. In order for a non-hominid species to be allowed on an ARM, there are expensive health checks to go through and we don't have the mono to pay for them. But if Zep and I do the pre-mission, we'll earn some of the contract fee up front, which would pay for Aum's checks. The pre-mission is basically to test out a Vimana 5.0 – the newest model of spaceship they plan to use for the main mission. Don't ask me how, but it's powered by some kind of gooey green astral algae. As someone who plans to study astrobiology at Kollege, that got me pretty excited.

So, long story short: I submitted my application this morning. The next stage is passing the Sirian High Kouncil's Aptitude Test, which involves a full screening process. As a chameleonoid, I have to be able to demonstrate a minimum of three shapeshifts: one mammalian, one reptilian and one non-sentient being. I can do a simple baboon for the first category no problem, but I'm still working on the reptilian one. I'm basing it on a kind of blue-skinned biped royal lizard from Alpha Draconis. The skin is basically the same colour as my eyes, but I can't quite get the gills working yet. As for the non-sentient, I still have no idea what to go for. Aum suggested I should do 'wormwood', which is a healing plant that grows on Earth, but Zep said I should go for slime. Revolting but novel ...

*

I passed! The blue lizard worked a treat once I'd mastered circular breathing, and the recruitment agents all said my electric slime shift was the best they'd ever seen. They said my baboon shapeshift got the lowest grade of the three, but they seemed particularly impressed by the fact I also had blue eyes, although I don't remember that being in the job description. So, I just have to get through the endurance tests now. The hardest part was getting back to my usual body shape and skin colour after doing the slime shift – my skin stayed gooey for hours. Plus, it made my hair full of static and even more frizzy than normal.

Luckily my Blocker successfully masked my real age, because there were no questions about my adult status, and they've told me to report to En.Ki's HQ tomorrow morning with Zep. He's having his operating system updated so he can control the Vimana 5.0's algae-based propulsion system. Aum is going to be part of the ground team for the pre-mission, which involves observing us operate in low orbit for the better part of two days. The vimana – or V5 as all the field agents call it – affects your sense of gravity and your muscles can waste away if you're not careful, which sounds pretty weird. We have to strap ourselves to the walls to sleep and eat freeze-dried food, but it can't be any worse than Ma's cooking. I told her at Rations last night that I'm going on a field trip with Ed, and that I'd been picked for the Elite Scholar astrobiology group, which she was thrilled about. I only lied a little bit. She thinks I'm taking part in a government project to study how life began on Sirius, when really I'm part of a galactic project to sort out some problems on Earth.

Nommo One, the Sirian High Kouncil Leader who has to sign off on the mission (I mean 'field trip'), says it can't go ahead until they've had a final meeting with someone from Earth called 'the Dogon Chief', who is basically the leader of an ancient mountain tribe that our ancestors first made contact with eons ago. Apparently, it was us

Sirians who taught them everything under the stars. Zep's datafiles say the Dogon people have been worshipping us ever since, which is probably why they're now appealing to us for help. Anyway, this meeting with the Chief is obviously a big deal, because stories about the Dogon are now all over the newscycle.

One thing they never talk about in the news is the fact that our mission is obviously black budget. At the end of my interview, they asked me if I had any questions, so I asked the panel how the mission was being funded, which I thought was a really grown-up question, but the Aptitude Board members just growled and grunted and wouldn't answer. I should have worked it out for myself – why else would the starting salary be 10 krates of monatomic gold? That's enough white powder to give my whole klan disease protection for life.

But that's not how I'll be spending it. Top of my list is to get my klan out of Relegation – it's become virtually uninhabitable. The air's so bad here in Relegation now, some people are resorting to using artificial breathers when they go out, and Ma has to double-filter all our water before it's even remotely drinkable. Last month, perhaps to make it up to Ma for falling out with my Pa, Uncle Jainko gave us a special monitoring device so Ma could keep track of radiation levels in our neighbourhood. Uncle Jainko is always talking about how the Sirian government is under-reporting radiation levels; he says they don't want us to realise how bad things have got on Nyan Tolo. Ma put the device under her kot, because no one in Relegation is supposed to have that kind of equipment. It was probably stolen by Black Khanus, who my uncle is part of. Black Khanus is the reason Pa won't speak to Uncle Jainko anymore and why Pa changed our family name to Urdinak. I bet my uncle knows all about black budget projects, but I can't ask him.

*

Yesterday was my 49th birthday celebration down at the Centre. Ma had tears in her eyes when she presented me with Pa's Chintamani, as per Sirian tradition when you reach 7x7. It's a beautiful dark green stone inscribed with ancient Sirian prayers and symbols. I was really touched. Ma says when I turn 50 and I'm truly an adult, I can have one of the ancestral symbols tattooed on my forehead like Pa and Uncle Jainko.

Ma also gave me a beautiful blue tunic she'd made out of a special fabric called 'silk'. She told me it was what Pa wrapped me in to bring me home when I was a baby. Zep told me silk is a secretion made by a worm. I know that sounds gross but, believe me, they do a good job! It's the softest thing imaginable. I slipped it on and lots of people commented on how it matched my eyes. Zep whispered, 'It's the same colour as Earth's sky, Kam'. I can't imagine what that's going to be like, to stare up at a bright-blue sky. Ours is always a dull, dirty orange.

Ma didn't make food for the party, which I was glad about because she's a hopeless cook. Instead she ordered in some really expensive-looking fruit from another solar system, and we drank a kind of mineral water that

I'd never tasted before. It was completely clear and had no bitter taste at all, unlike ours. After I'd opened all the gifts people brought, Ma made me give a speech, 'because that's what Pa would have wanted'. I could see that my younger siblings, Yuri, Tsygan, Dezik and Laika, were all waiting – their four pairs of brown eyes all staring up at me – for some wise sentiments, like I was their Guide or something and not just their eldest sibling. For Pa's sake I managed to say a few words, and then I proposed a toast to him, because he would have been celebrating his 11x11 birthday this year and should have been retiring.

Halfway through the toast, my ceph started throbbing and I felt gills opening on my neck, and I suddenly realised I was starting to shapeshift because of all the emotions running through me. I looked down at my hands and saw they were turning the same blue as my tunic, except that the texture was scaly instead of soft and silky. It was a horrible moment. I took a few deep breaths and then the gills in my neck closed and I could feel the air passing through my nose again. Fascinated, my sister Yuri got hold of my hand to examine it.

'What's the matter with your hand, Kam?' she asked, puzzled.

Uncle Jainko cleared his throat in case I wasn't aware I was shapeshifting and Ma gave him a funny look but didn't say anything.

My siblings don't know I'm chameleonoid – Ma says it's our little secret and that Pa said I mustn't ever tell them. I don't know why. I just know I'm a bit different to them. It didn't used to bother me, but recently I've been feeling frustrated that I don't really know who I am. I've realised that, as well as wanting to find Pa, I also want to find other people who are chameleonoid like me. I know it sounds a bit ungrateful when I belong to a perfectly nice family, but I just want to know who I am and where I come from, because I'm not sure I really belong here on Nyan Tolo anymore.

As I looked round the room at the faces of all the people I love, I suddenly realised that, however badly I want to go on this Mission, it comes with a huge risk: I might never come back, just like Pa.

Disk III

THE PRE-MISSION

Z EP'S NEW UPGRADE MAKES it feel like he's snooping on me. It's kind of annoying, because now I can hear all his anxious nerdy thoughts all the time. Right now, he's thinking over and over, *Is Kam OK?* Aum is sitting still with his ears bolt upright outside the vimana, looking a bit glum if I'm honest, but I'm feeling really buzzed. There are two En.Ki operatives coming with us, Enza and Bavat. They've spent the last two days putting Zep through his paces with the AI control systems aboard the V5.

I'm fine, I tell Zep, and realise I didn't move my lips. Enza helps me tighten my safety harness. I can sense that

Zep's counting on me to keep him from malfunctioning. He told me this morning that, since the AI upgrade, he now senses things a few moments before they actually happen. Like last night, when he went to check on the livestock in their byre, he said a message pulsed through him that one would give birth in a few minutes. As he tracked between the animals, sure enough, one of the females was calving.

Apparently, unless Zep's AI programme can make the plasma pulse through the five containers of green algae in the centre of the craft, the vimana won't take off. It makes my stomach lurch just thinking about it.

All checks are completed and hatches secured. Enza gives us the thumbs up, and Zep turns his attention to the first container. He told me afterwards there's this weird moment when he can sense his AI programming merge with the algae inside the container and fuse together, starting with the tiniest pulse of energy which then spirals up, at which point the plasma energy must pass into the algae, because that's when the vimana vibrated slightly, lifted and shot vertically upwards.

*

No one told us until after lift-off that I have to eat some of the monatomic gold we get paid for this pre-mission! I thought it was Enza's idea of a joke until Zep checked with En.Ki: in order for my hominid immune system 'to cope with the side effects of space travel, a small amount of mono has to be ingested'. This means I've got to eat these hard little dough balls, which Enza refers to as 'sho bread'. She gave me one and told me they're made from a combination of eight kinds of grain including millet and sorghum, some aloe vera, some bee propolis and a small quantity of powdered white gold. I made a face when I ate the first sho ball; it's worse than Ma's bread.

Nyan Tolo looks like a fuzzy grey ball from up here. I can see massive plasma filaments arcing between it and our three suns, Sigi Tolo, Emme Ya Tolo and Po Tolo, which then collapse into space in wide orange ribbons. There isn't much to do now we're in orbit; the vimana has been programmed to collect droplets of moisture and samples of anything that's present in the outer atmosphere of our planet – dark matter, stardust, space debris, organic particles, microbes, you name it – for us to study back on Nyan Tolo. Zep says the vimana's AI is so advanced it will have already processed and catalogued the samples itself by the time we get back, and then a team of astrobiologists will get to work on them. I'm going to have to get clued up on all this, especially since that's the reason Ma thinks I'm up here.

While we were up there, Zep got a couple of cute but mystifying messages from Aum:

Mission feel unsafe.
Friends fly up and sky bends down.
Test fur and fury.

Waiting, wondering
Time stand still, Sirius days
Dogon know the truth.

*

As soon as we returned from the pre-mission, we were told to report straight to the training suite because they were expecting an important virtual visitor. I was amazed how realistic this was: the elderly Dogon Chief slowly appeared as a three-dimensional hologram at the entrance to the High Kouncil Chamber, stooping slightly as he stepped off it. He carried a staff and a small bag and was wearing a long, frayed cape with a heavy adornment around his neck, strung with strange objects that glinted in the light. On his brown, leathery forehead was a symbol painted in thick white paint, similar to Pa's tattoo. He limped slowly towards the eight bearded Nommo of the Sirian High Kouncil, who sat in an arc behind an imposing stone levitable, their sinuous fishtails coiled in front of them. Before each step, the Dogon Chief prodded the floor with his staff, as if testing the firmness of the virtual ground in front of him. His dark eyes roved calmly around the chamber and his cape chafed against his legs as he walked. When he stood before the table, he bowed low and said, 'O Nommo, I beseech thee'.

As hired contractors, Zep, Aum and I were only allowed to witness this meeting from the training suite, which made it difficult for us to see everything or hear the whole conversation, but it was obvious that the mission is not quite what we'd been led to believe. For one thing, the Kouncil hasn't appointed a pilot yet, which is a worry, but even more ominously the mission has now escalated from All Risks to 'MM'. Zep looked alarmed when he heard this and when I shot him a confused look, he telepathed the words *'Mercy Mission'* to me. The thought of it made the training suite feel suddenly tense and airless, and the gills started to open on my neck. The eight Nommo looked about as nervous as I felt.

Then the Dogon Chief reached inside his bag and pulled out a scroll. He spread it out on the levitable in front of the Nommo and waited patiently for them to inspect it. It looked like a map marked with a circular target that had been partly erased. The Nommo leaned forward, their brows raised. Nommo One pointed to the circular mark on the map and an argument broke out, at which point the Dogon Chief reached into a pocket inside his cape and tipped a handful of golden sand onto the scroll. With a long, gnarled finger, he drew something in the sand.

'It is time,' he kept saying in a strange accent. 'It is time.'

The High Kouncil fell silent and stared at the Chief. He looked back at them gravely, bowed again and withdrew, leaving them poring over the grains of sand.

At last, with a bleak expression on her face, Nommo One stood up and ended the meeting.

'So be it. This is a job for Xnake Rapza.'

Disk IV

THE PILOT

THE PILOT THEY'VE SELECTED for our mission, Xnake Rapza, is nowhere to be found. Even though the High Kouncil put out a military summons, there was no response, and so now they've put our mission on hold. For some reason, they don't have an alternative pilot in mind.

I asked around in Relegation, but no one seems to know who this guy Xnake is. Not one to give up easily, I eventually found a report in the Bibliotek stating that someone by that name once served a lengthy prison sentence on a planet called Mars for mining illegal crystals on Earth. I also came across a story about a strange mythical eight-legged character called Xnake:

> *Deep in The Crease, a much-feared place in Sirian myths and legends, an electric storm was building.*
>
> *Xnake eyed the orange sky wearily and squirmed. He paused before a deep crevice, trying to get a better purchase on the rock face with his tentacles, eyes half-closed and tongue flicking. When the wind dropped for the briefest of instants, he quickly adjusted his position and cleaved open the crevice in the rockface to reveal a gleaming cluster of crystals. Scraping his way into the crevice using several tentacles at once, Xnake picked off the glistening loot and, stuffing it into his mouth, moved down to the next ledge, swallowing painfully.*
>
> *After several hours of vertical mining with no other means of support, his tentacles were slowly stiffening, and when he was almost at the base of The Crease he fell and slid across the rocky floor, then took a long draught of something from a flask and vomited the stash of crystals into a shallow metal crate.*
>
> *He sealed the lid and collapsed onto the ground. Stretching out all eight tentacles in turn, he coiled four of them around the crate and began the long, slow climb back to the surface.*

I went to see Zep down at the farm later that afternoon to discuss my plan. He was rolling through a barn, scanning and logging biodata from the new animals that had been born.

'Look, Zep, I'm going to ask around near the old prison tonight to see if anyone's heard of Xnake,' I announced in a wobbly voice, scuffing the ground with my foot.

Zep stopped what he was doing and was silent for a few seconds, his indicators flashing in a state of conflicted loyalties. But he knew better than to try to stop me.

'I cannot come with you, Kam.'

'Not even if Aum comes too?'

He fell silent again and then I faintly heard a thought pass between us.

-Take some mono with you, Kam, and your Ma's radiation detector.

*

The old prison is not somewhere you go without good reason and certainly not at night. You needed to be desperate, or fearless, or both. It's out past the edge of town, beyond Relegation. It was once a high-security facility, but after the Riots it became a no-go zone populated by the ex-inmates, who use the prison's surveillance and interrogation equipment for their own ends.

I have to find Xnake: Ma has started asking too many questions and I caught Yuri looking through my messenger today. Before long, the whole klan will have worked out what's really going on.

-Pa would be so angry if he could see you now – remember what he told you about this place, Zep keeps nagging in my head. I can still remember the day Pa got out of prison, his

face haggard and his body spent. It brings a lump to my throat even now.

It's going dark. I've got the radiation counter held out in front of me like I'm walking an invisible pet alongside Aum. I'm starting to wish I'd brought my facemask with me, because the air smells really bad, like ammonia only worse. Before I left home, I tucked my hair inside Pa's old Black Khanus cap and chalked a few white marks onto my forehead, thinking it might at least command a bit of respect down here.

Aum keeps trotting on ahead and then circling back to me, blinking fast. We're picking our way through street after street of ramshackle tents and dwellings, running along the edge of each dark alley and slowing up as we turn each corner. I'm painfully aware we have not been taking note of our route, so it'll be hard finding our way back. Suddenly Aum pulls up short by a pile of garbage, his ears pricked up vertically. The radiation detector is buzzing like crazy and the alley has petered out into a wide-open space.

I take another step forward and a load of floodlights flash on, casting shadows around us in four directions. I shield my eyes from the glare. I can see four watchtowers. A warning shot is fired from one of them and suddenly a couple of figures rattle down a ladder and start coming towards us.

I crouch down low, instinctively protecting Aum's little body with my own. The figures are moving quickly, but it's only when they are quite close and I can hear their breathing that I realise they are a couple of obese halflings who hardly even come up to my waist. I also know for a fact they can't see very well. They stop when the tips of their shadows reach a small dirt mound just in front of us.

Instinctively I begin to take on the appearance of the upright blue lizard. My additional height makes the halflings cower as they sniff the air and narrow their half-blind eyes. I slowly raise the radiation detector in the air as if it's some kind of exotic weapon. It's buzzing even more loudly now, perhaps picking up radiation from their clothes.

'I'm looking for Xnake Rapza,' I declare in a cloaked voice, my eyes slitting in the floodlit glare. The two halflings blink at each other halfwittedly and glance back at the watchtower.

'Mono?' one of them asks tentatively.

I throw a tiny pouch of it onto the dirt mound. They squabble over it, then, having eaten the contents, the one with the bigger nose, spluttering and sneezing, beckons us to follow.

As we leave the derelict compound and the floodlights at last flick off, I catch a glimpse of something peculiar in the contours of the landscape beyond the watchtower. It looks like a huge scar in the ground and, as we move closer, I suddenly realise we're standing at the edge of a dark, apparently bottomless abyss in the planet's crust.

The buzzing from the radiation detector grows more intense, and I now realise it's not coming from the halflings' clothes. I turn to see that they are hanging back, too scared to move any closer.

'Xnake down there,' one of them informs us.

'Down where?' I ask, pretending I hadn't noticed anything.

'Down The Crease.'

As the halfling utters these words, I feel a shudder rush through me, and I realise to my horror that The Crease actually exists!

*

The only way for me to climb down the vertical wall of The Crease is to revert to slime. The two halflings trot off, leaving Aum peering over the ledge, keeping watch while I descend. In slime form, I have no vision whatsoever, but a good grip on the rockface. All the way down I concentrate on keeping my slimy being connected as one gooey flow, in case, when I return to hominid form, I've lost a finger or a toe.

Several hours later, I finally reach the base of The Crease, and ooze my way horizontally until I find a smooth rectangular area where I decide it's safe to return to being a biped. Mid-shapeshift, I feel myself being shoved sideways.

'What in Saturn's name is going on?' demands a husky voice.

I start shuddering, like the algae in the vimana's tanks. My vision is returning, and I can see a large tentacled creature looming over me, clutching a rectangular krate and retching. This must be Xnake, and this situation is exactly like that story I read! In an effort to create a more favourable impression on my mission pilot, I adopt the blue lizard garb.

'Err, I've come to inform you, Komrade Xnake, Sir, you are required to report to En.Ki HQ to pilot our Mercy Mission to Earth. Sir.'

Xnake's double eyelids open and close several times before he coils up and around me, breathing rancid air into the gills on my neck. He smells of salt and dirt and ammonia. When his mouth is so close to my face I can hardly focus, he finally croaks.

'So, the Kouncil have changed their minds, have they? Think I'm fit for active service now, do they? And what use could a renegade like me possibly have for an immature shapeshifter like you on my crew?'

He spits on the ground and I spy a strange crystal glinting in the gob of dark saliva.

'I've passed the Aptitude Board, Sir. Mission is scheduled for 1st Paoni.'

I'm shaking all over, so the last syllable comes out as a weird stammer. Xnake withdraws, coughs and, with one tentacle wrapped around the krate, starts to claw and slither his way back up the rockface to the surface.

I have no choice but to follow him out of The Crease.

*

When we reached the surface, I realised we'd emerged somewhere different; neither the prison nor Aum was anywhere to be seen. Xnake was trying his best to shake me off, but I tailed him and the next thing I knew we had entered the city via a route I never even knew existed. We passed through a series of checkpoints, and each time just the sight of Xnake seemed to inspire such fear in the guards that not one of them stopped us to ask to see our ID. After the third one, I decided it was safe to go back to my usual hominid form and my blue skin faded back to its normal tone.

We were in a sort of shanty town full of dilapidated tents and huts, and after a while I realised it was where Uncle Jainko's underground network was based. I was still trying to work out how to steer Xnake out of Black Khanus territory when, to my surprise, I caught sight of Uncle Jainko some distance away, moving swiftly between the tents parallel to us. He appeared to be tracking Xnake's movements with some kind of device. I glanced at Xnake, but he hadn't noticed he was being followed.

I slowed down to watch what my uncle was doing. He had a steely, determined look on his face I've never seen before, and then I saw that Zep was trailing along after him! A wave of anger washed through me. What kind of AI bot goes running to Black Khanus the minute their komrade fails to return? Just then, Xnake pulled up sharply and turned right between two rows of tents. As Uncle Jainko followed, I decided to drop back, slipping between the tents to run along quietly behind Zep. As Jainko sped on ahead, Zep must have detected my presence and glanced back. Before he'd even reacted, I pushed him to the ground and, through gritted teeth, threatened to put him into shutdown unless he told me what he was doing and where Aum was.

It was only when we found Aum cowering under the table in Uncle Jainko's tent that Zep got over the shock of finding us both and started apologising.

'Zep, that's enough, let's not mess things up anymore, OK? We can't afford to get off on the wrong foot with our pilot.'

'That creature with all the tentacles is our *pilot*?' Zep asked, incredulous.

'Yup.'

Zep gave me that look that said '*Seriously?*'

'Look, Zep, it wasn't easy. I had to resort to being electric slime just to find him.'

'Shapeshifting should only be used in emergencies,' said Zep haughtily.

'I think you'll find it *was* an emergency!' I scoffed.

At that moment, Uncle Jainko was thrust violently into the tent by one of Xnake's tentacles. Jainko had hold of the rectangular krate and Xnake seemed to be very angry about it.

'I've made myself clear, Xnake: Black Khanus will only give you immunity in return for the contents of this krate,' insisted Uncle Jainko as he dumped the krate on the table.

'Why should I agree to a deal like that, Jainko? I owe Black Khanus nothing!'

'Once you cross us, you are always in our debt, you know that. This booty is ours now.'

'Have you any idea of the value of the contents of that krate on the black market?'

Neither of them had noticed the three of us watching the whole thing play out from under the table.

'I don't doubt you took extreme risks down in The Crease to procure it, but that's not the point. We both know the High Kouncil will never re-employ you unless

Black Khanus vouches for you. I am prepared to give you that one last chance.'

'No need.'

'What do you mean, "no need"?'

'A shapeshifting kid found me down The Crease last night, and said she's been recruited to a mission to Earth and that I'm required to pilot it. Not something you've ever been offered, is it, Jainko? What's the matter with you? Too incompetent to follow in your brother's footsteps, are you?' Xnake sneered.

Uncle Jainko was visibly shaken. He took a deep breath before replying, speaking each word slowly and deliberately, almost as if he wanted someone else to hear them.

'Whoever came to inform you of this mission has been badly misled. They are not even eligible for such a thing. I know for a fact that, even if they were the right age, they are hardly likely be allowed to follow in Pa's foot...'

'It's not your decision, Jainko. Out of your hands now. Kid passed the Aptitude Board.'

'If they had, I would know,' growled Jainko. 'We'll see about this.'

'Are you threatening me, Jainko?'

'Fifty-fifty, OK?' Uncle Jainko fired his weapon at the krate, splitting it open. He grabbed a handful of the contents, stuffed them into his coat pocket and left the tent.

Sighing, Xnake stooped down to pick up a stray crystal from the dirt floor. Aum flinched and the slight movement must have caught Xnake's eye.

'You lot, come out now!' he snarled.

Disk V

THE BRIEFING

I COULD TERMINATE ZEP for messing this up so badly. Not only does my uncle now know I've been recruited to a black ops mission but, worse still, it's being piloted by someone he regards as his arch-enemy. And because of him, Xnake gave us a real grilling. Aum was silent the whole way through, his cream fur all pricked up, while Zep talked way too much, blathering on and on until Xnake had heard enough and put him into shutdown mode.

He only asked me one question: which type of chameleonoid was I – type 1, 2 or 3? I have absolutely no idea, and said so, but he must have thought I was lying, because he kept asking the same question until I burst into tears and turned red, then blue, at which point he seemed to have his answer and left me alone.

Today we had another briefing session with our Case Officer, Savo, a wily little bureaucrat with a hairy face and a thick neck. I wish I'd paid more attention while I was at Ed, then I'd know what the deal is with Sirius and Earth. All I remember is that we're somehow connected and that their Moon once belonged to us. There was a song they taught us in Preliminary Ed that explained the whole story, only I can't remember the words.

Anyway, whatever is happening to Earth, the Dogon are expecting us Sirians to help sort it out. Their planet seems to be going through some kind of major upheaval – the climate has become totally chaotic and is going from bad to worse. Savo talks very fast so I may have got a few details wrong, but he says timing is everything – like for instance, we can only make the journey to Earth when our smallest sun, Po Tolo, is closest to Earth's Sun, which is about now.

Xnake sat at the back of the room throughout the whole briefing, scowling and spitting. He waited until the end before tackling Savo.

'I'm going to need to see these new recruits' casefiles, Savo.'

'Look, you might be reinstated as a pilot, Komrade Xnake, but that information is on a strictly need-to-know basis,' maintained Savo.

'I get that, pen-pusher, but I "need to know" about the crew I'm taking with me to Earth. Seems like this job is more like babysitting. I'm used to working alone; I don't do well in a team situation. And if I have to, I pick my own guys. I don't want some dumb furry creature, a wimpy third-grade bot and a moody female chameleonoid who doesn't know the first thing about risk management!'

'Like you have a choice,' Savo muttered under his beard.

At which point, Xnake stepped forward and swung for Savo's head with one of his tentacles. Savo leaned sideways and the tentacle clipped the edge of a door, slamming it shut and sending a loud gong-like echo down the corridors of the Sirian High Kouncil.

'Get out,' hissed Savo, 'before I fire you.'

'Don't I need to sign something first?' Xnake retorted, trying to play the bureaucrat at his own game.

Savo closed his eyes and pushed a scroll towards him. Xnake unrolled it, spat a gob of inky saliva next to his name and, flexing his tentacles, slid out of the chamber.

*

Denser than iron,
Po Tolo, our small black sun,
Heals like pure mono ...

*

Zep just sent me the latest datafile about Earth. It is full of holograms of a once-beautiful, verdant planet with a completely messed-up magnetic field being bombarded by photons and asteroids from interstellar space. On the surface, this is causing volcanic eruptions and earthquakes everywhere, as well as freak weather systems. Just like Savo said, it's total chaos. There's a place called Atlantis near where the Dogon people live, whose ruler knows they might not survive these extreme changes in their climate and is considering abandoning their city altogether. Most of the galaxy now regards everything inside the Solar System's asteroid belt as a no-go area and only the Trojan fleet, who are based on a planet called Europa near there, will go anywhere near Earth. There are even concerns that increasing coronal mass ejections from the Sun could lead to all-out nuclear war on Earth, just like the one that destroyed the surface of Mars the last time their solar system went through such changes.

I hate to admit it, but this mission is even more risky than I'd realised. I don't reckon much to our chances of survival on Earth, let alone getting back to Sirius in one piece. But deep down I know there's a reason they picked me; I have a part to play on Earth, and I think it has to do with my ability to shapeshift.

Disk VI

THE LAUNCH

Today's the day. Ma woke me up early with a special bag of snacks she's made for me, enough to 'last the whole field trip', she said. I'd only ever eat her snacks as a last resort, but who knows, I may find myself stuck in some place with only sho balls to eat, when even Ma's cooking would be a comfort. The bag reminded me I still needed to replace the mono we took from Ma's pot.

It wasn't until I was saying goodbye to Yuri, Tsygan, Dezik and Laika that I felt a sudden pang of guilt and sadness. Why was I doing this? What was I trying to prove? Could I count on Uncle Jainko not to tell Ma? Was this Xnake guy to be trusted?

'Pa would be so proud of you, Kam, getting this Elite scholarship when you've not yet come of age,' enthused Ma. 'He always said you were a restless spirit thirsting for adventure, just like him. So, he'd be thrilled to know you've settled down now and are taking a more sensible path. Have a wonderful time, my dear, be nice to Aum and Zep, and remember to eat properly. Now off you go! This is your last year of Ed. You don't want to be late.'

It was the most touching speech I'd ever heard Ma give. Even at my birthday party she didn't say that much. I gave her a big hug and kissed her bald pink head. Laika walked all the way to Ed with me, holding my hand and trying to get me to skip with her.

'Kam, you will come home, won't you?'

Laika was too young to even remember Pa, but she'd heard all the stories.

'Don't worry, Laika, I'm coming home,' I said, although at that moment I wasn't quite sure what or where 'home' really was.

I waited until she'd disappeared into class before I headed off in the opposite direction, to En.Ki HQ.

*

Xnake stood at the bridge flexing his tentacles as we climbed aboard the Vimana 5.0. He looked like he'd either hardly slept the night before or had downed too much mono.

Flicking his double eyelids open and shut a few times, he cleared his throat and slurred, 'Drop your kit over there – we'll sort out hammocks and lockers later.'

Our pilot obviously wasn't in the mood to give us a proper 'new crew' welcome. I noticed a large bruise on one of his tentacles. Savo was standing outside the craft, awaiting orders. He eyed Xnake suspiciously and started making some notes.

'So, newbies,' Xnake sneered as we strapped ourselves into our seats, 'I hope you're prepared for the boredom of space travel; the V5 might have the most advanced propulsion system, but 8.6 light years is still a shedload of space to cross. We have drugs to put you into semi-stasis if you want, or you can stay awake for the whole of the journey. Your choice. Semi-stasis is not recommended for small mammals, though.'

'I'd prefer to stay awake, for Aum's sake. And anyway, semi-shutdown is not an option for Zep, because of his recent AI upgrade,' I informed him.

'Suit yourself, but I'm opting for semi-stasis,' Xnake announced airily, turning to the control panel. 'Savo, we're ready for the off.'

'You go when I get the order and not before,' Savo replied testily, stepping aboard to hand us each a travel pack.

As he stepped out again, the V5's port whisked shut and a high-pitched droning noise started up. Xnake bunged some plugs into his gills. We covered our ears until Aum showed us we'd all been given earplugs in our travel packs.

-Good job we can telepath now, Zep thought, and I smiled back. Aum was looking agitated, so I picked him up for a cuddle.

Xnake bellowed at Zep to 'get going on the goo', and within a couple of minutes the vimana lurched violently upwards.

With Aum curled up in my lap, I stared out of my visor as we rose through the dirty Nyan Tolo stratosphere and out into the silent haze above.

Disk VII

THE JOURNEY

T HERE'S NO POINT IN counting time in Nyan Tolo days when you're travelling through space, so we're logging our progress in GTUs – galactic time units – instead. The last thing Xnake said before he conveniently put himself to sleep was that time isn't linear, and I need to get used to it.

We've clocked up 500 GTUs of space travel so far. That's equivalent to exactly 20 days on Mars, or 20.8333 Earth days, because Earth rotates a bit faster than Mars. I think that GTU should stand for gross tedium units, because it is spectacularly dull. I wish now I'd opted for semi-stasis like Xnake. Not only is the journey boring but the interior comfort and the catering standards on this vimana leave a lot to be desired. I never want to sleep in another fibre-gel hammock, and I've eaten enough sho balls to sink an intergalactic battleship. Aum has had to run healing protocols on me several times after I ate one of Ma's snacks, and there are strange smells emerging from the Urine Extraction Unit.

We'll be entering the Oort cloud soon, when Xnake says we'll be in for a bumpy ride. From this distance, it looks like a whitish fog surrounding Earth's Solar System, but it's actually a load of rocks, asteroids and space junk. It's been cool watching the stars rearranging their relative positions as we hurtle through space. Zep says the V5's navigation system totally relies on them: each star emits its own unique sound signal and light stamp and all stars are either expanding or contracting, apparently. Kind of like breathing.

We're not sure yet if Xnake can telepath or not. He must have quite a strong Blocker fitted, because Zep can only pick up his thought patterns every now and then, when he's in a lighter stasis cycle. He has a recurring, quite angry thought pattern about someone called Meth. Whoever that is, he experiences strong emotions about it. He also thinks about the illegal scalar weapon he's brought with him. I haven't seen it yet, but Zep says it's bigger than Uncle Jainko's. Let's hope he isn't tempted to use it.

*

Things must be bad because Xnake has brought himself out of stasis and is hissing and cursing into the comms equipment on the bridge. Not long after we entered the Oort cloud, the V5 lurched abruptly sideways to dodge an asteroid in its path. I went up to the bridge where Xnake was running his tentacles over the controls and rapidly scanning all the screens.

'What's up?' I asked sleepily.

'Can't connect to Base Control anymore. Guess that means we can do what we like. Fancy a little side trip?' he quipped, but I knew he probably wasn't joking.

'I'd rather stay on course for Earth if you don't mind, Sir,' I said, trying to keep my voice steady. He rolled his eyes and turned away. It was only then that we realised Aum was unconscious.

'What's the use of a healer that goes comatose at the first sign of trouble?' scoffed Xnake when we reported the situation.

'Give Aum a break! I'm sure it's just a side effect of his slow metabolism, that's all,' I protested.

'Shame you don't all have a slow metabolism,' Xnake muttered moodily. I could tell by the sheen on his skin that he was starting to lose it.

'Let's give Aum a shot of adrenaline, Zep,' I suggested, deciding it was best to just ignore our pilot for the time being.

There was another violent sideways jolt. I stumbled and crashed into the galley. As I slid onto my knees, I could feel strange vibrations coming through the deck of the ship – not bombardments exactly, but a powerful sort of electromagnetic buffeting of the outer shell. When the V5 locked onto a passing rock and flipped through 180 degrees, I must have passed out.

Disk VIII

THE DRACO

I REGAINED CONSCIOUSNESS HOURS later to find we were through the Oort cloud and now passing Neptune and Uranus. Both planets looked as if they'd been dragged sideways and had massive storms brewing, because their axes were tilted differently to what Zep's datafiles show. Xnake claimed it's a side effect of being bombarded by powerful cosmic rays from the galactic centre, but Zep isn't so sure.

As we drifted past Neptune's outermost moon, Zep got an SOS message and asked me if he should report it to Xnake. I told him to wait and see if it happened again. It did.

Xnake made him transcribe the message word for word, and when he saw that it contained the words 'Agartha Outpost', he practically jumped out of his skin.

'OK, crew, we need to go down there.'

'Our itinerary didn't include this side trip,' I said stroppily. 'Who's down there?' I enquired.

'It's a distress call from an old komrade of mine.'

Xnake instructed the vimana to change course and we plunged abruptly towards the surface of a moon called Proteus. I was expecting us to land, but instead Xnake made the ship hover above the surface in 'oblique' mode. Once he'd got a visual on his stranded friend, he piloted the V5 closer to the moon's surface and beamed down a powerful shaft of ultraviolet light. As we peered down into the deep gaseous gloom below, without warning, a charred figure was thrust upwards into the craft and landed beside Aum. I gasped and even Xnake reeled a little at the sight of his mostly dead komrade.

'Get to it, Aum,' he ordered and went back to the bridge to close the hole in the floor. We rolled the figure over. He looked in a pretty bad way. It was a ghastly sight to see so much burned flesh, but Aum instinctively seemed to know what to do, paws working away to heal the skin bit by bit.

Once Aum had repaired the guy's skin somewhat, we could see that he was not in any way Sirian or even hominid, if indeed this was his natural skin colour. He had dark-green limbs that faded to a pale yellow across his chest, and his back was scaly, not unlike a lizard, but with large octagonal plate-like folds of skin that lay flat against his back. When Aum laid him on his back he seemed unable to flip himself over, and we had to help him up. He was much smaller than Xnake but considerably taller than me. Xnake patted his komrade on the back and offered him a line of mono, but he declined, so Xnake helped this friend into his hammock and gelled him in.

'OK, back on course,' Xnake barked, waving a tentacle in Zep's direction.

'Should I report that we've picked up a passenger, Sir?' he asked tentatively.

'Negative.'

*

Komrade is hurt bad
Hard to heal bad soul, sore paws.
Meth evil Draco.

*

The atmosphere aboard the V5 has changed since we picked up Xnake's komrade. Even though he's been sleeping the whole time, everything seems much more tense. I hardly noticed the majestic flyby of Saturn until there was some turbulence as we passed through its outermost ring. I had been moping in my hammock all afternoon, peering out of my visor at the skeins of gas and debris arcing away from us and encircling the planet, and at the spaceships coming and going from a weird pentagonal opening in Saturn's north pole.

But I knew the exact moment the scaly guy finally woke up, because the background buzzing in my ceph suddenly started up. He claims he's over six hundred years old, which I don't believe for one minute. When I asked him his name, he said it was Methuselah Beltane, or Meth for short. Is this the same person Xnake has angry thoughts about? He kept staring at my face like he recognised me, and for some reason kept trying to impress me or get my attention. When I took no notice, he went up to the bridge and now he mostly plays hex with Xnake to pass the time. Zep asked him what he liked to eat and he said 'fresh female hominids – especially ones with blue eyes' and laughed. He's making me really edgy, but there's nothing I can do about it.

I don't think Aum likes him either, because he was supposed to continue the BAP – Burn Aftercare Protocol – for another few days, but he's stopped it. Aum won't have anything to do with cannibals, as it's against his belief system. Technically a Draco eating a hominid wouldn't count as cannibalism, but Aum is sticking to his principles.

*

Zep telepathed me urgently while I was dozing.

-*What is it, Zep? This better be important – I was enjoying that sleep.*

-*I got an alert from En.Ki saying there's an escaped prisoner somewhere around these parts.*

-*Is that all? Have they only just realised Xnake's piloting this mission?*

Meth sidled up to us as if he could tell we were telepathing. He has this creepy way of appearing from nowhere.

'What's up with you two?' he asked nonchalantly in his scratchy voice.

'My sponsor is warning us to stay away from an escaped convict,' Zep reported.

'It'll be the Trojan fleet stirring up misinformation. They patrol the whole area between Jupiter and Mars.'

'You mean the asteroid belt?' I asked. Meth raised his eyebrows.

'Who's been doing their homework, then?' He eyed me like I was I was some kind of juicy fruit and I recoiled. Zep started reciting info from his datafiles.

'Several races have strongholds in the asteroid belt. Most space travellers think the dangers involved in traversing it are to do with colliding with a stray rock, but En.Ki regards this area as a war zone.'

'Is that how you got stranded on Proteus?' I asked Meth.

'You could say, blue eyes.'

I stared hard at him, holding his vile gaze.

'You think I'm a loser, don't you, Kam?' Meth said mockingly as he tried to stroke my arm.

I pulled away and blurted out a stroppy comeback.

'That's because you *are* a loser.'

*

I woke to find a state of commotion on board the vimana. Zep was screaming in some AI language that just sounded like numbers and Aum had erected a full-on force field around himself that was blazing red at the edges. I had no idea why until I saw that Meth had Xnake pinned to the floor, the ends of his tentacles flailing around. Alarmingly, I could see that the plates on Meth's back had started to protrude and form into weird hexagonal flaps that looked like wings. Behind him, Xnake's krate had fallen on the floor, its crystalline contents strewn all around Xnake's tentacles.

I stooped down to pick up one of the crystals, but Zep telepathed to me.

-Don't touch them, Kam, they're radioactive. The whole place is.

-What happened?

-Meth and Xnake had a fight.

-About the crystals?

-I'm not sure.

Meth could obviously tell we were communicating, because he backed off Xnake at that moment and his wings subsided back into shoulder blades.

'Nothing to see, kids. Just an old score to settle between two old rivals,' he sneered.

Xnake didn't move. He appeared to have been knocked unconscious.

'Ship's under my command now,' Meth said airily, moving up to the bridge.

Disk IX

THE TROJAN

O UR VIMANA, NOW RED-HOT with radiation, must have been emitting an automatic mayday signal that was picked up by someone from the Trojan fleet, because they messaged Zep: '*Immediate status and destination required to avoid interception*'.

I convinced Zep not to report this message to Meth and told him to only tell the Trojan ship the make and model of our vimana, its point of departure and our destination. The ship's commander – someone called Nazar – told Zep they were under orders to put our V5 into 'toxic limbo' and call for backup.

Aum gave us iodine shots to prevent us from getting radiation sickness. When Meth asked what we were doing, I told him we were taking vitamins. Meth laughed and left us to get on with it.

'What about Xnake? Should we give him iodine too?' I suggested, yawning.

Aum shook his head and Zep put the rest away. The iodine was making me sleepy. Zep checked in again with the Trojans.

'*Backup arriving shortly,*' came the reply. The last thing I remember was Xnake stirring and edging over to Zep.

'Sure you know what you're doing, co-pilot?'

'Yes, Sir.'

That was the first time I saw Xnake smile.

*

When I came around from my iodine stupor, the vimana was in full toxic limbo and the Trojan ship had taken over control of all its operations. Unaware of what was happening, Meth was jabbing at the control desk and cursing.

Zep silently relayed to me the message he'd just received:

This is Commander Nazar, a pilot with the Trojan Paramilitary. After detecting a severe radioactive leak in your vicinity, I have been ordered to entrain your ship, impound her on Mars and detain all crew members at the Valle Marineris

prison camp, pending further investigation.
The Sirian High Kouncil has just confirmed to me
that your ship is being piloted by Xnake Rapza, who
is on record as being banned from active service. We
also have reason to believe that Dracos may have
tampered with this vimana. Are you carrying any
reptilian specimens or radioactive cargo?

Zep's datafiles stated that Valle Marineris was a scar deeper than The Crease, spanning a third of Mars' circumference, gouged out by directed energy weapons during the Great Martian War, which destroyed half the planet's surface and its atmosphere completely. Most of the Martian reptilian population was killed, and the few who survived, unable to live on Mars' devastated surface, either dug deep beneath the surface to survive or else relocated to Earth. I bet Meth was one of them.

Disk X

THE PRISON PLANET

I'VE BEEN SEPARATED FROM the others because the prison is gender- and species-segregated. The Martian ground staff seemed to regard Aum as extremely dangerous and shoved him in a cage as soon as we disembarked, right before they gagged and handcuffed the rest of us.

At first it was a relief to set foot outside the vimana after all that time, but I'm now locked up in another tight space with not enough air. My cell appears to have been carved out of the sheer red rock this planet is made of, just like the hangar where we arrived. There is no door, just a force field that's so painful on your nervous system I'm not going anywhere near it. Even crouched in the back corner of the cell with my spacesuit on, I can still feel it stinging my skin. They only drop the field to pass food in, which mainly consists of some green sludge and cloudy water. I haven't taken a single mouthful in two days because Zep keeps messaging me not to touch anything. So, I'm just sleeping as much as I can. And having weird dreams.

I know that voice … it's Pa!

His hair is greyer than I remember and there are lines around his brown eyes now.

Pa is telling me he has something he wants to show me.

Where is he taking me?

Pa, what are those green circles?

Pa calls them his 'crop circles'. I've always loved it when he chuckles like that.

As we walk closer, I realise the green circles are shallow tanks of green algae.

I turn to Pa to ask him about them, but he's gone.

*

When I woke, a woman was in my cell staring down at me.

'What's your name?' she demanded.

'Kam Urdinak,' I rasped, retreating to the far corner of my bunk.

'Urdinak?' she barked, as if she was deeply suspicious of anyone by that name. When I didn't answer, she tried another approach.

'I'm Commander Nazar. Were you on the vimana I brought in?'

I nodded, still avoiding eye contact.

'You look too young to have been recruited to an exomission.'

I hugged my knees and said nothing.

She moved a little closer, peering at my face, her voice quieter.

'How did the Draco get aboard your vimana, Kam?'

I shrugged and turned to face the wall.

'Don't be afraid – I can help you,' she said gently, sitting on the edge of my bunk. She reached forward and turned my chin so she could see my face.

'Oh!' she gasped, 'You have incredible blue eyes…'

A gaping silence opened up between us. Nazar seemed lost in thought; her dark eyes looked hollow but ruthless under her grey fringe, like those of a soldier who's seen too much but is forced to carry on regardless. She sighed and told me that both Xnake and Meth had managed to escape and that she needed me to tell her anything I could about the connection between them.

'I have no idea how they know each other.'

'Listen, Kam, your bot Zep is being examined by the Martian Military and your little creature Aum is currently in quarantine. Things are not going too well on Earth, and I know you're headed there, am I right?'

I nodded.

'It's a pretty dangerous mission you seem to have got yourself mixed up in. Look, I want to help you, Kam. But you need to help me, too.'

Eventually I relented and told her that Xnake had stopped to pick up Meth from Proteus. She thinks they must have barged through the force field guarding the entrance to their cell. I could tell Commander Nazar felt responsible for their disappearance and that by befriending me she thought she'd be able to get out of trouble. I still wasn't sure if I could really trust her, but when she said she'd contacted the chief vet on Earth's Moon and was arranging to get Aum released for me, I decided to cooperate. For some reason, she's also offering to be our pilot for the last leg of our journey to Earth if Xnake can't be found.

'Why do you want to go to Earth if it's not a good place to be right now?'

'I have some unfinished business there. Someone I really care about, someone who is like a son to me, has gone missing. I lost my own child to radiation sickness when I was a civilian living on Europa. After he died, to take my mind off the grief and heartache, I signed up to become a pilot with the Trojan fleet. But I can't bear to lose another loved one. I have to find him.'

When Nazar said this, for some reason I started to hyperventilate. The gills on the sides of my neck began to open and a vague memory of Ma's yam stew drifted into my mind. I pictured her hand stirring the pot with a wooden spoon and a tear started forming in the corner of my eye. Is this what being homesick feels like?

Disk XI

THE MOON BASE

NAZAR MIGHT HAVE SUCCEEDED in piloting the vimana, with Zep's help, to the Moon, but she forgot to tell us where to meet her after getting through toxicology. Being a Trojan Commander, she went through the 'Military Personnel' channel, which only involved a quick debrief by Moon Security instead of the four-hour grilling I got. Aum, Zep and I were all sent to different parts of the spaceport. Aum was taken straight to the Moon's quarantine unit as Nazar predicted and, because of the lizard shapeshift on my Profile, I had to go through the reptilian channel. Just before they took me off to toxicology, Zep telepathed me tersely.

-Kam, just do what they say.

The scrub-down afterwards was the worst thing I've ever experienced, and I have raw red weals all over my skin to show for it. Plus, they shaved my hair off, so now I'm completely bald, like Ma and Pa. Zep's was more of a mental scrub-down; they've basically wiped his entire memory. Nazar told us this might happen, so as a precaution she made a backup before we left Mars and stored it on the vimana's operating system.

There are some pretty weird-looking characters here in Arrivals, I can tell you, which is just as well, because I look pretty weird now too, without my red hair. Everything from analogue to digital, simian to reptilian, biped to milliped. They seem to have abandoned the idea of providing furniture, as there are too many different body shapes and sizes to deal with, so everyone is just standing around. There's a kiosk serving food and drink, but I don't have any means to pay, so I just gaze at the rows of imported beverages with names like 'Etheria Extract' and 'Rhesus Negative Power Shot'.

*

Moon and more bad news.
Heal a human, called kernel.
He's up to no good.

*

Zep and I have to appear in court tomorrow because we arrived on the Moon without our preassigned pilot. Nazar thinks it'll just be a formal warning, but it could be worse.

She told me that the Moon is a totally covert base, where all the facilities are located on the side facing away from Earth, so that everyone on Earth thinks it's uninhabited. No one is allowed up to the surface without express authorisation, and there are armed Draco guards stationed at all the exit hatches to the surface to make sure you comply. So even though we're within spitting distance of Earth now, I still haven't seen it with my own eyes.

The architecture here is all a bit basic, like they hollowed out the underground corridors in a hurry. There are masses of coloured tubes running in all directions loosely tacked to the ceilings of all the tunnels, which are lined with grey concrete. It's quite dimly lit, so I might have been imagining it, but as we were walking to Nazar's dorm, I think I caught a glimpse of Meth disappearing down one of the tunnels. Just the idea of running into him again makes my skin crawl.

Disk XII

THE GIANT

THE OUTCOME OF OUR court case was that we got off with a warning. But we were told that if there were any further deviations from our specified mission plan we would be instantly dismissed and sent back to Mars. Zep says we should stick to the script from now on. I've started to wonder if this is what happened to Pa: did he get caught improvising? Is that why he didn't come home when his last contract should have ended?

Now for the Mission Briefing. On the way into the Hall we were all given mission packs but told not to open them. The mission leader is a giant called Captain Tehuti, who's from Earth and who was apparently brought up by priests in Atlantis. According to Zep's En.Ki datafiles, Tehuti was initiated into the weird and powerful Black Sun brotherhood, which is some kind of secret underground organisation a bit like Black Khanus, only more extreme. There are also rumours going around that Tehuti controls our mission sponsor, En.Ki. Does that mean he's Pa's boss?

Whoever he is, Captain Tehuti is the first giant I've actually seen in the flesh. He's really, really tall. If I stood next to him, I'd feel like a little kid, because I'd just about come up to his waist. No wonder the Briefing Hall ceiling is so high. He has a very impressive, low-frequency voice that you just seem to feel in your chest rather than hear through your ears, and he has a way of casting his eyes around the room like a bird of prey so that when he looks in your general direction, you feel like he's about to devour you.

'Do I make myself clear?' Captain Tehuti's voice boomed inside my chest.

Lots of heads nodded vigorously. He seemed to want an audible response from his rather dumbstruck audience.

'OK. Open your mission packs now. On the first page you will find your arrival location on Earth.'

There was a lot of shuffling of hands and tentacles. I opened mine up. On the first page it said in bold capitals: ATLANTIS. I felt a strange fluttering sensation in the pit of my stomach. Wasn't that the city near where the Dogon people come from? All the recruits started muttering to one another, comparing notes on what locations they'd been given.

'SILENCE! There is no time for questions. Make sure you read your packs thoroughly and complete your health checks before reporting to the main hangar at dawn tomorrow. And for your information, there will be no passcodes to watch the Earth eclipse from up top later. The surface remains strictly out of bounds at this time. That will be all. Everyone except the Sirian unit is dismissed.'

Unsure why we'd been singled out, Zep and I lingered at the back of the Hall until everyone else had left. I scratched my bald head and waited until Captain Tehuti beckoned us forward impatiently and tapped the wall behind him. Maps started appearing that looked as if they'd been drawn from memory, or like illustrations in the Sirian Sagas I used to read to Laika. Finally, he stopped at one map in particular of a circular city that sat like a giant blue eye in the midst of a vast plain, with mountains to the north and sea to the south and west. He made it larger by gesturing with his huge hand in front of the wall. I noticed he had six fingers.

'So, my young Sirian recruits. You have been assigned Atlantis. This is one of the most unstable and volatile of all the mission locations, currently experiencing hurricane conditions which are blowing in toxic volcanic ash clouds as well as creating a high probability of tidal waves. Your unit has been selected because we need a small crew who can communicate non-verbally and change their form if needed, and are capable of coping with any issues, medical or otherwise, that might arise. Your combined chameleonoid, telepathic and healing skills will be vital if you are to succeed in Atlantis. Due to various recent calamities that I won't go into now, the whole city is in the process of evacuating. Be aware this is not an easy first posting.'

Captain Tehuti paused expectantly and eyed each of us in turn.

'Since your original pilot Xnake has – true to form – failed to report for service here, your mission will continue to be piloted by Commander Nazar. Your vimana is in the process of being refitted with gold exterior cladding, to be able to enter Earth's atmosphere. You will make landfall *here*, where the Dogon people live; their chief issued the mayday call to the Sirian government,' he said, indicating a range of mountains to the north of the city of Atlantis. 'You are to make contact with the Dogon, then proceed into the centre of Atlantis to make a detailed assessment of the current situation. Ensure the whole city is empty of inhabitants and then report to En.Ki's Atlantean headquarters *here* within seventy-two hours,' he said, pointing to a large facility on the outskirts of the city. 'Once we are satisfied with your report, you will be briefed on your next assignment. Do I make myself clear?'

I nodded, but it all felt far from straightforward. Captain Tehuti cleared his throat with a deafening rumble, turned his back on us and strode off the podium in two giant steps, stooping slightly to exit through the door at the back of the Hall.

*

Zep went to check if our vimana was ready, and I was walking back to Nazar's quarters on my own when I heard someone sneaking up behind me. I turned round and there was Meth, leering and panting slightly. So gross. I was trying to think of an excuse to get rid of him, but he didn't waste any time getting friendly with me.

'Hey, blue eyes, look at you with no hair. How about I make you a tempting offer?'

I was trying to play it cool by ignoring him, but he persisted.

'I know a way to get up to the surface to see the Earth eclipse.'

I know it was stupid, but I jumped at the chance. For one, you have no idea how claustrophobic it is down here, and for another I can't bear the thought that I'll have been here two weeks tomorrow and still won't have been up to the surface because of all the rules and regulations. Plus, I absolutely *love* eclipses. I'd stay up all night on Nyan Tolo to watch them with Pa when I was little. So, don't judge me, but I agreed to go with him.

Meth led me through a maze of tunnels, explaining that we had to get to the other side of the Moon to be able to see the eclipse properly. I was starting to doubt his intentions, when we reached a hatch that was being guarded by a pair of lazy Dracos. Meth flashed them his ID and they just opened the hatch for him. I guess it's because he's a Draco too, so they don't care. I followed him up the long metal ladder and he offered me his claw when I got to the top. The Sun was already starting to disappear behind what I assumed must be Earth. To be honest, it didn't look like the pictures I'd seen, because the side facing us was in deep shadow, so it looked grey rather than green and blue. The Sun edged further and further behind the planet until it was completely covered up and there was just a glow around the whole perimeter of Earth. It was only then that I looked around me at the dull dusty surface of the Moon, now bathed in a deep, gloomy twilight.

It would have been a really special experience if only Meth hadn't ruined it by draping a limb along my shoulder just as the Sun started to bleed round the opposite side of the Earth. I could feel his slimy breath right next to my ear as he stroked my bald head, and then, much to my horror, I started to shapeshift into the blue reptile. Unfortunately, this not only seriously impressed Meth, but it also made him think I was actually interested in his creepy advances. That was when he moved in for the kill, and I don't just mean that as a figure of speech. He actually meant to do more than kiss me. He was going to eat me, his teeth bared and his saliva dripping. In my state of abject fear, I felt myself turning into electric slime. It must have hurt to have all that voltage passing through his body. I oozed away and left him smoking like a bushfire as the Sun slowly re-emerged.

-*You don't mess with Kam Urdinak*, I screamed at him in my mind as I regained my biped form and ran off.

*

Meth attack my Kam!
Hear her crying, I can heal.

Put curse on Meth too.

*

I don't know how I managed to remember my way back to Nazar's dorm, I was in such a state. I didn't want her to see that I had been hurt, so I stopped at a vending machine and, using the token Nazar had given me, got a karton of Etheria Extract to numb the pain. It did more than that: within minutes I was practically hallucinating that I was in someone else's body. Kind of weird, actually. Perhaps it was because I'd just stung Meth, but it was like my arms and legs didn't belong to me. Maybe you shouldn't drink that stuff if you're chameleonoid.

When I walked in, Nazar was taking her weapon apart and putting it back together again, checking each component carefully. She paused and inspected me closely with her hollow eyes, like I was also part of her weapon.

'So, we got Atlantis. That's good. Did they mention anything about Agartha to you at the briefing, Kam?'

'No. But now you come to mention it…'

'What?'

'Well, I don't know if it's just a coincidence, but "Agartha Outpost" was Meth's callsign.'

'You mean the Draco that ambushed your ship?' Nazar shot back, looking suddenly stressed.

'Yes, that Draco. Why? What is Agartha?'

'An underground stronghold deep inside Earth where the Dracos are hiding out. The boy I'm looking for is lost somewhere down there.'

Disk XIII

THE VET

IN THE END I decided to tell Nazar what happened with Meth. She gave me a bit of a lecture about avoiding Dracos 'like the plague' and then lent me a navigation device to find my way safely to the quarantine unit to get Aum.

The vet's receptionist looked as though she'd been expecting me and asked me to follow her into the restricted area behind her desk. I could see Aum in the corner of a dirty cage, looking a bit distressed. There was an untouched bowl of reconstituted vegetables and a bowl of murky water. I opened the cage door and Aum climbed out and onto my lap for a cuddle.

'Can I speak to the chief vet, please?' I asked the receptionist. She nodded and went off to find him.

The vet's name was Colonel Askew and he had the same shocked reaction as Nazar had when she first saw me. He stared at my face and scratched his silver hair, and seemed at a bit of a loss for words.

'I've got to ask, um, d-d-did you know that this creature is a rare fennec fox, only f-f-found in the Atlas m-m-Mountains on Earth?'

'No, I didn't, actually.'

'If you don't m-m-mind my asking, how did you c-c-come to own him?'

'He was a present from my Pa.'

'And where is your p-p-Pa, my dear?'

'I have no idea. He never returned home after his last contract ended.'

'I see. Where is "home", exactly?'

'Nyan Tolo in the Sirius System.'

This answer seemed to make Colonel Askew more curious.

'I see. Indulge me for a m-m-m-moment, would you? I've only ever known two other people with b-b-blue eyes like yours. What is your name?'

'Kam Urdinak, Sir.'

There was a long silence.

'Did your Pa ever m-m-mention that he worked in Atlantis?'

I shook my head.

'Do you know who he was working f-f-for?'

'I believe he worked for En.Ki, Sir.'

Colonel Askew seemed to relax a bit then and began to open up.

'Well, k-k-Kam, there are some things I need to tell you. You might be surprised to know that I worked with your p-p-Pa on a research project in Atlantis. We were hired by En.Ki to develop and field-test some new Atlantean t-t-technology and, in the course of our work, your Pa and I unfortunately lost track of one of our assets. In an effort to locate him, we sought the advice of some mountain tribesmen called the d-d-Dogon.'

'I am familiar with the Dogon people,' I said, not wanting to give too much away.

'Is that so? Well, much to my delight, we travelled to their village by c-c-camel, an even-toed ungulate or dromedary, cleverly adapted for desert conditions with a well-developed hump on its back in which it stores water. M-m-marvellous creature. Anyway, where was I?'

'You said you went with Pa to see the Dogon?'

'Ah, yes. We rode out of Atlantis under cover of d-d-darkness, into the mountains, finally arriving at the village at nightfall. The camels were exhausted. The Dogon tribesmen were very tall, dark-skinned people wearing cloaks, hunched round a campfire. They somehow knew we were coming and when they saw your Pa's Sirian cloak and ancestral m-m-m-markings, they bowed down low and invited us to sit with them. Your Pa slid off his camel and we were given some animal skins to sleep in and a strange dark b-b-brew to drink that made me throw up most of the night. But as we lay looking up at the stars, the wind b-b-blew stronger and the tea gave your Pa visions, Kam, p-p-powerful visions, which he shared with the Dogon. Some of them seemed f-f-frightened by his words, but their elderly Chief, a stooped man with wizened skin, sighed deeply and began to d-d-draw in the sand with his staff.'

Colonel Askew paused and asked his receptionist for some water. He reached into a pocket for a small pouch of mono and took a couple of pinches. I had a million questions I wanted to ask him, but I didn't want to break the spell of his story. It was the first time I had heard anyone talk about Pa's time away from home. He had never spoken of the work he did on Earth. I always thought it was because things had happened there that he was trying to forget.

'Now, what was I s-s-saying?'

'About Pa and the Dogon…' I urged him gently.

'Ah, yes. I have no idea what it was he drew in the sand, b-b-but it had a profound effect on the tribesmen, as if they had arrived at an important d-d-decision. They said over and over again, "It is time, it is time".'

He paused again and looked at me carefully, as if hesitating.

'That's not all. I have s-s-something that one of you should have.'

'One of us?'

Colonel Askew unlocked a cupboard behind him and took out something wrapped in cloth. He unrolled it on his desk, revealing a deep-red crystal. When he handed it to me, a powerful buzzing energy began pulsing outwards from my heart and for a few seconds I had the sense I was connecting into a vast energy field.

'This crystal was one of your Pa's f-f-favourites. It's red j-j-jasper. I think you should have it.'

'What does it do?' I asked. I handled it gingerly, wondering if it was radioactive like the crystals Xnake had been scavenging for down in The Crease.

'It's supposed to give you psychic p-p-protection, it is useful for anyone facing new b-b-beginnings or endings, it helps with survival instincts and d-d-dream recall and anyone who wants to make ch-ch-changes in their life. I think it has a kind of homing instinct, Kam. Maybe it will help you f-f-find your way when you're down on Earth.'

'Thank you. I will take good care of it. But Colonel Askew, there's something I need to ask you: where is Pa now?'

'Well, you see, that's the thing. First, we lost t-t-track of the asset we call "Leon", but now En.Ki has also lost track of your p-p-Pa. After that night in the mountains, I returned to the lab and haven't heard from him since.'

There was a lump in my throat. Aum moved closer and the red jasper buzzed faintly against my fingers. A vivid image of Pa's friendly face appeared in my mind's eye, and it was as if he was trying to tell me something. I closed my eyes and clutched the crystal tighter to sense things more clearly. I knew my skin was starting to turn blue, but I couldn't do anything about it. I felt as though I was part of a triangle of energy being pulled towards a much larger energy field that was coming from somewhere on Earth. Who was this Leon and where was he? If I found him, perhaps I would find Pa too.

THE SPHINX CODEX

(PART 2 OF LEON'S STORY)

Tablet X

TUNNEL VISION

W HEN LEON ESCAPED FROM the base on the first
day of Paoni, I seized my chance to return to my
Trojan ship, which I'd hidden in a cove near the ocean,
several stadia to the west of Atlantis.

There was chaos at the base as Meth tried to work
out how Leon had disappeared, and if it was just another
disappearing trick he'd pulled, or if he'd really gone. With
Meth, everything is blame first, lash out, extract the truth,
move on to the next victim. I knew my turn was coming
and I didn't like what the other prisoners had told me
about his torture methods, so I fasted for two days, and on

the third morning waited until my daily 'fresh air break' and, instead of taking the riser to the surface, I decided to risk doing something Leon had taught me. It's taken me weeks to master the freeze-time thing he does and even now I can only do it momentarily when I've eaten no food for a day or two, but I knew I'd only need to maintain the timelock for the few seconds when the guards open the gate, then I could slip out behind them and head for the tunnel that Leon and I went down the time I took him to the ocean to check on my ship.

Knowing how quickly they figured out Leon was missing because his things were gone, I'd taken nothing with me except a canteen of groundwater. The tunnel system is dark and complex, and you need to tune in to microchanges in smell, dampness and air movement to navigate your way around. There are very few visual cues other than the marks other people have left on the rough walls, and these repeat but make no sense, so are completely unreliable. I kept telling myself, 'Nazar, it doesn't matter, you don't need to remember the way back, you're never going back there'. But it was hard to keep going deeper and deeper underground, not knowing if I'd ever reach the surface again, especially for a pilot who is used to running missions in the vastness of space, where the only things you needed to avoid running into are comets and asteroids. I tried to tell myself this was just a different kind of dark void, an internal one. After a couple of hours of virtual darkness, I decided it wasn't worth trying to see where I was going and shut my eyes and experienced the tunnel system like Leon, blindly groping my way along, encased in my own thoughts, with just my own breathing for company.

After a while, behind the close weave of my breath, I could hear a deep rumbling, rolling sound that convinced me I was getting closer to the ocean. At the next intersection I turned left, and the sound grew in volume, its texture dispersing into a series of thumping pulses. Air moved in stifling swathes over my face as I turned back down the tunnel, and if I turned to face the other way, it felt slightly cooler. I continued towards the cool air, imagining it was coming straight off the ocean and that soon I'd emerge to see my Trojan ship standing there on the sand just where I'd left it. My orders had been to infiltrate Atlantean society unnoticed, gather intelligence and relay it back to the Trojan fleet. Not only had I failed on all three counts, but I had been captured, tortured and identified. Everything else had been a disaster, and my reputation as a respected Commander had almost certainly been destroyed by recent events. The only good thing that had come of my time on Earth was meeting Leon. So why was I going back to Europa without him? Why was I going back at all? What did I have to prove?

I blundered on. The tunnel floor started to fall more steeply and sometimes I found that, without meaning to, I had broken into a slow trot. There was a new sound, a dripping. A crack in the tunnel wall was seeping groundwater. I pushed my canteen up against it and refilled the container. I ran my fingers over the wet, greasy surface of the tunnel wall and smeared it over my face, turning back to let the cooler air dry my skin. There was a fungal smell. I opened my eyes and here and there I could make out luminous mushrooms in the darkness, pale and delicate, growing out of the crevices in the walls. I stopped to pick one. I sniffed it cautiously, aware of my grumbling stomach, and then stuffed the whole thing into my mouth. There was a small plant growing next to it, and I ate that too. Suddenly I was overcome with hunger and my knees felt wobbly. I sat down and zoned out. I have no idea how long I was sitting there, but when I became aware again, I was lying face down in the tunnel. I stood up and felt all the blood rush to my head. It was as if someone was twirling me round and round. If the tunnel had not been sloping, I would have forgotten which way I was supposed to be headed.

A stomach-ache grew into a spiky beast inside me and, a few stadia further on, I threw up. I washed my mouth out with a swig from my canteen, and staggered on, my limbs weak and shaky. I realised it was the first time in my life that I was not acting under orders; I was in survival mode, just like they taught me on Europa at the Trojan training camp: 'Nazar, survival is a selfish act'. But behind this thin veneer of selfishness, there was another motive, a deep heartache. My training told me I had to find my ship and get away from Earth, but a deeper, more personal longing to find Leon was pulling me in the other direction.

Had Leon stumbled this same way? Had he sniffed out the potent mushrooms and greedily consumed them, just like me? Was Babi still with him? Instead of thinking of my ship in the cove, I began to visualise myself tracking his route, and each time a choice came up when the tunnels split, I tried tuning into Leon's consciousness and going the way I thought he would have gone. I told myself that, no matter what, I had to keep going, afraid that, if I were to stop and rest, he would get too far ahead of me.

*

My walking had slowed, and I noticed the tunnel floor was rising slightly. The rumbling too had changed: it was now more rhythmic and almost mechanical, plus the air was drier, fresher somehow, although it was still virtually pitch black. I blinked and tried to force my eyes to see a little better. The floor seemed to be cleaner, like it had been swept. I bent down to touch the surface and, as I did so, felt something slide across my hand – a snake. I gripped it firmly and stood up. The snake writhed against my wrists, trying to wriggle free. I was struck by the fact that this thing was alive, like me. It must also have found access to food and water, or it would not have survived down here. Then it occurred to me that the snake was a source of food for me if I could find a way to kill it, just like I'd shown Leon. But that was on the base, where I'd had a weapon and light to see by.

Then I remembered my Trojan leader telling us during training about the slots in the soles of our standard-issue boots – there is a blade concealed in the right boot and a pill in the left. I reached down to examine the sole of my right boot, feeling for the rectangular area with the fingernails of one hand as I continued to grip the snake with the other. I managed to peel away the rubber cover and pull out the slim ceramic knife. It was barely as long as my little finger, but it was immensely sharp. I brought it slowly towards the snake, aiming for its soft underside, and drew the blade along it in a line. The snake hissed and thrashed, and I could feel its cool blood trickle along my arm until the creature became limp and I relaxed my grip.

Perhaps drawn to the smell of the snake's blood or the sounds of it resisting my attack, at that moment something came scampering along the tunnel. The creature made a soft cackling sound and, as it came closer, I saw a blur of grey fur in the almost total darkness and a little pink face. Could it possibly be Leon's baboon? I called to the animal, realising that I must smell different now with the snake's blood on me. The creature crept cautiously towards me, and then leapt onto my shoulder, moving its hands playfully over my nose and mouth. I smiled.

'Babi, it *is* you! Where's Leon?' I whispered.

She jumped down and I followed after her, still holding the dead snake.

Tablet XI

———

STASIS GIANTS

T HE BABOON SEEMED QUITE adept at navigating the immense tunnel system. I followed, hoping that she had a better idea of her whereabouts than I did. She seemed to be bringing us closer to the source of the rumbling, because it was getting much louder. The tunnel also felt much more spacious in this section. I reached out my arms and could no longer touch the walls on either side. This made me feel nervous for some reason; I had got used to the false sense of security that the narrow tunnels gave me. In addition, the roof was getting much higher over our heads. Babi ran from side to side, rising halfway up the wall on one side and gathering momentum, then skipping across to the opposite side in a wide zigzag. I was having to run just to keep up with her but was brought to an abrupt stop when the baboon suddenly shrieked and stopped dead at the tunnel mouth. My stomach lurched as I stared down into a vast cavern. The space was lit by glowing specks of light that covered the cave walls. Down below, I saw massive creatures moving. They were thickset bipeds, lumbering to and fro. I realised the heavy footsteps and low murmuring voices of these giants were the source of the rhythmic rumbling sounds I'd been hearing, not the ocean.

Without pausing, the baboon clambered down the cave wall and I watched as she moved across to where the creatures were clustered. Pointing in my direction, Babi started chattering to the giants, excited about my arrival. There was no sign of Leon amongst them. I stood there panicking, wondering what the giants might have done with Leon, unable to decide if I should take the cowardly option and go back the way I had come or confront them now. Before I'd made up my mind, one of the giants moved across to the rock below where I was standing, reached up and lifted me down. It was terrifying, but I was powerless to do anything about it. The giant's fingers pressed into my ribs as it clutched me in its fist. When it brought me up to its face to take a better look at me, its breath stank. I stared back until it put me down on the rock and patted me on the head, as if I was a small child. Then it noticed I was holding the snake and indicated that I must hand it over. I bowed, hoping the giant would think it was a gift. The giant looked approvingly at the limp snake and withdrew.

Babi brought me a hunk of something strange and lumpy to eat and sat beside me while I tried to decide if it was edible. Although my hunger was intense, my need for sleep was even stronger. The warm, fetid air of the cavern and the sound of the giants murmuring was quite soporific and somehow I nodded off.

*

I woke to find I had been placed into some kind of coffin and someone was closing the lid on top of me. In a state of panic, I pushed back against the underside of the rough carved surface and managed to lift it open a crack. It seemed I was being taken out of the main cavern into a smaller side area. I waited until the box was still before trying to lift open the heavy stone lid again. It took all my strength to push it open enough for me to squeeze my way out. Looking around, I could see there were rows and rows of similar boxes – actually stone sarcophagi – all twice as long and twice as wide as my own body, some with lids firmly on and others off. Most of the open ones lay empty, but there were some that contained bodies, and as I looked more closely I could see they were giants, all snoring in unison, their jaws slack and their mouths open to reveal double rows of teeth and their hands, each with six fingers, clasped across their chests.

Not wanting to disturb these slumbering creatures, I crept to the mouth of the cavern where there was more light. It seemed to be coming from luminous specks in crevices in the rock walls. I could hear someone singing, a magical angelic sound rising above the deep drone of the giants' voices. It wasn't the only thing rising up: the sound seemed to be lifting all the small rocks and stones in the cavern off the ground, where they hovered motionless in mid-air. I followed in the direction of the singing and came into another cave flooded with a luminous blue lake. The water was warm, and I walked into it fully clothed, sinking down until I was totally submerged. When I came up for air, I heard laughter.

'What you doing, Naz?' a voice asked.

I spun round in the water, and saw Leon standing at the edge, Meth's black sword dangling from one hand, his head cocked on one side looking highly amused.

'Leon! You're alive!' I clambered out and tried to give him a hug.

'Too wet!' he protested, pushing me away, perhaps remembering the incident by the ocean.

Babi ran around our ankles as I tried to get some answers from Leon.

'What happened?'

'Ran away like we plan. Find big ones sleeping. I tired too. Fell to sleep.'

'Then what happened?'

'Babi wake all up. Big ones angry like Meth. I go bubble, wait see.'

I assumed Leon meant he had put himself in a timelock.

'Good idea, Leon. What did the giants do?'

'Big ones take my white crystal, now I mad too. I fight like this with Meth sword.'

Leon proudly demonstrated his swordsmanship.

'And?' I asked, edging away from the weapon scything through the air.

'I win. Big ones friendly now. Get crystal back. See?' He gave me a quick flash of the selenite crystal in his pocket. I laughed, imagining his triumph at winning the strange little battle he'd just described.

'Well done! I'm so happy I've found you, Leon.'

He beamed at me and grabbed my arm.

'Come, Naz – meet Jentilak.'

He walked off singing, and it was only then that I realised it had been Leon making the beautiful angelic sounds. I don't ever remember him singing when we were on the base, apart from the time I took him to the crystal beds.

It seemed Jentilak was the leader of the giants. He surveyed me with a curious disdain at first, just like the giant who'd picked me up, only this one kept his distance. He had dusty grey skin that hung in folds around his neck. Along both his forearms were huge open sores and burns and on his hairless chest he wore a snakeskin necklace, which I realised he must have just made from the one I'd killed and given to him. He saw me looking at it, pointed at the necklace and then at me and bowed his head in thanks and approval. I felt as though I had been accepted, and started to relax a little. Leon seemed completely at ease, sitting on the giant's foot and playing a clapping game with Babi, and I realised I'd never seen the child happy like this. Jentilak eyed him fondly and I was still taking it all in when suddenly Jentilak's booming voice rang out and echoed around his cavern. It was only when he brought his large eyeball level with mine that I realised he was speaking to me. He spoke in a guttural, resonant language similar to ancient Lemurian. I could only make out a few words:

Fire within. Water flood. Rock move. Humans die.

Tablet XII

AGARTHA OUTPOST

I SOON GOT TO experience at first hand the scale of the problem they were dealing with. I'd seen eruptions on Jupiter and experienced earthquakes on Europa growing up, but nothing could have prepared me for experiencing an eruption from deep underground and at such short range that my eyebrows and eyelashes were totally singed.

Jentilak walked slowly in front, his two brothers bringing up the rear, as we went to inspect the source of the intense heat. It was only when I saw the bright orange magma seeping out of a gap that had opened in the floor of the cave, that it occurred to me I was now several stadia into the crust of the Earth and beneath us lay only molten rock, which would find its way through any weakness, any rupture.

As a monstrous tongue of lava made its way towards us, I watched in awe while Jentilak and his brothers attempted to change the direction of its flow with large slabs of stone they'd brought with them, the molten rock hissing and spitting. Having got used to the dimness of this subterranean world, the intense orange glow was mesmerising, golden yellow at its brightest and cooling quickly to a hot grey sludge at the edges, forming into creases and folds as it pushed its way along the tunnel. They succeeded on this occasion in stemming the flow and blocking its route, sending it off down another tunnel that led away from their lair, and returned triumphant but exhausted, their arms red raw. Now that I knew the cause of the burns, I had a new level of respect for these giant creatures.

*

Judging by the petroglyphs and paintings on the walls everywhere, it seemed the giants had been down here for a very long time – centuries, if not millennia – driven underground by vengeful enemies, forced to lie in wait until such time as they would be tolerated again on the surface. I got the impression from Jentilak that they regarded Leon's unexpected arrival as a sign they should commence their return. They are some kind of builder race, responsible for constructing huge megalithic temples, walls and strongholds on the surface. Jentilak must have been born in an era before the Lemurians, before the Earth's surface iced over completely and they were forced to hollow out all these underground tunnels and caverns to live in. The petroglyphs show that the giants survived a previous catastrophe, despite regularly coming under attack from Draco factions who also dwelt below ground, while the humans on the surface were virtually wiped out. My guess is that, without the help of this ancient builder race, humans would not have been able to come back from the brink of extinction and create new civilisations like Atlantis. Now it seems everything is under threat all over again.

I understand now why the Trojan fleet is on high alert, why there is such a tense atmosphere out in the asteroid belt, and why there is so much talk of the need to redevelop the prison facilities on Mars. No wonder I was sent to do undercover surveillance of Earth. Meth knew I was a spy, but it's only now that I've been able to gather any intelligence that the Trojan fleet will find useful. However ashamed I am of messing up this mission, I need to get a message to them. I need to return to my ship urgently and tell them it's time to intervene. Earth might be about to bear the brunt of this catastrophe, but it also means our whole solar system is vulnerable.

Jentilak is feeling this sense of urgency too. He told me in stilted words that the giants must now return to the surface via an old trade route that will bring them out in

Khem, a place a long way east of Atlantis, where they are needed to complete a long overdue building project. I had been planning to take Leon with me, but Jentilak insisted Leon must go with them.

'Leon is kahuna, is wizard,' Jentilak explained patiently as he chewed a hunk of rock in his double row of teeth. 'He sing, he lift rock.' Jentilak picked up another piece of rock and held it in the air to demonstrate. 'Leon!' he commanded.

Leon flashed a smile and obliged us with a beautiful high note. When it reached a crescendo, Jentilak let go of the rock and it stayed suspended in mid-air, only dropping to the floor of the cave when Leon's voice faded.

Jentilak got up and took me to see an elaborate circular calendar that he'd drawn on the cave wall to explain the unfolding of events from his perspective. I could see that he had a totally different sense of time than me, having lived for millennia. To the giants, Earth had now reached a part of its cycle that required action on their part; a key turning point that their ancestors had faced many times and, if handled right, heralded the beginning of a proud new era, which Jentilak called 'the Age of Leo'.

Pointing to one section of the circular calendar, Jentilak became quite emphatic.

'Leon is lion, he is sign for Age of Leo!' Jentilak insisted, pointing at a picture of a lion crouched on its haunches, which represented the constellation Leo marked in the sky above its head. I nodded. Then he pointed to a drawing of three triangles on a horizon, adjacent to the picture of the lion. Jentilak pointed at the triangles and began making a sequence of gestures with his big hands, counting the tasks off on his six fat fingers.

'We pack up, go to Khem, finish pyramids. Leon sing, make energy flow, then water rise,' Jentilak assured me, thumping his fist on the ground and making me jump.

From what I could tell, the giants' job is to encase these unfinished pyramids in white stone, so they are able to capture, store and emit energy, giving humans on the surface a way to survive the Earth changes and a place to keep their precious records and artefacts safe. The timing of these tasks is linked to the rising of Sirius in the eastern sky and the flooding of the River Khem, which runs past a vast statue of a lion that the giants also built.

I could see there was no way Jentilak was going to let me take Leon back to Europa. But I could also see that coming to live with me was no longer what Leon dreamed of, either. He had found his niche with the giants and he was happy. Although it saddened me, I actually felt quite proud knowing he now had a purpose and a tribe. Maybe my idea of adopting him was crazy anyway. I'd got used to losing a child once before, so I suppose I could get used to it again.

*

Cutting short what little time we had left together, while Leon and I were sleeping, a rebel Draco faction descended into the cavern on fine cords like dark, silent spiders. By the time Babi raised the alarm and woke everyone up, the Dracos had us surrounded. The giants were incapable of moving quickly, and so it fell to Leon, Babi and me to attempt to take control of the situation. At first, none of the Dracos had noticed us among the giants, so we had the advantage of surprise. In addition, both Leon and I had experience of dealing with angry reptilians, and these rebels were neither as skilful nor as canny as Meth, so it was not going to be difficult to outwit them.

Leon told Babi to scale the wall of the main cavern up to the tunnel mouth where I had arrived. The baboon obligingly ran up and crouched at the top, taunting the Dracos until a small group of them started firing in his direction. When they had expended most of their ammunition, I attracted their attention and lured them towards the luminous lake.

Dracos don't like water, so all I had to do was wade into the lake until they were taking aim at me from the water's edge, and that was when Leon came from behind them brandishing Meth's sword. There was an awkward moment as one of the soldiers leapt forward and tried to grab the sword. Leon tussled hard, and Babi came to his rescue, clambering up the soldier's back and wrapping herself around his face so he couldn't see.

Leon then ran into the tunnel that was now blocked by the most recent lava flow and put himself into a 'bubble', as he calls it, to wait for the Dracos to come after him. But something that none of us could have foreseen ruined Leon's quick thinking: the surface of the lake started to ripple and bubble and, out of nowhere, an octopod rose to the surface and wrapped a tentacle around me, preventing me from escaping. The Dracos turned back to the water and started firing at me and the octopod. Hearing me struggling for breath, Leon tried to push past them to get to me. I sank underwater to avoid their ammunition, but soon realised that the octopod was the Dracos' primary target, not me. And now I was in its clutches. Wriggling hard against the octopod's tight grip, I managed to get my head above water. Leon stood knee-deep in the water and let out a mighty roar, while Babi, picking up on his stress, ran up and down the water's edge, cackling manically.

'Just go, Leon! You have to go with Jentilak, don't worry about me,' I spluttered, just as one of the giants grabbed Leon in one fist and Babi in the other, at which point the octopod made a revolting noise and regurgitated a whole pile of crystals in front of the Draco rebels. This seemed to be the real reason for their invasion and they started scrabbling on the ground, trying to gather up as much of the sparkling haul as they could. While they were distracted, Jentilak gave the signal and the giants departed with Leon and Babi, leaving me to fend off the octopod myself.

The movement of so many heavy footsteps put further stress on the surrounding rock strata, and soon the giants' thundering feet were drowned out by the creaking and groaning of the Earth. Slowly but surely, the bottom of the lake started pushing upwards, taking me, the luminous water and the octopod with it.

THE DOGON SCROLLS

(PART 2 OF MEL'S STORY)

Scroll VIII

HOME

W HEN THE SUN COMES up, we pause our journey into the mountains and rest. No one is in the mood to eat. Miss Mel sits beside the elephants in silence, watching the first rays of light fall across the marooned city of Atlantis, now far below us. The houses look like tiny boats drowning in a huge sea. As the Sun rises higher, we can make out families huddled on the roofs, gripping onto chimneys or clinging to each other for dear life. The Temple in the middle of the Palace grounds is the only building left that's above sea level.

'Everything is flooded, Mama. What will Grandpa do

if our house is flooded too? How will he get up on our roof, Mama? Can you see him?' frets Mintaka between bouts of coughing, as she stares hopelessly at the scene of devastation that was once her home.

I cannot answer her. Nor can Miss Mel. I don't have the heart to tell my daughter that my father most likely drowned in his sleep. It feels like my insides have also been torn apart by the earthquake – just like Atlantis – and now there is a tidal wave of tears inside me. It is taking all my effort to keep them at bay. I must not cry. Mintaka has enough to bear without seeing my grief.

*

The Sun is setting as we enter my childhood village after travelling all day. The Dogon Chief is there to meet us. Miss Mel is exhausted and Mintaka is coughing up blood. She desperately needs to rest. None of us has ever walked so far. Not even the elephants. Nor have we ever witnessed anything as shocking as our whole world falling apart. Seeing Atlantis being engulfed by those huge waves was utterly devastating. I can't help thinking if people had listened more to Miss Mel's nightmares and predictions, none of this would have happened.

I help Miss Mel down from Elisha's back and the Chief leads her into the Togu Na – their meeting hut. Elijah trots in behind us. It is dark and smoky inside. The Dogon Elders sit around the edge of the hut, passing around a steaming gourd of tea. All I can see is the white markings on their foreheads. The Dogon Chief invites Miss Mel to sit with him on the raised platform in the centre. He speaks to her in Atlantean. First, he expresses his condolences. He tells her that the Dogon people knew that bad things would happen. He tells her it is time.

'I believe you're right, Sir,' Miss Mel murmurs. 'We've come to seek safety here among the Dogon. My life is in danger; the same person who killed the King and Queen also wishes me harm. And now that Pa has gone too, there is no one left in Atlantis I can trust.'

'I understand. You should know that two men arrived a short time ago seeking our help, just like you – a Sirian scientist, who we've helped before, and a zoologist who also works for En.Ki. They were looking for someone else with blue eyes, just like you.'

'Who were they were looking for?' Miss Mel asks softly.

'A boy called Leon.'

Miss Mel is silent. The Dogon Chief carries on speaking.

'The changes that are afoot will affect not just your life, nor even just the people of Atlantis, but the whole world. We must all seek a place of greater safety.'

Miss Mel nods.

'The scientist – where did he go?'

'He went to look for Leon in Agartha, a place deep underground. He said that if he failed to find Leon, he was going home.'

Miss Mel looks devastated. She walks away and stands in the entrance of the Togu Na. She looks down into the valley below. The sky is turning a deep dusty pink over what little remains of our once beautiful city. Suddenly Miss Mel breaks down in tears and I go to comfort her. She wipes her eyes and is silent for a long time. Then she whispers to me.

'Listen, Saha'Ra. If Pa planned to return "home", he did not mean En.Ki or Atlantis, did he? Home to Pa means somewhere much, much further away and much closer to his heart. Home means Sirius.'

Miss Mel turns to face me, her blue eyes clear and intense.

'I have nowhere that I call home, not like Pa. I know that Atlantis is not my real home. And yet the people of Atlantis, whose home it is, are now forced to leave. We are all homeless, we are all refugees. I need to help us all find a new home. That's what Pa must have meant about finding my way home when he gave me the crystal!'

She is shaking from head to toe. She grabs my hands, like she does whenever she is excited about something.

'Don't you see? I need to make sure we carry out King Atlas's plan for the New Atlantis. I am the one who needs to lead the Atlanteans there. I will be their queen from now on!'

*

Today a few brave Dogon men went down into Atlantis to rescue any survivors from the flood and bring them up into the mountains. My father is not among them. Mintaka is still hoping she will find him, but I know he didn't make it.

*

It is now three days later and we are preparing to leave the Dogon village. Altogether, the Chief has calculated there are no more than a thousand of us making up the caravan of Dogon and Atlantean people: men, women, children, horses, camels and elephants. Everyone is in mourning. Only the Black Sun priests will stay in Atlantis to bury the King and Queen in the Temple of Enesidaone. No one wants to leave, but we all know we have no choice. We have all seen the ground shake and the storms getting worse. The Dogon people also know that this is not the first time. A long time ago, our ancestors fled too. And because of that, they survived.

As we are about to leave, Miss Mel tells me about the dream she had last night. She was standing in front of a big statue of a lion. Behind her were three huge pyramids. She was facing the same way as the lion statue, towards the sunrise. The Sun had not yet come up, but she could see a bright star. There was a huge crowd around her. She said everyone had been waiting for that star.

'Saha'Ra, the star was Sirius, Pa's home star!' she says excitedly. 'It's a sign, don't you see? And there was a statue of a lion. I think it's a sign we are going to find Leon. Wherever this place is, that's where we are going to find him and Pa.'

I can only hope for her sake that she is right.

*

We are making our way slowly east. It is not easy walking so far each day in the fierce wind and heat. Miss Mel and my daughter Mintaka are riding the two elephants. I have no more mono to give to Mintaka and I am worried she is getting sick again. My people are frightened; the women wail in despair while the men walk in silence by their sides, trying not to show their fear. Only the Elders and their Chief, who lead the caravan, walk with dignity, but I know their hearts are just as heavy.

We camp each night and the Elders keep watch. We have few possessions and not much food or water. When there is water to drink, we stop. Or if we find anything growing. Eating leaves and even soil is better than eating nothing.

Miss Mel is having visions all the time. She tells the Dogon which way they should go, what lies ahead, and where there is water. At first they did not believe her, but they soon found out that she was right every time. Like the Queen's soothsayer, she can see into the future.

Tonight we have camped by a small lake. I am sitting on the ground next to Miss Mel, unable to sleep. She tells the Dogon the place is not safe, but the people are tired, and the Dogon Elders decide to stop anyway. Mintaka is curled up in my lap. I hear a low rumbling sound in the distance, like thunder or animals' hooves. It gets louder and Mintaka moves closer to me. Miss Mel sits up straight. She stares into the darkness. The edges of the lake start to shudder. Then there is a deafening noise and in an instant, the water sinks into a deep hole. Suddenly everyone is awake and on their feet. There is a lot of shouting and before long we are on the move again.

When we reach the pass that leads into the next valley, the Dogon Chief comes up to Miss Mel, who is riding Elisha. He reaches up and gives her his carved staff. Then he bows and says,

'I humbly beseech you, Princess Mel. We acknowledge you as our supreme guide and leader. Your knowledge is our protection, and in return we will protect you. You are our Queen now.'

Miss Mel bows her head and graciously accepts the Chief's staff. When he walks away, I see he is limping. He is very frail now; I don't know if he will survive the journey. I don't think Mintaka will, either.

Scroll IX

STAMPEDE

SOME DAYS, WHEN MISS MEL lacks the energy to see into the future, we find that our way is blocked. Deep cracks have opened up in the ground or new ridges have formed where before there were none. The Dogons' ancient trails no longer exist and they have come to depend entirely on Miss Mel's sense of direction. Without the well-worn nomadic paths, the ground we are walking on is rough and painful.

Every night there are terrible sounds like animals dying. But the sounds are not coming from any creature – it is the Earth itself groaning because it is being ripped apart. Often there is a shimmering red or green light in the sky. The Dogon women think it means the Nommo are coming back, but I don't believe the myths anymore. No one is going to come down from the sky and save us. We have to save ourselves. That's what Miss Mel says.

Tonight, the groaning is so loud that no one can sleep. We have set up camp on a ridge and the Elders are keeping watch. They sit in their cloaks, passing round their strong herbal tea. The Chief sees that Miss Mel is still awake and invites her to join them. When the tea comes around to her, Miss Mel takes a slow sip like the Dogon.

'What does the Queen see?' one of them asks softly.

Miss Mel closes her eyes and is silent for a few minutes.

'I see sand billowing up near the western horizon, like a dark wall, and the ground around us is starting to shake, the rock becoming liquid and flowing downhill, folding all the trees and bushes into itself as a dark, unseen force moves up the valley. I see a thin orange line appearing, engulfing the hillside as it splays out like a giant fiery tongue. I hear the sound of many stomping, stampeding hooves moving in the same direction as the sandstorm. A huge army of terrified animals is coming in our direction.'

Suddenly, Miss Mel stumbles to her feet, confused about what is real and what is a vision. She points to the horizon.

'Look, they are already here – we must go quickly!'

The Elders look up in alarm and begin to gather their belongings. We can see a cloud of dust coming towards us. Our own animals can sense something is very wrong and are becoming restless. Suddenly, hundreds of fleeing elephants, buffalos, lions and gazelles are upon us. They are running for their lives, shoulder to shoulder. There is pure fear running through their bodies. Some of our animals bolt with them. Elisha looks confused, sniffing the air anxiously with her trunk, while Elijah cowers between her legs, trying to suckle her for comfort. Many of our people are crushed underfoot as they try to get away from the panicking animals. The stampede is united by one idea: to find solid ground. Just like us, they have been thrown into a state of confusion and were forced to leave their homes.

*

Our whole world has been turned upside down. It's horrendous. Half our people have been trampled to death, but there is no time to stay and bury them. We just fold their arms across their hearts, close their eyes and leave them where they lie. It feels all wrong. As we leave, birds of prey are already gathering in the scorched branches of nearby trees, waiting to feast on their bodies. It breaks my heart.

Those who have lost loved ones are begging Miss Mel to let them stay and wrap them in shrouds and perform their funeral dances. But even the Dogon Chief insists that in the present circumstances, we must break with tradition. Sadly, Miss Mel agrees we have no choice but to move ever onwards.

Miss Mel's visions have become a heavy burden that she struggles to understand. The Elders know that she has visions whether or not she drinks their tea. A few nights ago, she woke to tell them that the valley where we'd camped was about to crack open, which of course it did. We could feel the heat from the lava burning our backs as we hurried away. No one could run because our feet were too sore.

This morning, Miss Mel asks me to come with her to talk to the Dogon Chief. He is washing his face and arms in a stream. The bottom of his cape is wet and his face is streaked with the white paint of his tribal markings. He stands up stiffly and smiles at us. Miss Mel wants to show him something. It's the black crystal her Pa gave her. Shaking, she places it in the Chief's gnarled old hands.

'My visions make me afraid to sleep, Chief. Is my ability to see the future because I have this?' she asks him. He slowly turns the crystal over and closes his eyes.

'This is a powerful obsidian, Queen Mel,' he murmurs. 'My mind is weak, but I can tell it is charged with ancient energy. The keeper of this crystal is more blessed than most mortals. Use it well.'

He hands it back to her and bows deeply. Then he suddenly collapses in the shallow water. We try to help him up, but he has passed out. Despite his frailty, his wet robes make his body heavy. I call to the Elders and eventually they help Miss Mel and me lay him down beside the stream. We have no mono left to revive him and there is a storm brewing. As lightning flickers on the horizon, we manage to make a rough shelter over where he lies. Soon there are rocks, hail and ice bombarding the ground, making circular hollows all around us. There is nowhere for our people to shelter from the storm so they cower on the ground like wretched animals.

When the hailstones stop, something else falls from the clouds. It is a swarm of reptilian drones. They circle around us like huge vultures, as if they know the Chief is about to die. The drones land and a band of Draco rebels armed with scalar weapons start rounding up the few hundred of us that are left. But Miss Mel refuses to leave the Dogon Chief's side, and she begs Mintaka and me to stay with her until his last breath.

Elisha and Elijah know the exact moment the Chief passes and begin to wail. The Dracos keep their distance but their weapons are pointed straight at us. Miss Mel stands up with tears streaming from her blue eyes and confronts them. She holds the Chief's staff out in front of her to try to stop them coming any closer and scans their faces. I know she is looking to see if one of them is Meth.

Menacingly, they start coming towards to us. Elisha rears up on her hind legs and Elijah copies her. When Miss Mel realises they are about to shoot her baby elephant, she cries out.

'Please, spare him. Take me. I am the one Meth wants.'

Scroll X

GOLDMINE

T HE REPTILIAN GUARD ON duty at the mine-head stops when he gets to Miss Mel and cracks his whip. She is waiting in line in front of me. He stands very close to her and leers in her face.

'I've heard good things from Meth about you, blue eyes. I could do with some of that, too.' Then he pulls her out of the line and pins her arm behind her back.

'The rest of you, get to work!' he yells and walks off with her. There is nothing I can do.

This has been going on for weeks, but I am just a slave like all the rest of the survivors. Every morning since we were captured by the Dracos, we have been forced to go down that dark mineshaft. All you can hear is the clanging of tools – no voices. It's so hot and the supervisor barks orders all the time. Each slave is given a hammer and a basket. We hack at the rockface for hours. There is nothing to eat and only the dirty water they give us to drink. I work most days beside a skinny black woman in filthy overalls. She is not that old but she has calloused hands and broken teeth. I don't know what I am supposed to be scraping from the rockface, so she points to new areas I should work on, trying to be helpful.

While I am down there, Mintaka is lying in our shabby little hut with no medicine. I know that somewhere above ground they turn this rough gold ore we are scraping into pure monatomic powder. If only I could find a way to steal some mono for Mintaka. It's all I think about until the siren goes off and the slaves put down their tools and shuffle back towards the shaft. We are stuffed into the cage and hoisted back up. The woman in the dirty overalls stares at me and smiles. This is what passes for kindness in these dark days.

*

When I am reunited with Mel, her blue eyes are bloodshot and her lips are split and quivering. She doesn't say anything but when we get back to our tiny hut, she shoves a pouch of mono into my hands. I am too afraid to ask her what she had to do to get it.

I am thankful that the Dogon Chief did not live to see his people become the Dracos' slaves, forced to mine gold and satisfy their appetite for pleasure, while Dogons and Atlanteans alike are sick and dying. Disease is rife in the mining camp and many people are sick now, not just Mintaka. It makes me so angry to think that the valuable mono we are producing is just for the Dracos' own amusement and none of it is being used as medicine by people who really need it. Mintaka is not the only child wailing in the night. Miss Mel is not the only one to go without food in the morning. The elephants are treated even worse. The Dracos whip them mercilessly to make them drag the gold ore up to the place where it is turned into mono.

Mintaka is delirious with fever now. The mono Miss Mel got helped a little, but she needs more. I am praying every day for a miracle. Sometimes I think we should have stayed in Atlantis and died there along with my father. It's hard to recall life at the palace when we had everything: clear, fresh water, all the fruit and vegetables you could eat, all the comforts and delights – all now gone.

Miss Mel still has vivid dreams, but strangely they are now less fearful and more fanciful. They are all she has to cling on to. When she describes them to Mintaka, they sound like fantasies; none of them will come true, no matter how beautiful they are. Her last dream was about a shining object that came out of the sky and rescued us.

'Oh Min, it was so beautiful! It hovered above us in the sky and started sending down bright balls of light that danced across the surface of the lake, and the lake was full of crystal-clear water, which made a strange symphony of sounds, just like when we used to play the kamelan! Sparks of energy flew across the lake and seemed to suck up the water, making rainbow-coloured shafts of light that criss-crossed the space between the surface and the shiny object in the sky. It seemed to be making a kind of web out of the sticky shards of light, and when it had finished there was a lovely diamond pattern hanging in the air above the lake.'

'What happened next, Mel?' Mintaka pants softly. She is so weak and pale now. She hardly even opens her eyes anymore.

'Well, there was an eerie silence as the shimmering object in the middle of the lake began to change shape. And then a new energy filled the air, pulsing through all of us, so that we all felt it at once. Then the object in the lake began to open up like a flower and some beings emerged. One of them was a strange little furry creature with long ears who had healing powers. It won't be long now, Min, you'll see – they're on their way.'

I don't know how she can still have such hope. It breaks my heart to see her blue eyes lose their sparkle every morning when she wakes up and remembers we are just slaves now. By the time we are herded off to the mine-head, those big blue eyes are as dull and lifeless as the rest of us.

From: ian.clyffe@queensland.edu.au
To: camille.warden@ucl.ac.uk
Date: 20/2/22 06:11
Subject: RE: 'Operation Chameleon'

Dear Camille,

It is really very kind of you to persevere with a sad old sceptic like me, who has had a lifetime of being harangued by colleagues and the media because of my obstinate refusal to accept that climate change is entirely induced by humans and my constant questioning of their definition of the Anthropocene.

I was most intrigued by your last instalment of 'Operation Chameleon', particularly the account of Mel's flight across North Africa in search of the Nile valley. It is a poignant tale of human hardship, and I have to admit it had me hooked. The descriptions of rapid terraforming are consistent with what we have seen happening recently to a lesser extent along the New Zealand coast and in western Japan. It is a well-known fact that aviation authorities the world over are having to adjust the coordinates of landing strips on account of this constant tectonic creep.

I have done some background research of my own and wonder if the location of the City of Atlantis that these documents suggest is, in fact, the Richat Structure in Mauritania, otherwise known as the Eye of Africa, regarded by many geologists as a collapsed caldera. Based on current computer modelling of the probable extent of inundation of the Earth's surface, it would only take a modest tidal wave bearing a quantity of mud and debris to have completely deluged Atlantis and its surrounding plain in this location, leaving behind a vast barren area covered in sand and mud that later became the Sahara Desert. We know from other studies that the Sahara region once supported a temperate climate and verdant habitat. In addition, asteroid impact craters recently discovered as far apart as Greenland and Chile are now thought to have been the cause of rapid widespread flooding and freezing around the world, leading to the last mass extinction event, which roughly correlates to the presumed time frame of your documents: the end of the last mini ice age or Younger Dryas period, around 10,000 BCE.

The evidence you've now shown me has without a doubt given me pause for thought. It is remarkable to think that, if it were not for En.Ki's genetic experiments, we would not have any of this material. Not that I am advocating this kind of nefarious scientific endeavour – in fact, if this information gets into the public domain, human nature being what it is, the powers-that-be will inevitably seek to deny the technological implications of your findings and at the same time secretly look for a way to profit from them. I have seen this happen time and time again.

Your documents inspired me to re-read Francis Bacon's unfinished utopian novel 'The New Atlantis' as well as Plato's writings. He also wrote of the unexpected rapidity of events, whereby Atlantis disappeared in a single day and night. Having read your documents, this now seems much more plausible. One section from his dialogue 'Timaeus' seemed particularly pertinent:

'And when, after the usual interval of years, like a plague, the flood from heaven comes sweeping down afresh upon your people, it leaves none but you the unlettered and uncultured so that you become young as ever, with no knowledge of all that happened in old times in this land or in your own.'

It seems to me that your findings offer us a choice, Camille. We can either succumb once again to severe climate change and get left literally 'high and dry', to emerge – if we're lucky – to find nothing remains of the past. Or, we can pay heed to these discoveries and act on the profound insights they contain. I therefore think your idea of a trip to London is not a bad idea. Any further electronic communication might be unwise.

I have taken the liberty of booking a flight and will arrive on March 1st. I will be staying with my good friend Major Jonathan Edwards, curator of the Petrie Museum in Bloomsbury. Would you would care to meet me there at 6pm? Perhaps then over dinner you can show me the rest of the Sirian Disks and we can discuss what is to be done.

Yours,
Ian

THE SIRIAN DISKS

(PART 2 OF KAM'S STORY)

Disk XIV

CHAMELIENSIS

Z EP INFORMED US WE were over the landing site. The vimana descended slowly through Earth's atmosphere, which was a dense fog of dust and ash. When the portal in the floor opened up and the vimana projected its violet-white beam of light downwards, all we could see far below us was a vast expanse of mud. No sign of the Atlas Mountains or the Dogon village, no sign of any people, not a single living thing. Just slow-moving, brownish-yellow mud.

'This can't be right, Zep,' said Nazar, looking down.

'I've checked the coordinates three times, Commander Nazar. We are right where we should be, just north of

Atlantis, but I will check again if you want me to,' Zep offered. 'Wait, I have new instructions. We're being diverted to land in the centre of Atlantis now, directly in the palace grounds.'

After Zep changed the destination coordinates, the vimana began to skim over the sea of mud until eventually I could make out a circular roof with gold pinnacles standing proud of it. As the vimana dropped lower, I could see that the building occupied a patch of dry ground and told Zep to land there. Leaving Aum and Zep in the vimana, Nazar and I exited into the shaft of light, wearing our spacesuits for protection from the strange, unstable conditions. We found ourselves ankle-deep in sea-water in a courtyard in front of a ruined circular temple with tarnished silver walls. A huge tapering obelisk that presumably used to stand on a plinth in front of the building had been knocked over and lay in pieces. Waves lapped against the steps leading up to the temple and there was a lot of static in the air. Every so often there was a sharp surge of electro-magnetic energy that made my skin tingle, sending a pulse through my body and making the silver coating on the building's outer walls tremble.

The circular roof of the temple had fallen in and like everything else was covered in a thick layer of ash. There was a fountain in the courtyard full to the brim with dead birds and rotting vegetable matter. The whole place stank and was eerily silent except for a buzzing sound, which turned out to be clouds of insects feeding on anything dead or dying. There was nothing left of the palace gardens surrounding the temple except a vast inland lagoon. The ring of water that used to surround the royal compound must have flooded its banks, and all you could see of the ancient arboretum Zep had described to me were a few broken trunks and branches standing clear of the grey water.

I waded towards the temple steps. So much for the blue skies I'd been dreaming about; the sky above the temple was alive with weird rippling bands of green, red and purple light.

-What's going on up there, Zep? I telepathed.

-That is Earth's Aurora, Kam. Charged particles from the Sun are affecting Earth's atmosphere. It usually only occurs at the poles; something must be very wrong for it to be visible so near to the equator.

More concerned with what was going on closer to hand, Nazar drew her weapon and pushed open the ornate temple door. Inside there was a strange sickly smell, and on the altar lay two plain copper coffins, their lids lying open. Nazar peeped inside and then quickly backed away, gagging even with her helmet on, and waved her arms to keep me from coming any closer. Zep received another download, which he dutifully relayed to me.

-Bodies identified as Atlas and his wife. Deceased 21 days ago. Funeral abandoned due to severe earthquake. Air quality currently unsuitable for respiration, advise masks fitted with grade 9 filters. Risk of tsunamis in this area 80%. Risk of aftershocks 100%. En.Ki recommends immediate relocation to their Atlantean headquarters.

Even after a quick look at what remained of the Royal Palace, Zep's message made complete sense: for a start, all the guard posts around the perimeter wall had been long abandoned and the gates looked like they had been forced apart. The Hall of Records was standing open and had been stripped of all its contents; there was no sign of any books, scrolls or tablets – all that remained were the Atlantean laws inscribed on the stone walls, which were now turning green and slimy. Inside the palace, the kitchen was deserted but still had pots and pans on the cooking stoves and rodents were climbing in and out of them, looking for any remaining scraps of food. The sumptuous carpets in the banqueting hall were sodden with sea-water; it looked like a tidal wave had burst through, shattering the large windows and sweeping furniture into mangled piles in the far corners.

Nazar and I climbed the staircase up to the King and Queen's chambers. Laid out on a desk in the antechamber I found plans that the King had been working on, entitled 'The New Atlantis'. They showed a large, circular city, similar to how Atlantis must have looked before it was destroyed, with thousands of houses arranged concentrically with radial avenues intersecting them at all the cardinal points, like a huge wheel. Next to this the king's mapmaker had drawn a broad rectangular platform labelled 'power plant' on which he'd marked three squares of different sizes that almost lined up, but not quite. At the edge of this platform, facing east, was a small irregular shape marked 'The Great Statue of Leo'. An arrow pointing to its chest was clearly the main entrance, and another pointing to the side of its left paw indicated a smaller entrance. I pored over the drawings, wondering what their significance was, and on a whim, decided to take them with me. I rolled them up and moved on. The next discovery was the most shocking: entering the King and Queen's bedchamber and seeing the silk sheets stained with blood. They must have been killed while they slept.

We left the room in silence and climbed the last flight of stairs to the King's observatory, where precious telescopes, astrolabes and the remains of an orrery lay strewn in pieces. I noticed the King's robe was draped over a chair by the window. I picked my way through the debris to the window and stared out at the abandoned, ruined city. I turned as Nazar bent down to examine the shattered pieces of a blue orb from the orrery, which must have once been the Earth.

'Come on, let's go,' she muttered, 'I think we're done here.'

*

The wind had started to howl when we returned to the vimana and flew the short distance across the flooded city to En.Ki's headquarters on its northern edge. The building was like a bunker, with a landing area and an entrance on the roof. The lower floors were completely flooded, but the upper floor was dry and still had power.

It was a strange sort of set-up, with rooms in which there were human-sized cages, surrounded by testing equipment that looked a bit barbaric. There were rooms full of smaller cages containing various little mammals that had all now died. There was a storeroom full of different kinds of crystal, although none of them was like Pa's that Askew had given me. Nazar seemed very curious about these and began to open the chiller cabinets to take a closer look, but it was the office doors on the other side of the corridor that had caught my attention: one had a name plaque bearing the words 'Colonel Askew' and the one next to it said 'Dr Jainko' – Pa's old surname before he fell out with his brother, my Uncle Jainko, and changed it to Urdinak.

It felt strange pushing open the door to Pa's office. I tried to imagine him sitting at this desk, sending those few precious messages to us back in Nyan Tolo, asking how big Laika was and if I was keeping out of trouble.

I opened drawers, hoping to find something personal of Pa's from home that I would recognise. But I could only find files stuffed full of project notes, all kept in that haphazard but attentive way Pa did everything. There was one filename that caught my eye: *Kam-Mel-Leon*. I pulled it out and laid it on Pa's desk. My heart was thumping. Inside were detailed case notes about a strange-looking white kid called Leon Urdinak who scowled in every photo, and another set of notes about a gorgeous young black woman called Mel Urdinak. I hardly dared look inside the last section of the file, because it bore my own name: Kam Urdinak.

With a strange, unsettled feeling, I turned the page, expecting to find a case study about me, but it only contained one item: a picture of a baby with bright blue eyes and reddish hair, wrapped in blue silk. When I looked closer, it wasn't Pa who was holding the baby, but Colonel

Askew. And the room in the background looked familiar; it had been taken right here in the En.Ki lab, in front of a wall of medical equipment! I turned the picture over, and on the back was a date that I knew to be when I was born and the words 'Homo chameliensis 1.0'.

I didn't know what to make of it. Had Pa named me after this baby? Or had I been adopted here in Atlantis and the picture was actually of me? My mind ran in circles around all the possibilities. The baby certainly looked a lot like me. But the words on the back bothered me. I flipped back to the other two sections in the file, 'Leon' and 'Mel', to look for clues. In the Leon section, there were growth charts and the results of fitness tests, measurements, graphs, minutes of various meetings about the project, and a section marked 'field notes'. In the section labelled 'Mel' were accounts of several visits to the Royal Palace, a gilt-edged invitation from the King to attend a special banquet, and a copy of an employment contract for someone called 'Saha'Ra'. I flipped back to the field notes about Leon, which contained a top-secret specification document about an underground military base, some medical notes about some ongoing behavioural issues, and a page of Pa's scrawled handwriting that made me stop in my tracks: it mentioned the squadron leader of the underground base, whose name was Methuselah, and the fact that Leon's minder was someone called Nazar. Was the asset Colonel Askew said had gone missing and the boy that Nazar was looking for the same person: Leon?

'Nazar!' I yelled across the corridor. 'You might want to come and look at this.'

Disk XV

INQUISITION

"YES, LEON IS THE person I'm looking for, Kam. I used to take care of him when I was being held prisoner by the Atlantean Royal Guard. These must be the notes Dr Jainko kept on him. May I have a look?'

Nazar had a strangely excited look on her face. I passed her the file and she started scanning the pages. She could obviously sense I was scowling at her and looked up.

'Kam, I know what you're thinking, but I honestly had no idea there was any connection between Dr Jainko and you, otherwise I would have told you.'

'So, am I related to this Leon Urdinak? His last name is the same as mine. Is he my brother or a cousin, or what?'

'I don't know, Kam. I never knew Leon's surname. I only knew that Dr Jainko was concerned about Leon's welfare on the base and that everyone went crazy when Leon vanished. He was a bit of a handful.'

'Do you know anything about Mel Urdinak?'

'No, I've never heard of her… although now you mention it, there was one time when Dr Jainko brought someone else to the base for Meth to meet. A girl. Perhaps it was her.'

'I have another question for you, Commander Nazar,' I said testily, 'because this is all getting a bit weird, don't you think?'

'I know how it must look, but I assure you…'

'When you intercepted our vimana out in the asteroid belt, did you already know we had Meth on board?'

'I had my suspicions, which you confirmed when you told me his callsign was "Agartha Outpost". That was his nickname for the base.'

'What about Xnake? Did you get him thrown off as our mission pilot just so you could get back to Earth?'

'I was mixed up with him once before. But that's a whole other story.'

'I think it's time you told me it, don't you?'

'Look, everyone in the galaxy knows that Xnake is notoriously unreliable. I did you a huge favour when I took over as your pilot.'

'There must be a pretty good reason why he was assigned to us by the Sirian High Kouncil. They were adamant no one else would do.'

'I'm sure they had their reasons, but if I hadn't been in the area and intercepted your vimana, you'd never have got this far, Kam. You'd still be in a prison cell on Mars.'

Zep could hear our raised voices and came to see what was going on.

-*Is everything OK, Kam?* he telepathed.

-*Not really, no.*

-*Do you need Aum to do a healing on you?*

Aum brushed up next to me with his tail. I reached down and stroked him, feeling my heart rate drop a little.

-*Not now, thank you Aum. We've got to find Pa. I want to get to the bottom of this. I don't even know who I am anymore.*

I sniffed, feeling angry and sorry for myself at the same time.

-*Kam, don't forget we have a mission objective to complete,* Zep objected.

-*I know, but it's not my top priority right now.*

Nazar could tell we were telepathing and rolled her eyes.

-*Just tell me one thing, Zep – can Nazar be trusted?*

*

Kam feel confused with
Woebegone thoughts, dark ideas,
Taking their toll now.

*

I took the *Kam-Mel-Leon* file from Pa's office with me and we returned to the vimana for Zep to transmit our initial report to Captain Tehuti on the Moon. I asked Zep not to mention some of the personal information we'd found at En.Ki's lab in his report but he said that went against his 'transparency protocol'. I rather stroppily told him to get over himself, and when he said he didn't understand what I meant, I persuaded him to omit anything about Pa for now, until I figured out this *chameliensis* business.

The more I read of the *Kam-Mel-Leon* file, the more I began to see there was a connection between Pa's work here and me being chameleonoid, because, whoever they are, it seems that Mel and Leon are most likely chameleonoid too. I remember when Xnake found us in Uncle Jainko's tent and demanded to know which type I was, 1, 2 or 3, I had no idea how to answer him. If I am the baby in the picture, then it seems I am type 1. But what does that mean? Maybe Mel and Leon are the other types. Did En.Ki mess with our DNA before we were born? Did Pa *design* us? Did he *plan* for me to have shapeshifting skills? I decided to press Nazar some more.

'Could Leon shapeshift like me, Nazar?'

'Not exactly, no.'

'What do you mean, "not exactly"? Either you can, or you can't.'

'He couldn't change shape, but he could alter where he was in time.'

'Like how?'

'He tried to teach me how to do it, but it's tricky. It's all about being able to manipulate your vibrational frequency so you can switch briefly into another timeline. Leon got really good at it and it drove Meth mad.' Nazar paused and looked at me, perhaps trying to decide if I was less angry now.

'Did this time-shifting require any tools or equipment?' I asked.

'I don't think so. But Leon did have a white crystal that Dr Jainko gave him. I don't know what its powers were, but he was very attached to it.'

'Hmmm. Colonel Askew gave me a crystal that used to belong to Pa,' I said, hunting in the locker beside my hammock for it. I unwrapped it and passed the red jasper to Nazar, but she wouldn't take it from me.

'You should be careful with that, Kam – crystals can have a very strange effect on you if you're not in the right place mentally. I don't think I should handle it.'

'I see. Is there anything else I have in common with Leon that you can think of?'

'There's one very obvious thing, yes.'

'What's that?'

'The blue eyes. Yours are just like his. They were the first thing I noticed when I met you. All the humans I've ever met have brown eyes. I figured at first it was some kind of genetic aberration that you happened to share. Of course it could have occurred naturally, but it's much more likely to be the result of deliberate tampering with the standard human genome.'

'By En.Ki, for instance?'

Nazar nodded.

'But what for?'

'I don't know, Kam. Everybody likes novelty features. You said yourself that you think Meth was attracted to you because of your eyes.'

A flashback of the moment during the eclipse skirted the edge of my consciousness, but I pushed the memory of Meth's lewd act away.

'So, does Leon look exactly like me?'

'He has the same blue eyes and fair skin, but he has white hair, not red. He's virtually blind and he has a very different personality to you. He's on the deviant spectrum in terms of behaviour. Leon could get very agitated, and often that's when he'd do the time-shift thing. It was a bit like passing out, I guess, but instead of going unconscious he literally became invisible for a time.'

I mulled over this new information, wondering what kind of skills Mel had, as the third of Pa's case studies. Did I have another sister somewhere out there? Was she living at the palace at the time of the King's death? And if so, had she been killed too?

I suddenly remembered the moment in Colonel Askew's quarantine unit when I'd felt that strong tug from an unidentified energy field, pulling me towards someone or something – had it been leading me to Mel and Leon? Was this energy field what connected the three of us? Were they feeling it too? And, if I paid attention to it, would it lead me to them, and perhaps even to Pa?

I was completely lost in thought when I suddenly realised Zep had started up the vimana and we were ascending into the ash cloud over Atlantis. Through my visor, I caught glimpses of what remained of the city, the curving contours and slight indentations of its former canals now buried in mud, and the Temple in the centre, like the dark pupil of an enormous eye in the landscape.

Eye of Atlantis,
Blind like Leon, lost like Mel,
Closes now on Kam.

Disk XVI

GOBERO

Z EP WOKE ME TO tell me we've been ordered by
Captain Tehuti to abort our mission.

*-What does that mean? That we have to return to the
Moon? Go back to Nyan Tolo?*

*-No. Captain Tehuti says he's got what he needed from
us about the state of Atlantis. He wants us to stay down here
and carry out extensive aerial surveillance. He wants me
to compile a datafile on the exact number of survivors left
on the surface and to log the direction in which they are
moving. He has forbidden us to perform search-and-rescue,
just surveillance for now. He is sending down two more*

AI-controlled vimanas, which have gold cladding like ours to withstand Earth's volatile atmosphere, and they will be covering the area to the north of us. We've been assigned a wide band that stretches west to east, all the way from the ruins of the Atlantean archipelago as far as Khem.

-Can you show me a visual?

Zep projected an animated map of a massive green area of land covered with towns, farms and villages that was smothered with a mixture of ash, mud, sand and debris when the tsunami swept through.

'What exactly are we looking for? There's nothing left. Surely no one has survived!' I blurted out loud as the extent of the damage finally dawned on me.

'I know it seems pointless Kam, but our orders are to scan the whole area for Atlantean refugees. If we find any, Captain Tehuti wants me to report it immediately. We are only allowed to intervene if war breaks out.'

'How many people lived in Atlantis before it was destroyed?'

'A hundred and forty-four thousand but, according to Tehuti's last update, the majority of them died before they even had a chance to leave the city.'

'How?'

'After news got around that the King and Queen had been killed by the rebel Draco army, riots broke out and the next day there was a huge earthquake, followed by a massive tsunami. A thousand or so survivors were rescued by the Dogon and taken into the mountains, but it's likely that most of them have now also perished either due to fierce storms, earthquakes or stampedes of fleeing animals. There are new risks every day. Right now, a giant rift valley has opened up, running north to south across the land mass, splitting it in two. If there are any refugees on the move, it will block their progress as they move east. Our mission is simply to observe. We cannot risk being detected at this time. Those are Tehuti's orders.'

'You mean we're not allowed to help these poor people in any way? That seems so heartless, Zep.'

'Standard operating procedure, Kam,' Nazar butted in. 'I'd been tracking your vimana for days, but it was only when the ship started emitting the mayday signal that I was allowed to make contact with you and intervene.'

'I see. But it still doesn't seem right. I mean, it was the Dogon who made contact with us Sirians, so it's not as if the people down there don't know we exist.'

'Orders are orders, Kam,' Zep said obstinately, putting the vimana into cloaked mode. Nazar assumed night duty on the bridge and I retired to my hammock with Aum.

*

We flew for days, skimming the surface of the desolate continent, looking for anyone or anything that was moving or alive. There were dried-up lake beds where herds of animals had died when they got trapped in the mud trying to find water. We saw deserted towns and villages that were still flooded up to their thatched rooftops, forests flattened by storms or consumed by fire and thick smoke, and strange circular holes where the ground had been impacted by something or had just caved in. The only places that were left unscathed by Earth's rapidly deteriorating climate had also been abandoned by whoever had once lived there, leaving crops unharvested in the fields and small enclosures where a few farm animals still wandered around, untended and unfed.

During my watch the vimana slowly drifted over the snowy peaks of a mountain range and, as we descended on the other side, up ahead I saw the giant rift valley Zep had mentioned. It was like a jagged scar where the skin of the Earth had been ripped open to reveal its guts. We dropped a little lower and tracked back, following Zep's grid meticulously, and finally I detected something moving – something alive! It turned out to be a column of several hundred people descending from a steep mountain pass, among them a few 'camels' (the animal with humps Colonel Askew had talked about) and two other beasts with long trunks that Zep's datafiles identified as 'pachyderms', commonly known as 'elephants'.

'Wake up, guys – look!' I yelled to Nazar and Aum, who were both taking a nap.

Zep steadily piloted the vimana until we were overhead, and we followed the column's progress for several hours until they came to a small lake, which Zep's files identified as Lake Gobero.

'I think we should help them.'

'It's not necessary – they look like they know where they're going.'

'But they're not going to be able to make it across the rift, Nazar,' I argued.

'They are not at war, Kam, so we can't help them.'

'I don't care. These might be the only people left alive on the whole planet. Don't you think we should at least let them know what's up ahead?'

'Captain Tehuti has forbidden us to approach anyone,' said Zep mechanically.

'Listen, Zep, I know you're programmed to follow rules, but this is a Mercy Mission; I say we show those people down there some mercy!'

No one spoke after my little outburst, but to my surprise Nazar stepped up to Zep and put him into shutdown mode and then reset the controls to put the vimana into limbo over the lake.

'Better put on our spacesuits before we go down,' she advised.

The UV portal opened up. Aum went first and then Nazar and I jumped down into the water after him. When we surfaced, bobbing in our large semicircular helmets, I saw a long line of dark, sombre faces staring at us from the water's edge.

I swam towards them, hoping they would not try to attack us, because I had no weapon and it would be impossible to run in the suits. To be honest, they looked utterly worn out rather than aggressive – as if they'd seen just about everything and our arrival from the sky in a strange spaceship was nothing out of the ordinary. There was some murmuring and pointing from the younger ones, and the camels shied away. But the tallest and the eldest stood their ground and waited patiently to see who we were and why we had come.

A short distance from the shore I stopped swimming and floated in the water, waiting for Nazar and Aum to catch up. There were just two elephants; a little black girl was riding the smaller one, and a young woman who could have been her older sister was on the larger. She wore a strange hooded cloak, rather like the one I'd seen the Dogon Chief wearing when he met with the Sirian High Kouncil. A large group stood huddled around the woman on the larger elephant, and I took that to mean she was their leader.

Once the water was shallow enough to stand up, I began to wade out to meet them, thinking that the sight of another regular biped would put them at ease. The young woman on the larger elephant nudged her animal forward, and she dropped the hood of her cloak to her shoulders. She had dark skin and black hair tied up in an elaborate style, and held her hand above her eyes to get a better look at us as we approached.

I looked back at Nazar and realised that, with our helmets and breathing equipment on, we looked as if we had trunks too, just like elephants. I decided to respond to the woman's gesture by removing my helmet, even though Zep had warned me not to. I held it by my side and waded to the water's edge. I could feel a cold wind moving over my stubbly ceph and I was suddenly conscious of my white skin. Worse still – now that I wasn't breathing through my suit – the gills in my neck were opening up and I was starting to turn blue. I willed myself to regain control of my body, and then walked up to the leader with a smile on my face.

There was total silence among the people as I approached. The young woman slid elegantly down her elephant's neck, then took off the cloak and handed it to someone standing behind her. As she dusted herself down, I noticed she was wearing a loose-fitting ragged blue dress. But it wasn't the only thing that was blue: when I stood within arm's reach of her, I saw that she had vivid blue eyes. I took another step forward, with Nazar and Aum right behind me. Was this the person in Pa's file, the one he'd placed in the Royal Palace for 'field testing'? Had she fled all the way from Atlantis with these people?

'Mel?' I asked softly.

She looked confused for a moment and turned to the woman standing just behind her, as if needing her support. The latter shrugged as she helped the little girl down from the other elephant. Then the young woman with the blue eyes turned back to face me.

-*Leon?* she replied in a silent voice in my ceph.

Disk XVII

UNITED

I'M KAM. BUT YOU'RE *right, there is also a boy called Leon who went missing. My pilot knows him and is trying to find him,* I telepathed back, gesturing to Nazar behind me.

-*Yes, I also know he is missing. The Dogon Chief, may he rest in peace, told me Leon had disappeared underground. I fear he may not have survived. Thousands of my people have already been lost. We are all that is left.* She gestured sadly to the people huddled around her. -*We are lucky to be alive. I must lead my people to Khem and build the New Atlantis, just as King Atlas wished.*

-*We have just come from the palace in Atlantis, Mel. We saw that the King and Queen had been killed, the palace ransacked and the city abandoned. It must have been hard for you.*

-*Did they bury the King and Queen?* she asked anxiously.

-*They were… laid out in two coffins in the Temple.*

Mel looked away, her face laced with grief.

-*This place you call New Atlantis – I have the plans King Atlas made – I don't know why, but I took them from his chamber – but you should have them. They're in the vimana.*

I turned and pointed over my shoulder and got a shock when I saw the vimana hanging there above the lake, shimmering in a sort of golden haze. It really did look strange and unreal.

-*A 'vimana' – is that what it's called?* Mel asked dreamily. -*Kam, where are you from, and how did you know my name?*

I stared deep into her blue eyes. There was kindness and a strong feeling of empathy there, but, even more than that, I felt a strong energetic connection to Mel tugging me closer. Whatever our relationship to one another, Mel deserved to be told the truth.

-*I have come from the Sirius system, from a small planet called Nyan Tolo. I was recruited to a mission to assist your planet as it goes through this catastrophe. We were supposed to assist with the evacuation of Atlantis, but we arrived too late.*

-*Too late to see Atlantis in its prime, but not too late to help us start again.* Mel smiled and embraced me.

-Welcome, it is an honour to meet you, Kam. My father told me a great deal about his home planet, and it is wonderful to finally meet someone else who comes from there.

-King Atlas was from Sirius? I asked, somewhat surprised.

-No, the royal household was my adopted family; Pa sent me there to live. He's called Dr Jainko and he worked for En.ki. He is my real family.

I started shaking when Mel said this, and my skin went blueish for a few seconds. I took a deep breath and grabbed both her hands.

-Mel, I know this sounds strange, but I think somehow you, Leon and I are connected. You see, Dr Jainko is part of my family also. And for all I know, Leon's too. I found a file at En.Ki's headquarters with detailed notes about both you and Leon. There was no information about me, just a picture of me as a baby.

-It is not so strange to me, Kam. You see, I have been having dreams about you and Leon. I didn't know your name and I could never make any sense of the dreams, but when I finally realised I could see into the future, I expected that one day I would meet you. Mel paused and beckoned to the woman behind her, who stepped forward and bowed low to me.

-I want you to meet Saha'Ra. She was hired by Pa to look after me and to attend me when I went to live at the palace. She's been like a sister to me, and this is her daughter, Mintaka. She is very sick.

Aum made a low, sympathetic noise in his throat. I picked him up to show him to Mel.

-Since we're doing introductions, this is Aum. Pa gave him to me when I was very little. He is a fennec fox with healing powers – perhaps he can make Mintaka better.

Mel turned to Mintaka and said something in Atlantean. It was only then that I realised no one around us had heard our conversation. In stilted Atlantean, I spoke to Mintaka.

'Would you like to meet my fox?'

The child nodded, her big brown eyes wide. She sat on the ground with Aum on her lap, stroking his long ears as he got to work.

'Mel, this is my pilot, Nazar. She comes from one of Jupiter's moons called Europa.'

'Jupiter,' Mel breathed as Nazar greeted her with a formal Trojan salute and began to ask about the elephants.

'I've never seen anything like them before. Are they fierce?'

'They are when they have to be, but they are really kind and gentle by nature. Aren't they adorable? The baby elephant is called Elijah – he was a present to me from the Queen – and the adult one is his mother, Elisha,' Mel told us. She patted Elisha's flank. 'We wouldn't have got this far without the animals,' she added softly.

Mel's people started settling for the night by the lake shore, gathering water, making small fires and laying out their blankets on the rough ground. I scanned the valley and estimated there were maybe two or three hundred of them left. None of them looked in the least bit healthy or hopeful about the outcome of this endless journey. Nazar was helping Saha'Ra set up a makeshift tent for Mintaka and Aum. I could tell Aum had already made a difference to Mintaka's state of health by the field of energy glowing around the child.

-How long have you been travelling like this? I asked Mel.

-For weeks. There were thousands of us when we set out. Many of my people were trampled to death or got sick and died. The Dogon Chief also passed away. We have all suffered greatly. It breaks my heart just thinking about it. These men are the Dogon Chief's brothers. She indicated a group of tall, dark men who sat nearby, drinking tea beside their camels.

-I'm so sorry. I feel as though I met their Chief. He sent a message to the Sirians to tell them Earth was in trouble. We wouldn't be here if it wasn't for him.

I was feeling quite overwhelmed. There were a few too many tragedies and revelations for my brain to untangle. I needed Zep. Maybe his datafiles would help us piece all this information together.

-Listen, Mel, we've got a lot of things we need to discuss – in particular I need to work out how to help your people make the rest of the journey. We've been surveying this whole area looking for survivors, and you're the only ones we've found. But that's not all: not far on from here is a huge rift that lies right across your route. There's no way you'll be able to get across it, even with the animals, to reach the place you're calling New Atlantis. So, would you mind coming aboard my ship to speak with my AI bot, Zep?

-Of course, I will do whatever it takes to make sure my people make it to Khem.

Mel took my arm and we started walking towards the vimana.

Disk XVIII

RESCUE

CLOUDS WERE GATHERING IN the sky now, enveloping the vimana in a strange golden haze above the lake. When we reached the water's edge, I thought I would have to carry Mel back to the ship, but she suddenly rose above the water and floated across to it. I was just about to make a comment about her unusual ability when she drew attention to something weird that I was doing without realising.

-Your skin is turning blue, she commented, peering at me curiously.

When we entered the vimana and I brought Zep out of shutdown, my bot was behaving a little strangely.

Whether it was because Nazar had accidentally messed up his protocols, or because he was in the presence of royalty, Zep went slightly went over the top with his welcome speech.

'Princess Mel, how gracious of you to honour us with your presence aboard this Vimana 5.0, the most advanced ship in the Sirian fleet. May I offer you a sho ball?'

'Not now, thank you, Zep – perhaps later,' she giggled.

As my skin returned to normal, I gathered my thoughts, which were all over the place. Mel and I look nothing like each other except for our blue eyes, but somehow she feels like my sister – much more than my adopted sisters Yuri, Tsygan, Dezik and Laika back home.

-*I think there's a reason we have been brought together, Mel. I've been feeling a connection to something bigger than me for a while now, like an energy field drawing me down to some place on Earth. I know we're supposed to do something important and I have a strong sense that if we find Leon it will all slot into place. There's got to be a reason why Nazar came back to Earth to look for him, why she picked up my ship and then became our pilot, otherwise this is too much of a coincidence – do you think King Atlas could have planned for all this to happen in some way?*

-*I don't know. He was a very wise man who would do anything to save his beloved Kingdom, I know that.* Mel looked thoughtful for a moment. -*Can you do anything else, Kam? I mean, other than changing colour?*

-*Why, can* you?

-*I have a few strange traits. Like how I can pull myself free of gravity.*

Mel wriggled slightly and, more for Zep's benefit than mine, she drifted up towards the ceiling of the vimana, as if the ship was in interstellar space and she was no longer bound by the pull of Earth's magnetic core.

-*Wow! My other trick is a bit gross: I can turn into slime. I had to be able to do three shapeshifts in order to get recruited onto this mission. I can also do a baboon.*

-*Show me!* Mel commanded, clapping her hands together.

I grinned and focused very hard on growing a tail; then I could feel the fur happening, hugging me like a cloak around my shoulders. My face got longer with whiskers at the sides, and before I knew it I was swinging from hammock to hammock. Mel laughed and floated up beside me.

'Can you stop behaving like a child and focus on the matter at hand please, Kam?' Zep trilled, not amused. We both reverted to our normal appearance and Mel's face was serious again, as though she had the weight of the whole world on her shoulders.

-*Have you always known you could do these things, Kam?*

-*Yes, but I never knew why. It's called 'chameleonoid'. Before I left Nyan Tolo, it was really starting to bother me that I was different from my siblings, and that I wasn't supposed to tell them. That photo of me in Pa's lab said my date of birth and 'Homo chameliensis 1.0' on the back of it – like that's my body type. I think you're chameleonoid too, Mel.*

-*Sometimes I have visions about things before they actually happen, Kam. What I mean is, I can see into the* future. It's quite scary sometimes. I knew, for instance, that the King and Queen were going to be murdered, but I didn't have enough time to prevent it from happening. I ran to their chamber as soon as I saw what was about to take place and found them both already dead. It was awful.* She looked at me with tears in her eyes. *-Sometimes the dreams are just weird, though. Like I've had vivid dreams about some strange giants and a boy that seemed very significant, but I don't know how. Then, when your vimana came down over the lake, I recognised it, because I once had a vivid dream about that too.*

-Do you think the boy in your dream about the giants could be Leon?

-I'm not sure. But if he's like us, he must have some unusual powers too. I always knew I wasn't like anyone else in Atlantis and that Pa regarded me as special in some way. I used to feel a bit of a freak, to be honest, when other scientists used to visit the lab, and I was expected to sort of ... perform. The worst time was when Pa took me to the underground base and introduced me to the reptilian squadron leader there, a revolting character called Meth.

-Did you say 'Meth'?

-Why, have you met him?

-It sounds like the same person! He's got to be the creepiest individual I've ever come across. He assaulted me when I was at the Moon base. I've still got the bite mark to prove it. I peeled back my clothing to show her the long gash across my left shoulder.

-You're lucky he didn't kill you. I am certain he murdered Atlas and the Queen.

-Meth? That would explain why he was hiding on Proteus… Our original pilot, Xnake, got a call to rescue someone he said was an old komrade, and it turned out to be Meth. I think they had some score to settle, because almost as soon as Meth came aboard our vimana, they were fighting over a krate of crystals, which split open and made our ship radioactive.

-That's got to be Meth – he runs all of the illegal gold and mineral mines this side of Atlantis. When his Dracos captured us and forced us into slave labour, Meth came to the goldmine and assaulted me, too. I never want to see him ever again as long as I live.

-How did you manage to escape from the goldmine, Mel?

-One night there was an almighty earthquake and the mine collapsed, trapping all the Dracos who were on duty that night inside the mine-head. We'd heard them talking about invading a stronghold of stasis giants living way below ground, who they thought were guarding a strange creature down there. The Dogon Elders thought the earthquake was caused by the giants waking up, but I'm not sure.

-So, what happened?

-It was the elephants that raised the alarm. They both knew instinctively that the earthquake was about to happen and started wailing. They were chained up, exhausted from hauling gold ore to the surface. But Elisha must have been so scared that she somehow broke free and then freed Elijah and they both came running to find us. Unfortunately, many of my people had fallen ill from drinking the contaminated water at the mine and were too weak to come with us, so we had no choice but to leave them there.

-*What do you think happened to Meth?*'

-*I know I shouldn't say things like this, but with any luck, he was crushed in the quake too.*

Zep interrupted our telepathed conversation with a message from Captain Tehuti. I was curious if Mel could hear what he said to me, but from her expression I could see that he was talking to me on a different frequency that she was not receiving.

-*Kam, we are being told to expect the arrival of two V6 vimanas before nightfall. We've been ordered to fly with them overnight in cloaked mode all the way to Khem.*'

-*I see. Is there any way we could commandeer them and bring Mel's people with us?*

-*I don't think that's wise, Kam. You have already gone against the rules by making contact with Mel. That was strictly prohibited…*'

-*Listen Zep, I don't care what the rules are. Right now I'm not going anywhere without Mel and her people.*'

*

Nazar worked out that the combined passenger capacity of two V6s and our V5 was just about sufficient to transport a couple of hundred Atlantean and Dogon people to Khem, but to do this we would have to somehow gain control of the other two ships, disable all three AIs, and pilot all three of them ourselves with Zep offline. We were just discussing how this could be done when Mel thought of something else we'd overlooked.

'What about Elijah and Elisha and the camels?'

'Oh. I was forgetting about the animals…' I faltered.

'There's no way there'll be room for them too, Kam,' Nazar said, running over the calculations one more time.

After much discussion, it was finally decided that Mel and the Dogon survivors, plus Saha'Ra and Mintaka – who was still very poorly – would come in the vimana with us, and that we'd leave Nazar, the Atlantean survivors and the animals behind, and return for them the following day.

'Are you sure about this, Nazar?'

'Absolutely, Kam. You and Mel know what you're doing, and it's important to get these people where they need to be one way or the other.'

Later that evening, Saha'Ra, Aum, Mintaka and the Dogon people joined us aboard our vimana with their few remaining possessions. We bade farewell to Nazar and the Atlanteans, leaving the elephants and camels drinking from the lake, oblivious of what was going on. As the Sun dropped below the mountain range to the west, we were promptly joined, as advised, by two V6s, both larger than our V5 but of the same square-based prism design sheathed in gold, which hovered above the lake while they synced with ours. Then the three vimanas shot off vertically in a tight triangular formation.

I noticed we were trailing some way behind the two V6s. Zep admitted to me that our algae had lost a lot of its power, so we were not able to maintain the same speed as the others. I had no idea what we were going to find in Khem when we arrived, or even if we would be welcome there. The only thing Mel knew was that King Atlas had visited the place several times to carry out a progress check on the construction of New Atlantis, but when I showed her King Atlas's plans, she had no idea how much of it had been built.

A quick look at Zep's datafiles confirmed that our best route would be to go north into an area called Libia, and from there turn east towards Khem, to avoid a particularly intense hurricane that was showing up on En.Ki's current meteorological data. Owing to the weather conditions, we were forced to fly below the base of the storm clouds, which meant two things: first, there wasn't as much turbulence, and second, we were flying too close to Earth's surface for cloaked mode to work.

Halfway through the night, Zep received a warning that there were enemy craft in the area and they were moving in our direction. Once all three vimanas rose higher into the turbulent storm cell above to avoid detection, Zep struggled to maintain contact with the other two AI pilots. Neither of them was showing up on our comms deck, but we knew one of them was in trouble when debris came hurtling through the air. Communication with the other vimana became extremely intermittent, and then we came under intense fire from whoever was pursuing us.

Zep dodged the worst of it, but there was a strange pulsing feeling sweeping through the cabin from one side to the other, and then from top to bottom, like we were being scanned remotely. The next thing I knew, Meth's scratchy voice came through the comms deck. Both Mel and I recognised it straightaway and looked at each other in horror.

'Well, what do you know – two blue-eyed playthings for the price of one!'

Disk XIX

AMBUSH

I STARTED HUNTING IN all the storage lockers on the vimana.

-What are you looking for, Kam? Zep enquired.

-Xnake's scalar weapon. I think we're going to need it.

The vimana was ducking and lurching but some ammunition found its mark. Our poor passengers were screaming with their hands over their ears and it was impossible to calm any of them down, until Zep had the idea of putting everyone except me and Aum into mass semi-stasis.

-Sounds a bit drastic, Zep.

-*It's for their own safety*, he assured me, booting the programme.

Immediately, the Dogon Elders, Mel, Saha'Ra and Mintaka slumped and fell silent.

Meanwhile, I'd found what I was looking for – but I hadn't realised Xnake's weapon was more than half my weight and I could barely lift it.

Between the three of us, Zep, Aum and I managed to slot the weapon into its mount and figure out how it worked. As I was about to test-fire it, I felt something lodge itself in the vimana's outer shell and we could hear a loud whistling sound as the craft lost altitude.

-*That was a direct hit!* Zep informed me.

-*No kidding! Just keep going, Zep, whatever you do!*

-*I'll try, but we're expending valuable power just by taking avoiding action whenever they fire at us.*

I looked over to where Mel was lying. Her eyes were closed and she was clutching a black crystal. Then I had a sudden realisation: Meth only wants to scare us, not take us down.

-*Don't worry, Zep – Meth wants Mel and me alive.*

-*But their firepower is deadly, Kam. The scalar weapons they're using are much stronger than Xnake's. Look at the ground below us!*

It was true. Something strange was happening to the Earth's surface every time Meth's rebels fired at us from above and missed. Whatever they were firing must have been sophisticated nuclear weaponry because it was more than just scorching the ground – it was *melting* it! Any loose material on the surface was instantly fused into glistening translucent clumps wherever a directed energy beam had hit.

Inside the vimana there was also a peculiar acrid smell that was making me feel dizzy. Within minutes, I passed out.

*

Meth's rebels continued their aerial assault on our three vimanas until they had us surrounded by their drones and forced us down in the middle of a wide empty expanse of Libian desert about a hundred stadia west of Khem – the perfect place to leave the last remaining survivors on Earth to die unnoticed in searing heat in the middle of a hurricane. I knew that if I let this happen, we'd never be found alive, not by Nazar, not by anyone.

As they forced Zep and the other AIs to open the hatches to the vimanas and the sand blew in, Meth stood outside on the ground and directed operations with an electric prod, bundling the Dogon refugees off the craft and ordering them to lie face down in the sand. Meth then ordered his rebels to board each vimana to check there was no one hiding and disable the AI systems controlling them. Meanwhile, Meth moved up and down the rows, flipping over the prostrate bodies with his foot as he searched for the only two he was really interested in – Mel and me.

But I wasn't one of the ones lying in the sand. Instead, I was slowing oozing my way along the barrel of Xnake's scalar weapon, waiting for Meth to realise I wasn't there. I knew he'd soon be heading my way and I just had to hope that my body weight as slime would be sufficient to trigger the weapon when the opportunity arose. As I predicted, Meth found Mel quite quickly, stripping the Dogon cloak off her. He then continued looking for me until he came to a stop at the end of the row of terrified people, when he turned and strode across to our vimana, dragging Mel along behind him by her hair. I waited until he walked into the crosshairs of Xnake's weapon and then fired directly at his face. His skin melted away into a translucent green mass just like the desert sand, leaving one yellow eye with its vertical pupil glaring at me. He flexed his wing flaps, gripped Mel around her neck and, using her as a human shield, continued walking into the wind towards our vimana.

If I fired again, I knew I would hit Mel, so I bided my time. As Meth reached the vimana, he tossed Mel back onto the sand and walked around the craft to enter via the hatch. He spotted Xnake's weapon almost straightaway, and I knew I had one chance. It was almost as though the anger I felt inside turned into electricity rippling through me, and when he grasped the weapon to lever it off the mount, the voltage I delivered in that sting should have been enough to kill him. There was a revolting smell of burning flesh, and he looked almost as charred as when Xnake found him on Proteus. But somehow Meth regained consciousness and half-crawled, half-fell out of the vimana right onto Mel, who was trying to stop him from inflicting any more harm on her people. I knew I didn't have much time to stop him getting away, but reverting back from slime is a slow process and, before I managed to regain hominid form, the Draco rebels had gathered up Meth and Mel and got away in their fleet of drones, leaving the rest of us in the middle of a desert storm.

In a state of shock, I picked up one of the pieces of melted rock. It looked like a pale green crystal and it was still hot. The wind was roaring in my ears and sand stung my eyes, but I remember looking up and seeing Saha'Ra and Aum run over to where Mintaka lay. Saha'Ra crouched down and was calling out 'Mintaka, wake up!' When the child didn't stir, Aum put a force field round all three of them and Saha'Ra started pushing against the child's chest, trying to force her to breathe. When nothing was working, Saha'Ra sat rocking backwards and forwards, clutching Mintaka's limp little body to her heart and sobbing inconsolably.

The Dogon Chief's brothers began uttering incantations in low voices. Slowly they moved in a circle around the mother and her dead child, collecting any larger stones they could find and standing them upright around Saha'Ra and Mintaka in a wide circle until they were surrounded by twenty or thirty small standing stones, creating a sacred space in which to pay their last respects.

As if in sympathy with Saha'Ra's anguish, the earth around us started quaking and rumbling. I watched as the sand began to vibrate, making a strange humming sound and lifting off the ground. I knew that, if we stayed there any longer, the whole area would soon become quicksand and swallow us all up.

'Get in the vimana!' I yelled, but my voice was drowned out by the wind and the resonant frequency of the humming. I started to move between the survivors, pushing them in the direction of our vimana, until eventually everyone got the idea and started moving. I climbed inside our craft and brought Zep out of shutdown.

-Fire up the other two AIs, Zep. We need to get moving NOW!

I went back to persuade Saha'Ra that we had to go, and watched as the Dogon Elders solemnly wrapped Mintaka in their Chief's cloak and slowly carried her back to our vimana, leaving a small flat stone in the place where her body had lain.

By the time all three vimanas finally pulled away from the surface, the combination of our vertical propulsion and the strange humming quicksand left a series of strange circular impressions in the Earth's surface that reminded me of the overlapping pitted craters I'd seen on the Moon's surface the night of the eclipse. Zep did a head count.

-Where are Mintaka and Princess Mel?

-They didn't make it, Zep.

Disk XX

CAPSTONE

T HE DRACOS MUST HAVE extracted from Mel where she was planning to take her people, because when we arrived at the place Zep assured me was Khem, there were drones everywhere. However, with the storm now over we were flying higher and therefore in cloaked mode, so they had not yet detected us as we flew back and forth over the area again and again, unsure where to land or how to thwart another ambush.

I kept looking for the concentric streets of a city with radial avenues leading to a grand central temple, just as King Atlas had shown on his drawings of New Atlantis.

However, there was nothing here except a broad stone platform with the three squares he'd drawn, but these weren't courtyards; they were towering pyramids, each one missing its apex. Then I spotted something else I recognised: the statue of a lion lying down with its paws stretched out in front of it. I took the drawings out of my locker and unrolled them to compare what we were flying over with what Atlas had marked on his plans. I remembered that there was a discreet entrance beside the left paw. Perhaps we could find a place to shelter there, beneath the lion statue. I was about to instruct Zep to land just in front of the statue of the Great Lion, when he began to receive a message through the vimana's comms system.

-It's Captain Tehuti, Zep said.

-What does he want?

-For some reason he wants us to land the vimanas on top of the three pyramids. We are to land ours on the smallest one.

I consulted Atlas's plans again. None of the pyramids had been named, but the smallest one had a letter M beside it. Was it an M for Mel, perhaps?

I looked across at the blank expression of pure shock on Saha'Ra's tear-stained face. No, not M for Mel. We should name this pyramid after Mintaka.

I went over to her, crouched down and put my arm around her.

'Saha'Ra, we have arrived. Your people are going to be safe here,' I assured her.

'They are Miss Mel's people, not mine. To me, this journey has all been for nothing if we have arrived here without her and without Mintaka.'

'I know. It's not much consolation, but remember how upset Mel was that the King and Queen did not receive a proper burial ceremony?'

Saha'Ra nodded.

'Well, I promise you we will give Mintaka one. And then we'll do everything we can to find Mel.'

Zep and the other two AIs coordinated with each other to land the vimanas as instructed on top of the pyramids, and even peering out of my visor it was quite a sight to see, as the golden prism-shaped crafts docked, perfectly topping out the three pyramids. I had no idea what they were for, but they were more impressive than anything I had ever seen on Nyan Tolo, or anywhere else for that matter. I wondered if there were pyramids like these anywhere else on Earth and who could have cut and moved and placed so many pieces of stone so accurately.

Before Zep had given the vimana any kind of command, the UV portal just opened up and a violet-white column of light beamed straight down into a long vertical shaft inside the smallest of the three pyramids, right below where we'd landed. Almost as soon as the shaft opened, a powerful charge of energy pulsed right through the vimana and up into the sky. As I looked at the faces around me, I could sense the energy field around us getting stronger and brighter. I can't explain it, but it felt like coming home.

I gathered my belongings together, including my blue silk tunic and the red jasper crystal that Colonel Askew had given me, as well as the fused Libian rock, and stuffed them all in a bag. I could feel the jasper's gentle energy responding to the light flowing through the pyramid, and I took it out again. It felt calming and soothing as I weighed it in my hands. I looked up and saw that Saha'Ra was waiting for me.

'Have you got everything, Kam?' It was as if, now that Mel was no longer with us, Saha'Ra had decided it was her duty to serve as my companion.

'Yes, I have, but this is for you, Saha'Ra – I want you to have it. It might bring you some comfort.'

I gave her the red crystal, wrapping her fingers around the pulsating stone. She closed her eyes for a brief moment.

'Miss Mel had a special crystal too, that her Pa gave to her, but hers was black. I hope it is keeping her safe, just like her Pa told her it would.'

'This one also belonged to Pa, and I was told it would help me find my way home. It brought us safely here, so maybe Mel's will, too.'

Saha'Ra gave me a weak smile, which soon faded when she realised the Dogon Elders were lifting Mintaka's body down into the shaft that led down into the bowels of the pyramid. I put Zep into shutdown and, closing the hatch, climbed down after them.

The shaft was very narrow and had small ledges jutting out from the sides that served as hand- and footholds. After descending quite a distance, we came to a long sloping gallery leading into a larger chamber lined with granite. There was nothing on the walls, floor or ceiling, but at the far end of the chamber was a large rectangular stone vessel, beautifully cut from rose-pink stone. The Dogon Elders gently lay poor Mintaka's body inside it, wrapped in their Chief's cloak. We stood in silence around the vessel, paying our last respects to the child, while Saha'Ra sang a beautiful incantation and the Dogon performed a slow funeral dance around the stone vessel.

The atmosphere inside the chamber was very spiritual, and all the grief and exhaustion we were feeling somehow fell away, replaced by a renewed sense of hope and optimism. The sound of Saha'Ra's voice rising and falling in this cavernous space seemed to penetrate the stone walls around us, and set them humming too, although not in an audible way – it was more something you could feel in your bones or a slight tingle running across your arms and down your back.

As the sounds built to a crescendo, it was as if the whole pyramid was starting to buzz like it was a living thing. I closed my eyes and could sense tiny particles expanding and moving into formation, then flowing as one, rising up through the stone roof over our heads, and new energy flowing up through the floor to replace it in a constant cycle, until my body and my mind felt completely saturated and aglow.

When I opened my eyes again, I realised we had all changed. This whole experience had changed us from suffering victims into a united band of survivors, strong in spirit if not in number. Everyone had become in a sense 'chameleonoid' now, even if their outward appearance was the same. I waited as Saha'Ra blew her daughter a final kiss and then moved away from the vessel, her head bowed as the Dogon Elders closed the stone lid.

As I led the way out of the chamber and back into the long gallery, I could hear noises coming from somewhere below us in the pyramid. Was it the Dracos? I had no idea what we were about to face when we emerged from this huge structure.

Disk XXI

MEETING

THE DESCENDING SHAFT LED us into a vast underground hall directly underneath the three pyramids. A narrow channel of water ran down the centre of the hall, and one or two Dogon stooped to drink from it. Soon everyone was washing their faces and filling their gourds. Aum climbed right into the channel and gave himself a bath.

After we'd quenched our thirst, we sat on the stone floor to rest. I could sense a warm, loving energy moving through us, and it felt as though I could telepath with everyone in that moment. It was quite dark and as we all fell silent, I noticed the noises again. But this time, rather than coming from beneath us, it sounded like heavy footsteps and low, booming voices on the other side of the walls surrounding us. There were no obvious openings, and whoever it was seemed to be trying to hammer their way out. I got up from where I was sitting with Saha'Ra and moved slowly around the edges of the hall with one ear close to the smooth stone surface, listening intently. Aum followed just behind me, scanning the lower part of the wall, his huge ears bolt upright.

The sounds were definitely louder at one end of the hall than the other. I thumped on the wall from my side, and the sounds fell silent. Then the booming voices started up again, and suddenly there was a louder cracking sound. I stepped away from the wall, and part of the smooth surface flaked off, exposing a layer of rougher stone behind it. The voices sounded different now, closer and less echoing. Whoever it was struck the wall a few more times, until a whole heap of larger stones was dislodged. I knelt down and saw that a gap had now opened up at the base of the wall. Somebody prodded into the gap with a tool, scraping away the rubble to clear a path.

'Go, Babi!' said a shrill voice, a little impatiently. I heard a strange scuffling, scampering sound, and a small creature ran out of the hole. Aum barked and ran behind me. The creature, which I realised was some kind of baboon, paused on its haunches and started scratching itself.

'Babi, come back!' the voice on the other side of the wall commanded.

But it just sat there, head on one side, as if taking in my appearance.

There were more scraping sounds on the other side of the wall, and I took another look through the hole out of which the creature had emerged. The gap was now wider still and, as I peered into it, I saw a pair of bright blue eyes staring back at me.

'Mel?' I called out in amazement.

'No, I'm Leon!' the voice said indignantly.

Disk XXII

TRAPPED

WITH NOTHING OTHER THAN their bare hands, the Dogon helped me open up the gap until it was wide enough for Leon to squeeze through. The baboon was cackling and leaping around with excitement that her owner was about to appear, but I was even more excited. Had I really found Leon?

When he finally crawled out and stood up, he was a skinny, scrawny boy not much older than me, with white blond hair and very pale skin, perhaps because he'd been underground for a very long time.

'Naz?' he enquired quietly.

He seemed to sniff the air, and then reached out and started to feel my stubbly head, my shoulders and my face, and I realised that being underground must have made him go blind too.

'Not Nazar...' he muttered, disappointed.

'No, I'm Kam. I'm Nazar's friend. She's... I'm...'

What *was* I to Leon? Why had I agreed to leave Nazar behind? Were Leon and I meant to find each other like this? While I was still thinking what to say, Leon pressed something into my hand – a gleaming white crystal.

'What's this, Leon?'

'Present from my Pa. It's mine. You like it?'

'From Pa? I... I love it!' I gave Leon a big hug. He laughed and then pulled away, reaching for his crystal and grabbing at my hand.

'Come meet my big friend Jenti, Kam.'

Leon felt his way back towards the gap in the wall. The Dogon Elders had come to see what was going on, but kept their distance, not sure whether to be concerned. When Leon disappeared back through the hole, without hesitating I got on my hands and knees and crawled after him. It was even darker on the other side, and the air was cold and dank. It took my eyes a moment or two to adjust, while Leon was muttering away to someone.

'Urdinak?' a voice boomed in my ear so loud it hurt. I heard someone take a large stride in my direction and suddenly I was face to face with the ugliest set of features I'd ever seen; the nostrils were wider than my hand and breathing loudly, with wiry hairs protruding from each of them. When they breathed out, it released a horrendous stench. I reeled backwards and hit my head against the wall we'd just come through.

'Yes, Sir. My name is Kam Urdinak.'

The giant, who was considerably larger and wider than Captain Tehuti, came closer and bent down to get a better look at my face while I shook from head to toe, not knowing what he was about to do to me.

'Blue eyes like Leon,' he noted with some satisfaction. 'Must be chameleon.'

'And who are you?' I asked, trying to sound authoritative despite my relatively small size.

'He my giant friend, Jentilak,' Leon said proudly, reaching up and patting the giant's thigh. Jentilak gave a throaty chortle and, picking Leon up, stood us side by side as if we were a couple of dolls. Then I noticed there were several more giants standing further back in the dark cave. Leon made a funny little bow in their direction and pulled my arm so I would do the same, and they all started clapping. Then the clapping turned into a rumbling, and before I could work out what was happening, boulders started coming loose as the applause got louder, dislodging more rubble around the hole in the wall and closing up the gap. Suddenly I was on the wrong side of the wall – and there was no way back.

Disk XXIII

BUILDERS

JENTILAK WASTED NO TIME in tackling our situation. He picked away the jumble of stones like anyone else might pick bits of food out of their teeth, removing the ones that blocked the area around where the gap had been, then working his fingers into the gap to dislodge some of the larger ones and wriggling each one free, until Babi managed to squeeze back through and jumped into Leon's arms, cackling and shrieking with delight. I yelled through the gap for everyone to stand well back and then the giants gently pushed against the wall to make a much larger opening, which they quickly tidied up, laying the rocks in a neat pile beside where we stood.

'You first, Kam,' Leon urged, pushing me through the now much grander entrance. I picked my way across the gap, Babi following at my heels, and Leon clambered over right behind me. Everyone looked dumbfounded as Leon and I stepped into the light, and they could see how alike we were, what with our blue eyes and our white faces. But then I realised it was more likely that they were dumbfounded by the dozen or so hefty giants who followed after us. When Jentilak finally stood in the great hall, he rolled his shoulders back a couple of times, pulled himself up to his full height and looked around approvingly, running his hands first over the surface of the ceiling, and then over the walls and the floor, and I took his satisfied grunts to mean he was admiring the workmanship.

'Jenti's uncles built it,' Leon informed me, and I saw he was feeling almost as proud as the giant. 'Long time go.'

'Did they build everything here?' I asked him.

'Yes, pyramids too,' Leon said gesturing over his head as if he already knew what was above us, even though he couldn't see it. 'But not the lion. That made by Tehuti. He the boss giant.'

'Oh, I see,' I said, wondering if this Tehuti was the same giant as our mission Captain.

'Are you thirsty, Leon?' I asked him, taking his hand and leading him to the channel. Babi started drinking from it, and Aum crept up shyly to see what sort of creature she was. Leon crouched down and splashed his hands into the water.

'Leon, how did you get here?'

'Walking,' he replied, doing the action with his wet fingers.

'Do you know where Pa is, Leon?'

Instinctively he hugged himself for protection and rocked on his heels for a moment before answering me.

'Don't know. You know Pa?' he replied, turning his head away from me.

'Yes, but I haven't seen him for a long time.'

'I never *seen* him,' Leon announced and I realised he was trying to make a joke, so I laughed.

Then I touched his arm.

'He's my Pa too, Leon.'

I watched his face as he tried to process this piece of information. He obviously found it difficult, so he changed the subject.

'Kam, where Naz? She my friend.'

'You mean Nazar? She's coming, Leon, with the elephants. Have you ever seen… I mean, have you ever met an elephant?'

'With trunk like this?' Leon made his arm into a trunk.

'Yes,' I chuckled, 'Just like that.'

'Naz like animals. She like Babi too. And me.'

Nazar had only told me about Leon's time-shifting skill and had said nothing about Leon's lack of language, but despite his limited speech, there was something confident and optimistic about Leon's manner that I had already warmed to.

*

Jentilak, helped by some of the other giants, wasted no time in checking the doors to the other chambers that opened off the main hall. He was particularly concerned that one his uncles had built, called the Hall of Records, was properly sealed. He told me it was stacked from floor to ceiling with all the ancient documents that had been brought here for safekeeping from Atlantis over a period of many years.

'This must have taken a lot of work, Jenti,' I said.

'Before stasis, much effort, yes. Then long sleep. Now ready for final part,' Jentilak informed me, flexing his knuckles and looking very satisfied when they all clicked, and the sound echoed like a series of bullets going off around the chamber.

Then he led Leon and me up a long sloping ramp towards what seemed a dead end. It was a bit of a squeeze for the giant and, when we reached the blank wall, I could see it was a very well-made pivoting stone door. Hunched over, the giant leaned against it with his shoulder until he felt it give and it swung open. We emerged between the paws of the Great Lion statue. It was much larger close up than it had looked from inside the vimana but, compared to the giant, the lion was completely in proportion. Jentilak patted its broad stone head.

'This one very, very old,' he told me.

'How long ago was it built?'

'Before last flood.'

'So, there have been other times when Earth was flooded like this?'

'Yes, many. I was child-giant when last one came.'

'I see. How old are you, Jenti?'

'One Great Year.'

I decided that giants must have a very different way of measuring time than humans.

'And how long is a Great Year in Earth years?'

By the way he was hopping around, I could tell that Leon knew the answer and was eager to share it with me. The giant touched him on the shoulder to let him go ahead.

'Twenty-five thousand, seven hundred and seventy-two,' he recited proudly.

Jentilak laughed and then, without warning, picked Leon up and placed him behind the lion's head on its back.

'Great lion, great Leon!' he roared with laughter.

I looked up at Leon towering above me and behind him at the vast stone plateau and the three huge pyramids silhouetted against the setting sun. There was a strong wind blowing, making dust and debris swirl in eddies towards us. I blinked and shielded my eyes from the grit. Then I noticed there were drones circling in the sky, and beyond them a much larger ship that appeared to be coming in to land.

'Look at me, Kam!' Leon shouted down triumphantly.

'Jenti, what's that in the sky? I think the Dracos have come back, look!' I said, trying not to sound panicked.

'Tehuti arrive,' Jentilak remarked casually when he saw what I was pointing at. 'He always come with Draco drones.'

The giant was about to lift Leon down when something strange happened. Leon just disappeared. I blinked, thinking I must have something in my eye. But he still wasn't there. I looked up at Jentilak to see what he made of it, but he just stared at the space where Leon had been.

'Wait, Kam. He come back.'

Jenti crouched down between the lion's paws and waited. Suddenly, Leon was right next to me, brandishing his white crystal and doing a little victory dance.

'Enough, Leon,' Jenti said sternly, sounding like Ma when she told me off. 'Time to meet Tehuti.'

*

Captain Tehuti dismissed his convoy of drones and then strode towards us between the pyramids, leaving his huge spaceship parked alongside the largest pyramid on the platform, almost as though it had been designed for that purpose.

'Good work, Urdinak,' Tehuti exclaimed when we were within earshot, much to my surprise, as he glanced approvingly at the three gold capstones that were now in place thanks to the vimanas. 'We can now commence the activation sequence.'

I had no idea what he meant, but he was pleased and that was the main thing; he was not the kind of giant you'd want to disappoint. Tehuti then toured the remaining work that needed to be done with Jentilak. Leon and I had to run along beside them just to keep up.

'Captain Tehuti, what are the pyramids for?' I asked, a little out of breath. 'They don't seem to have enough space inside for all the survivors to live comfortably.'

Tehuti looked down at me and frowned.

'Survivors? According to my Draco informants, there are none. In any case, these pyramids were not built to house humans. They have been painstakingly constructed over many centuries by the Builders to protect a vast area of Earth's surface as well as deep below. They will boost the fertility of our seeds and therefore our crops, enabling them to germinate in low levels of daylight, should conditions on Earth deteriorate further. But, most importantly, they have the power to siphon off the energy caused by the impending impact event, strengthening Earth's magnetic field, which, when it is connected to the other pyramids we are currently constructing around the planet, will activate a protection grid for Earth. This was the solution Atlas and I worked out to ensure that humanity would survive the Changes this time around. Did you not read your briefing pack?' He was sounding annoyed now.

'I see, Sir – sorry, Sir.'

'Now that you and Leon are here, I will instruct Meth to bring Mel. We need all three of you for the activation to work.'

'So she's alive?' I gasped.

He flashed me a look of utter disdain, and I suddenly realised that not only had Captain Tehuti no intention of building a new city as Atlas had shown on his drawings to replace Atlantis, but he also had a very different project in mind where Leon, Mel and I were concerned.

'You went against my express orders when you intervened to help Mel, but I am prepared to let it go on this one occasion. However, no matter what Mel has told you about New Atlantis, I am in charge now. Your work here is done, Urdinak. You and the rest of your Sirian crew members are to return to the Moon tomorrow aboard my ship. You will be paid your salaries and transferred on the next scheduled service back to Nyan Tolo.'

He fixed me with an icy stare, clearly forbidding me to challenge him any further. There was something in his manner that made me very suspicious. I could feel the gills in my neck opening and reached up to cover them with my hands.

'Yes, Sir, as you wish. What about Nazar?'

'What about her? She is an escaped Trojan pilot caught spying, and her conduct will not look good when her case comes up for review in due course. If she is court-martialled, she will have to return to Mars.'

This was also news to me. Did Tehuti mean she had escaped from Meth's base here on Earth, or had she actually been a fellow prisoner on Mars and had somehow escaped with me?

*

While Tehuti and Jentilak finished their meeting, Leon and I returned to the lion statue. I had a strange sinking feeling.

'Leon, what do you know about Mel?'

'Who is Mel?'

'She has blue eyes like us, and the same Pa.'

'She our sister?' Leon stopped in his tracks and crouched down, sensing that Babi was coming towards him.

'Sort of… Listen, I don't trust Tehuti, I think he's a bad giant.'

'All giants good. Jenti my favourite,' Leon assured me.

'Tehuti is not like Jentilak. I think he's deceiving us, Leon. I think he wanted Atlantis to fall and arranged for the King and Queen to be killed so that he was the one who ended up in control of New Atlantis. Maybe he ordered that Draco Meth to murder them both and I'm worried he's going to order Meth to kill Mel too.'

'Meth? Meth kill our sister?'

Leon became suddenly very angry and stopped in front of the lion statue, stroking the baboon and mulling over this possibility. I remembered from Pa's notes that Leon had been placed for field-testing on Meth's base. Leon had obviously not got on with him.

'You know Meth, don't you? Well, he hurt Mel and me. And now he's taken her somewhere. We were ambushed by his Draco rebels in the desert when we were on our way here and, even though I injured Meth quite badly, he got away with Mel and his rebels. It seems as if Meth is working for Tehuti…'

'I hate Meth. He hurt me too. Where he take her? I have Meth sword. I kill him.'

Leon looked stony-faced and utterly determined all of a sudden.

'I don't know where he took her, maybe to another underground base somewhere. Mel told me the Dracos control all the mines and underground facilities.'

'Not all – giants fight them, get gold, keep safe.'

'I know, but now that the giants are coming to the surface, maybe they are taking over their territory underground.'

'Like Black Sun?' Leon asked me, his mind evidently racing to put the pieces together. 'Pa's crystal keep us safe, Kam, I no worry,' he assured me, patting his pocket.

'What is Black Sun, Leon?'

'They no good. Maybe Tehuti work for them. Meth make mono, get blood too. Give to Black Sun. Black Sun my enemy, like Meth.'

'It all makes sense now. But we have to work out a plan to get Mel back in one piece before Tehuti returns.'

'Naz help us,' Leon suggested brightly. I admired his confidence in such slim possibilities.

'Yes, but she's not here, Leon.'

'Pa?'

'I've no idea where he is, either. We're going to have to figure this out ourselves.'

Disk XXIV

———

TERRAFORMER

I TOSSED AND TURNED all night in the hall beneath the pyramids along with the other survivors, and was eventually woken by a tremendous din above our heads, high-pitched whirring and grinding, clanking and chugging. I left the others sleeping, including Leon, who was lying curled up with Babi and Aum, and wandered out into the morning sunlight.

The first thing I realised was that Tehuti had gone, presumably he'd returned to his base on the Moon in his spaceship, having given his orders to the giants and left them hard at work. I felt a sense of relief wash over me;

we were safe for now, even if we still didn't know where Mel was. I watched as the giants set about making the stonework to complete the largest pyramid, which Tehuti had instructed was to be covered in a fine white stone. There were several huge lathes and circular saws, and the giants were deftly pushing through slabs of the white rock, guiding it skilfully with their enormous hands, until what came out the other side were precisely-cut slivers of rock, which another team of giants collected and carried across to where a third team were kneeling down, applying a fine layer of mortar and carefully slotting the white stone slabs into position into what looked like a vast three-dimensional puzzle.

I spotted Jentilak supervising some repair work to the back of the lion statue and went over to talk to him. There was no wind and the giants were already sweating in the heat. I watched as they skilfully hoisted a stone into position, and stared up into their faces; their brows were furrowed as they grunted and pushed and pulled the rock into the right place, while the Sun blazed down on them out of a clear blue sky. In their hands, each rock took only a minute or so to place but even so, I calculated it had taken hundreds of thousands of rocks to build all three pyramids, so the giants must have been working on them for a long time.

'Good morning, Jentilak. Did the giants make all of this?'

'All you see,' he replied, waving his huge palms in front of him in a swimming motion. 'Here to river,' he added, sweeping his arms towards the morning Sun.

'Kam thirsty?' he asked, slicing off the top of a large green coconut with a knife and handing it to me.

'Thank you, Jenti,' I said, taking it from him.

I heard chattering behind me and turned to see Leon emerging from the left paw of the lion statue with Babi and Aum.

'Come with me, Leon!'

'Where going, Kam?' Leon shouted.

'To the river.'

As we approached the banks of the mighty River Khem, I heard strange trumpeting noises, and wondered what kind of gigantic machinery could be producing them. Perhaps there was more sawing equipment being used down by the water's edge. The banks were steep and Leon and I slowly zig-zagged our way down through the bushes, as Babi and Aum trotted on ahead of us. Leon was feeling his way quite confidently, considering he was used to solid walls, not vegetation, to get his bearings. I took his arm and steered him round a large boulder. Suddenly Babi came running back up the bank, making a racket. She seemed very agitated and climbed up Leon's body to sit on his shoulder, as if needing his protection. The trumpeting had stopped but I could hear Aum barking and wondered if he was hurt. I half-ran, half-tumbled down the last part of the river bank, and finally saw what Aum and Babi were making all the fuss about: around the next bend in the river there was a wide beach and standing up to their knees in the water were two elephants, covering themselves with mud to keep cool.

As I got closer, I could tell the little one was Elijah! He lifted his trunk out of the water and gave a loud friendly cry and promptly fell over in the mud as he tried to run towards me. Then I noticed something even larger than the elephants right behind them: a strange battered-looking military vehicle parked on the beach. And there, in front of it, sitting on a rock eating breakfast, were two people with their backs to me. One had long grey hair, the other was bald.

I stopped to wait for Leon and Babi to catch up and reached out to make them stop.

'What that noise, Kam?'

'Elephants.'

Leon laughed, and tugged my arm to take him closer. Then he heard someone else's laughter reverberating off the undercliff.

'Naz?' he breathed, then again, 'Naz!' this time at the top of his lungs.

The woman with the long grey hair turned around.

'Leon!' she yelled, dropping her plate of food and running towards him.

Leon stood stock still with his arms outstretched, waiting for her to come to him, while Babi ran in and out of his legs, clapping her hands in excitement.

Nazar didn't even see me – she only had eyes for Leon – and as they embraced each other, the other figure turned to see where his companion had gone. And that's when I started running. Because it was Pa!

*

I never knew it was possible to feel this happy. Or why, when your whole being is smiling, you cry so much! Pa's face when he realised it was me is something I'll never forget. There was a sadness in his eyes, a look of total disbelief – like he'd totally given up any hope of ever seeing me again – or, more likely, that he'd lost all hope of anything. I wanted the tears to stop so I could see Pa's face properly; he was just a blur of wrinkled brown skin. I ran my hands over his bald head, and he did the same to me, kissing my scalp and saying over and over, 'What happened to your lovely red hair, Kam?'

What a strange scene: four crazy people being reunited with each other, while two elephants, a baboon and a fennec fox watched in amazement. There was so much to say and ask, but somehow there was no need for words at that moment; the reality of each other's presence was enough. Eventually Nazar started to describe how she'd been down by the lake with Elisha and Elijah, when suddenly this huge machine came thundering towards them, just as it was going dark.

Pa took over the telling of the story.

'Kam, getting that thing going again was quite a feat, I can tell you! My advanced Ed on Nyan Tolo finally paid off – that's why you need to get back home and finish yours. Whatever were you thinking, coming on a mission like this?'

'Pa, let's talk about that later – carry on with the story!'

'Yes, so I found the Terraformer abandoned in a newly dug tunnel system deep underground. I'd almost given up trying to find Leon. I was planning to return to the surface and ask En.Ki for a dishonourable discharge and then go back to Sirius. But when I found the Terraformer and managed to get it up and running, I decided to keep looking. I knew that if I stayed below ground I would be safe, and besides, that thing can tunnel through anything. I must have destroyed a fair few goldmines along the way, but I kept going, and eventually a tunnel led me back to the surface. I had no idea where I was, and then I spotted something moving up ahead beside a lake, and when I got closer, I could see it was a couple of animals. I don't know why, but my heart leapt with joy just seeing signs of life. I waited until it was getting dark and they were resting, because I didn't want to scare them off. By then I knew they were elephants and, as I approached, I could see that there was someone with them. I got a bit of a surprise when I discovered it was Nazar.'

'I was just as surprised to see you, Dr Jainko!'

'So what did you do? How did you manage to avoid the rift valley, Nazar? And where are the others?'

'I… no – let your Pa tell the story, Kam.'

'So, Nazar told me you'd found Mel and taken her to Khem, and were planning to come back for her and the Atlantean survivors. I said, why wait, we can take everyone in the Terraformer – including the elephants – and I knew it could get through all manner of obstacles. So we got everyone inside and set off, confident we would find you soon enough. But then we heard on the Terraformer's military comms system that Dracos were patrolling the whole area around Khem, including Libia, so we didn't know if you'd made it. We were terrified they'd spot the Terraformer. Everyone was bracing themselves for the worst the whole way here.' Pa gestured back to the Terraformer, where the Atlantean survivors were obviously still sleeping. He turned back to look at us and beamed.

'What a relief! Oh Kam! Leon! Look at you! Come here, both of you. My goodness, how beautiful you are, Leon, and you too, Kam – even without your hair. You're as bald as Ma and me now! But where is Mel? Is she still sleeping?'

There was a silence, which Leon decided to fill, stating the situation as plainly as it was true.

'Mel not here.'

'Oh!' said Pa and Nazar in unison. 'What happened?'

I drew a breath, not knowing how Pa was going to take the news, and not knowing where to start with my questions about the *Kam-Mel-Leon* file.

'Meth got her!' Leon blurted out.

'Meth?' yelled Nazar.

'Captain Tehuti seems to think she's still alive,' I said quietly, 'it was awful. Meth ambushed our vimana and took Mel prisoner.'

Nazar and Pa both stared at me open-mouthed.

Disk XXV

RECOVERY

'**P**A, WHY DON'T YOU leave the survivors sleeping while you and Nazar come and meet the Builders? They will be able to tell you what Tehuti's plan involves and perhaps then we can work out how to get Mel back,' I suggested.

'Will the elephants be alright here too, Kam?' Nazar asked me.

'You'll be fine, won't you Elijah?' I replied, giving him a playful pat.

'What should we do with the Terraformer?' Pa fretted, as he pocketed its portable comms tablet.

'Don't worry, Pa, Jenti hide it,' Leon reassured him.

'Who's Jenti, Leon?' I heard Pa ask as they walked off arm in arm up the riverbank, with Babi running on ahead of them.

Nazar waited until they were out of earshot.

'What do you think Meth has done with Mel?' she asked.

'I've no idea. I tried everything I could to stop him, believe me. I even pulled my electric slime stunt on him, which left him in quite a mess, but we've seen him heal pretty quickly once before, haven't we, Aum?' I stroked Aum's pale cream fur. 'So no doubt he'll survive.'

'Did he just take Mel, or Saha'Ra and Mintaka too?'

'Just Mel. Saha'Ra is here, but there's something else: Mintaka didn't survive the ambush. We brought her body here.'

'Oh my god, the poor little thing.'

Nazar's eyes welled up and she brushed away the tears as quickly as they formed.

'Did everyone else make it?' I asked, gesturing towards the Terraformer.

'Yes, just about. When did Leon and the giants arrive?'

'Yesterday, but there were a lot of other giants already here working on the project. Yesterday Captain Tehuti came to check on their progress. The pyramids are incredible, but there's no sign of the city of New Atlantis that Atlas planned for his people, and I don't even think Tehuti has any intention of building homes for them.'

Nazar was silent as she took in this new information.

'Pity Xnake isn't here,' she muttered.

'I thought you said we were better off without him!'

'We are, but he'd know how to confront Tehuti. And where to find Meth.'

'Tell you what, Nazar, so will Zep.'

*

We'd been instructed by Tehuti to leave Zep and the other two AIs in standby mode inside the vimanas when we landed them on the pyramids, but I was determined to get Zep back up and running. That meant getting back inside the vimana via the shaft inside the smallest pyramid. I wanted to do this on my own, but Pa insisted Leon should go with me. Then Pa took out a little kit from his pocket that contained some medical swabs and needles and a set of tiny scientific instruments. He used one or two of them to fiddle with something on Leon's forehead and, when he switched on the Terraformer's comms tablet and set it to a particular frequency, the screen showed a view of whatever direction Leon was facing. Then he took a blood sample from each of us and checked something in the back of Leon's neck.

'Etheria levels and bloods are fine. Leon's good to go. What kind of Blocker are you fitted with nowadays, Kam?'

'It's that recon one that came from an elderly Sirian hominid, remember? Is that a problem?'

'You'll probably be OK. Those old Black Khanus models are pretty effective.'

'At what?'

'Avoiding detection. They were invented to stop the Alpha Draconis government stealing Sirian technology.

Leon has one too. It also stops anyone hooking you into their Hive Mind.'

'But Pa, if we had a window into Meth's Hive Mind, we'd know what he's done with Mel.'

'That's true, Kam, but also highly risky. It will bring Black Khanus online, and I don't think that's a good idea. I take it my brother doesn't know you're here?'

'Uncle Jainko had his suspicions, especially when he ran into our pilot, Xnake Rapza, but I managed to convince our klan I was going on an astrobiology field trip. Ma thinks I'll be back by the end of Koiak.'

'But that's only three days away! Kam, this is very irresponsible of you. You're not even the right age yet, and then to accept a mission piloted by a renegade like Xnake Rapza, well…'

Pa seemed at a loss for more words.

'I'm not a child anymore, Pa.'

There was a long silence.

'And I'm not *your* child, either.'

He looked at me sharply.

'I saw the file, Pa. In your office at the En.Ki lab. I know about field-testing Leon and Mel. I saw the picture of me as a baby at the lab in Colonel Askew's arms. I've met your colleague too, Pa, and I've also figured out a few things.'

'Kam, I…'

'Let's talk about this another time. Right now, I want to find out if Mel is still alive and figure out a way to bring her here.'

'Yes, Kam, you're right, absolutely,' he said with a weak smile.

*

With Leon accompanying me with that thing on his forehead switched on, I was aware that Pa could now see my every move. I was determined to show him that, even if I wasn't technically a full-grown adult, I was not only responsible but also experienced and capable of handling myself. I'd got this far, and I couldn't see any reason why I couldn't finish what I had come here to do.

Then it occurred to me that I had already achieved that more or less: I'd come on this mission to find out who I really was, to find out why I was chameleonoid, and to find Pa. So now what?

Those were things I wanted for myself – selfish things that caused me to act selfishly, like leaving Nyan Tolo in the sneaky way I had. Since I'd arrived on Earth, I had started to see the bigger picture and how things are all interconnected, that it takes more than the actions of a single individual – or even a single species – to succeed. The cataclysms that Earth was going through now seemed like a physical version of the inner turmoil I'd felt all my life. It wasn't just a case of surviving it, but of understanding it and helping others to do the same.

I realised I still had work to do. There were now other people involved, people I loved. I turned round and looked at Leon's white face, his wavy white-gold hair and his unblinking blue eyes. I thought of how beautiful Mel was, and how brave she'd been, bringing the survivors of Atlantis across a whole continent, determined to honour King Atlas's wishes about establishing New Atlantis. I realised how brave Leon had been, too, surviving the ordeal of Meth's underground base, then finding a way to escape into a subterranean world, befriending the giants and accompanying them all the way here. That took guts.

Whether or not Leon, Mel and I had been programmed to act this way, we'd all passed countless field tests, aptitude tests and initiative tests. We were now in a situation that neither Askew nor Pa could possibly have envisaged when they engineered our gene sequences. One thing was sure: we were not following a script anymore. We were now fully field-tested and battle-ready. The only problem was, I had no idea what kind of battle we were getting into.

-We take the battle one step at a time, Kam. Don't worry, we can do this.

-Leon, is that you?

-Yes.

-So you can telepath too?

-Of course I can.

-Your thoughts sound different compared to how you speak.

-Yours do too, Kam. It's because we're chameleons.

-Chameleons?

-That's what the giants call us people with blue eyes.

Leon began to sing in a beautiful clear voice as we moved steadily up the steep shaft to the central chamber inside the smallest pyramid. The sound of his voice somehow made the dust lift off the surfaces. It started to glow and dance in the air like tiny specks of light. As we crawled through the entrance into the chamber, Leon's singing reverberated off the smooth walls so loudly that at the far end of the chamber the heavy carved lid lifted up and hovered above the stone vessel where we'd laid Mintaka's body.

'How are you doing that, Leon?'

He shrugged and continued singing. It seemed as though someone else had joined in, harmonising with his voice.

-Shhh, Leon, I can hear something.

Leon stopped singing and the lid lowered back onto the stone vessel. Above it was a shimmering patch of light. I walked towards it and realised it was Mintaka's voice I could hear, singing the beautiful incantation Saha'Ra had sung when the Dogon Elders laid her daughter in the vessel.

'Min?' I whispered into the void, a strange feeling passing through me.

-It's not a real person. It's a spirit, Kam. Did someone die here?

-Yes, a little girl called Mintaka. We laid her body in here.

-Don't worry, Kam, if her spirit is singing, she's alright. I used to hear spirits singing every night whenever there was a death in Pa's lab.

-Why, did Pa make lots more of us chameleons?

- No, it was the little lab animals. When they were dying I used to sing to them to cheer them up. They lived such sad lives, but after they died, their spirits were much happier, and then they sang too.

*

The next part was almost impossible. Zep was stuck inside the vimana in standby mode and I couldn't get his attention telepathically, so I couldn't ask him to open the portal to enable us to get back inside the ship. In the end, I had to revert to slime and perform the Crease trick in reverse, oozing my way up the vertical shaft and into the vimana, while Leon waited in the chamber below.

I found Zep docked to the comms deck, where we'd left him.

-Zep, come online now. It's Kam. Zep?

There was no response.

I detached him from the dock and improvised some straps from the webbing of my hammock, then hauled him onto my back and descended into the shaft.

'Coming!' I bellowed down to Leon.

I don't know if it was the tone of my voice, or the fact that 'coming' sounded similar to 'come in', but at that moment the vimana's comms deck sprang into life and a voice spoke.

'This is the En.Ki command centre. Please state your mission name and recruit number. All Earth mission crews are grounded at this time, pending further instructions from Captain Tehuti. Take cover immediately. High levels of plasma energy and gamma rays inbound, solar storm commencing in twenty-four hours, mass coronal ejections, flares and severe seismic activity are expected.'

None of the message made sense to me, beyond sounding serious.

-Did you get that, Zep?

-Your AI bot is not functioning, Kam. En.Ki must have disabled him remotely. Pa might be able to fix him. Let's go.

I led the way out of the chamber and back down to the base of the entrance shaft. Just as we were nearing the gallery that led to the great hall beneath all three pyramids, a violent jolt threw us up against the wall. There was a flicker of electricity, like miniature lightning running from floor to ceiling, that made Leon's hair stand on end. Mine would have done too, if I'd had any, but I could definitely feel a prickle pass across my ceph.

-What was that?

-A solar flare, maybe. The whole solar system is unstable right now, that's what Jenti told me. That's why he didn't want to come above ground.

Disk XXVI

BLOOD RITUAL

FOR SOME REASON, WHEN we arrived back in the great hall the place was all lit up with flaming torches mounted on the walls, and a long red carpet had been rolled out leading all the way from the entrance steps into a circular chamber at the far end. There were no giants in sight, although I could hear their pounding footsteps overhead. Spaced at intervals along the red carpet were Draco guards standing to attention. Then I noticed that the Atlanteans had joined the Dogon survivors, but they had all been gagged and tied up next to the water channel.

-*What's happening, Kam?*

-*I'm not sure, but it doesn't look good. The survivors have all been gagged and I can't see Pa and Nazar.*

-*Can you timeshift?*

-*No.*

-*Then let me. I'll telepath you when I need your help.*

Leon stood very still for a moment and then vanished. In less than a few seconds, he reappeared.

-*Pa and Nazar are in that circular chamber over there, but I'm going to need your help freeing them, Kam.*

-*Kam, is that you?* Mel's voice came through in our heads as a terrified rasp.

Suddenly I realised all three of us were communicating.

-*Mel! It's you! Where are you? What's happening?* I asked her.

-*Oh Kam, please help us. Meth and his rebels brought me here to perform some sort of gruesome blood sacrifice, and then Pa and Nazar arrived, and now they've tied us all up and gagged us, Saha'Ra too. I think Meth is going to kill me. He's hurt me so much, Kam!*

As soon as Mel started crying I could feel myself turning blue with stress and I was breathing through my gills.

-*Where's Meth's sword, Leon? I need it.*

Leon nodded, timeshifted and returned with it a few seconds later.

I walked up to the first Draco, hoping that in this poor light he might just mistake me for a high-ranking blue lizard from Alpha Draconis and follow my orders. I stood up tall and commanded them to leave immediately. With no hesitation, all twelve of them marched in lockstep out of the hall and up the steps, while Leon and I ran into the circular chamber to find Mel tied up and laid out on a white stone altar wearing a red dress. I started untying Mel while Leon worked at freeing Pa, Nazar and Saha'Ra who were tied to the three columns that surrounded the altar. I had just freed Mel when I caught sight of Babi lying next to the altar in a pool of blood. Mel followed my gaze.

-Don't look, Kam. Meth killed the baboon to show me what he planned to do to me. He was going to kill Aum as well, but he was clever and put a force field around himself before Meth could catch him.

Hearing what Mel had just telepathed, Leon starting growling as he groped around on the floor looking for Babi's body. Then with his hands covered in her blood, he stood up with the animal in his arms, threw his head back and let out an angry roar. Above our heads, the giants' footsteps stopped. They obviously recognised Leon's distress call and knew he was in trouble.

But giants don't move quickly, and Meth was one step ahead. He'd worked out that Leon and I would arrive soon enough and try to find a way to stop him committing another murder. I could hear Meth's footsteps approaching and when I turned, there he was, standing in the entrance to the circular chamber, his head covered in festering wounds where I'd blasted him with Xnake's gun, his own scalar weapon raised and pointed in our direction.

'How nice – a proper family reunion,' he simpered mockingly. 'Leon the idiot, Kam the traitor, Mel the spoilt little princess, and, what do you know – Commander Nazar is here too! I hear you've been fired from the Trojan fleet. And let's not forget Dr Jainko. Isn't this nice? It's the second time you've been present for my audience with your delectable creation, "Princess Mel". And sadly, the last. I'm dying to taste this new prototype's blood; I've heard it's a great delicacy. I've tasted Kam's, but it's a bit sour. It's royal blood I like the best – preferably Atlas's, but the King's dead now, so a princess will have to do.'

As Meth made his depressing little speech, Leon slipped his hand around my back and loosened the sword from my grip. He edged round me and waited until he sensed that Meth was facing away from him, then raised the tip of the sword and placed it between Meth's wings. Meth wheeled around instantly, but Leon was too quick for him and he stepped out, winding the clock back to the moment just before Meth entered the chamber. I felt the room spin slightly as this small reset took effect. Leon then gave the signal.

-*Chameleons, we need to act fast. Are you ready?*

-*He means us,* I telepathed Mel. *Quick. Do your gravity thing!*

Mel grabbed hold of Saha'Ra and made her body rise to the roof of the chamber, where the two of them hung, looking down. Before I'd had time to think, I found myself shapeshifting into a baboon and clambering up the column above Pa's head, where I waited to see how the next few moments would play out.

Meth strode in, expecting to see the baboon's corpse lying just where he'd dismembered it and Mel tied up, awaiting her terrible fate. Instead he found that Mel had gone, the baboon – which was actually me – was still very much alive, and Leon had somehow appeared from nowhere, wielding the black sword that had once belonged to Meth! Leon sparred and roared, forcing Meth back out into the great hall.

Pa and Nazar watched in awe from a distance as Leon manoeuvred Meth to the bottom of the steps and then gave some kind of signal to Jentilak, who was now standing in the entrance between the paws of the lion statue. Jenti rolled one of the circular saws down the steps, its diamond-tipped blade flashing in the torchlight as it came thundering towards Meth. Everyone gasped, thinking it was about to slice him in two, but he somehow managed to dodge out of its way by half-opening his wings and flying sideways. The saw blade rolled into the corner of the hall and wedged itself in the opening where the giants had broken through from the underground tunnel.

Meth turned around only to find that Leon, Mel and Nazar now had him surrounded. I was running around his ankles with Aum, tying him in knots with one of the ropes, while Jentilak thundered down the steps. Weighing up his options, Meth made a strange menacing noise in the back of his throat, his remaining yellow eye flashing and waving his weapon in the air.

-I know that sound, Kam, he made it when he was teaching me sword-fighting and I tricked him. Meth knows I can move into another moment in time, but he has no idea how I do it. He's very angry – we need to be careful.

-I know, I've heard him make that noise, too.

As if there wasn't enough sense of drama, the Sun's

rays suddenly shone through the entrance, reaching down the steps and almost to the back of the hall, illuminating the terrified faces of the helpless bound survivors. Meth turned into the sunlight and narrowed his one eye, preparing to take on the giant single-handed. He took aim, but the glare of the Sun and his poor eyesight were making it difficult; before he'd had time to adjust to the brightness, Jentilak had slunk into the shadows. I managed to tie Meth's feet together and then tie the other end of the rope around the nearest column before I reverted to hominid form. Just as I was shapeshifting, the ground shuddered and the column buckled suddenly, and a diagonal crack appeared around its circumference making the upper half of it slip sideways. Several other columns also cracked and buckled, causing two or three stone panels to drop down from the ceiling and crash onto the floor right next to the nearest group of survivors, and knocking the weapon out of Meth's grip. I moved quickly and tied Meth's arms behind his back. Once the Draco was no longer a threat to any of us, Leon, Mel and I set about freeing the survivors, working our way down the row, Leon cutting the ropes with Meth's sword, and Mel and I pulling the gags from their mouths. Nazar ran back up the steps to check that the Draco guards had not returned in their drones, and Pa stumbled out after her.

There was another massive jolt and a series of minor tremors, and this time there was no mistaking the fact that we were in the middle of an earthquake. A huge crevice appeared in the stone floor of the hall, wider than the water channel and running in the opposite direction. With all the earth movement that was taking place, the large stone door at the top of the steps suddenly pivoted shut, leaving Pa and Nazar on the outside and the rest of us stuck inside. The gust of wind that it created when it slammed shut snuffed out all the flaming torches, leaving us in complete darkness. Leon worked quickly, not affected by the loss of vision, and told all the survivors to shuffle to the end of the hall nearest to the steps. I picked up my poor inert bot Zep, moved him to the steps and told Aum and Saha'Ra to stay with him. Meth was trying everything he could to work himself free of the ropes, including beating his wings, but nothing was working. Jentilak walked up and down the hall, checking each section of the ceiling with his hands, obviously worried the whole thing might collapse on top of us at any moment. Inside the hall there was an eerie silence, and then slowly there began a strange gurgling, whooshing noise, which seemed to be building up from below our feet.

Disk XXVII

DELUGE

WITHIN A FEW MINUTES, water started gushing up through the crevice in the floor. In a panic, everyone was feeling their way in the darkness towards the thin crack of daylight around the edge of the pivoting stone door, climbing the steps to get away from the water that was flooding the hall. As the channel overflowed, I ran towards the steps and stumbled into the new crack that had opened up, cutting both my shins, at which point I could feel myself becoming distinctly slimy as I crawled my way to safety.

In the end, only Meth was left standing in the middle of the hall, tethered to a column, up to his waist in water and yelling like a maniac. There was another shudder, and a new crack opened up in the ceiling, letting a shaft of light through. I could now see that the opening in the wall where the saw blade was wedged had started to collapse under the pressure of the water, dislodging the circular blade. It was just about to roll free when something behind it reached out to halt its movement and then slithered across the wet floor.

Whatever it was had long, tapering tentacles, several of them.

'It's Xnake!' Nazar screamed.

Meth turned to face the octopod as it reared up out of the water and wrapped two or three tentacles tightly around his torso. The water was now up to Meth's chest, and Xnake moved slowly but deliberately, pushing down on his heaving body, crushing the air out of his lungs, and curling a tentacle around his throat. With another tentacle he brought the saw blade right up to Meth's face.

-*That thing is going to kill him*, Mel remarked, a look of horror on her face.

-*It's revenge for something Meth did to him,* I replied, unable to take my eyes off the scene that was unfolding.

I don't think Xnake was even aware how many eyes were watching. The water was halfway up the steps now, and for some reason the giants had stopped trying to free the stone door. Jentilak was bellowing at them from the inside, but was getting no response. By now, all the survivors were either crammed together near the top step or forced to tread water in the hall which was three-quarters filled like a vast underground tank.

Above the sound of the torrent of water flooding in I could hear a familiar voice. It was Captain Tehuti.

'You will follow my orders, you useless creatures, do you understand? Everything has gone exactly according to plan, don't you see? Even the earthquake is right on cue. The final pyramid must be finished by dawn, when we will witness the heliacal rising of Sirius. The great River Khem will then flood the entire valley and wash away any remaining traces of life, flush out any survivors hiding out in caves and tunnels, and I will have completed Black Sun's mission to wipe everything living off the face of the Earth, so that Agartha can take back control. New Atlantis means new rules. My rules. Tehuti the Atlantean. Now get to work!'

We all listened in stunned silence to this speech, and the trumpeting that followed it sounded as though Tehuti had already begun his victory celebrations, until we realised the noise was coming from a couple of very angry and determined animals. I heard a huge thud as they ploughed past Tehuti and rammed the door between the paws of the Great Lion statue.

'Get out of the way!' I shouted. 'It's the elephants, they're trying to break through!'

Nazar and Mel started swimming hard to get the survivors back against the side walls. There was another tremor and a further surge of water filled the hall almost to the ceiling, with many of the people now struggling to breathe as they became submerged by the swirling water. The elephants rammed the stone door again and cracked it in two. I caught a glimpse of Elisha's trunk as she waved Elijah away and let out a loud cry.

Sodden with water and utterly exhausted, the Atlantean and Dogon survivors crawled out through the doorway one by one, leaving Xnake and Meth to fight it out in the murky depths behind them. I could picture Meth still trying to escape Xnake's clutches under the floodwater, and Xnake retreating back to Agartha once he was sure the Draco had finally given up the fight to live.

In the courtyard outside, the giants were standing around, totally stunned. At first I thought it was because of what Tehuti had decreed, until I noticed that it was something else entirely. It appeared that, in her determination to break down the door and free us, Elisha had taken Tehuti by surprise and pushing past him, she had knocked him over and left him unconscious. When we emerged, he was still out cold, lying face down in front of the lion statue. Jentilak was the last to emerge. He took one look at Tehuti and with fierce determination on his rugged grey face, began to drag his master's body back towards the entrance between the lion's paws.

'Jenti need a hand, you boys!' Leon yelled at the giants, and they stepped into action, pushing the unconscious Tehuti into a watery grave and then efficiently blocking the entrance back up using the broken stone door and any remaining slabs and boulders that were lying about. It would take the combined strength of Tehuti, Meth and Xnake to get out. And I could not imagine that happening any time soon.

I watched as Mel and Saha'Ra went up to all the survivors one by one to check they were alright, and saw Leon being comforted by the giants when he told them what had happened to Babi. Pa was shaking his head in disbelief and Nazar was praising the elephants for coming to our rescue. Mel then turned to the giants and thanked each of them in turn. After she'd graciously thanked Jentilak, who stood at the end of the line, she went up to Leon and introduced herself formally.

'My dear, courageous brother Leon, thank you for your perseverance and your kind and selfless acts of service.' She hugged him tight.

Then it was my turn.

'Kam, I am so happy to know someone like you – one on whom I can depend, and who I know will fearlessly search out the truth and not rest until you have found it.'

She hugged me too, and finally she turned to Pa. What she said to him totally took me by surprise.

'I am overjoyed to see you again, Pa, and at the same time I am sorry you had to witness all of this. But as you can see, the people of New Atlantis are survivors and, contrary to what Tehuti has just said, we are the rightful heirs of Khem, not Black Sun. I am sovereign of New Atlantis now. As my creator, you shall be given the keys to this new kingdom, but as engineered humans, Kam, Leon and I also claim back our personal sovereignty. You will no longer manipulate our bodies, our minds or our destinies. I would ask that you remove Leon's Remote Viewing device and any other devices and entities you have incorporated into our physical, mental, emotional or energetic bodies immediately, so that when Sirius rises tomorrow morning, we will no longer be under En.Ki's control. Everyone has the right to be free, even genetically modified experiments such as us.'

She bowed low and then kissed Pa on his forehead. He had tears of shame and gratitude running down his wrinkled face.

'I will do exactly as you ask, Mel. Perhaps, if I might suggest it, your majesty should have a coronation at dawn tomorrow?' he replied, proud but chastened.

*

Later that day, as the giants laid the last of the casing stones onto the largest pyramid, Jentilak called Leon, Mel and me over to show us something he'd found that Tehuti had left behind. It was written on a fresh sheet of vellum in a very old-fashioned script, and appeared to be either a set of clues he intended to hide with a view to being discovered at some future time, or the outpourings of a guilty conscience who feared their end was near:

Hear ye, and list ye,
O children of Khem...

Wisdom we gained
From the star-born races,
Wisdom and knowledge far beyond man's...

Know ye that in the pyramid I builded
Are the keys that shall show ye the way into life.
Aye, draw ye a line
From the great image I builded,
To the apex of the pyramid, built as a gateway.

Draw ye another opposite
In the same angle and direction.
Dig ye and find that which I have hidden.
There shall ye find the underground entrance
To the secrets hidden before ye were men.

Aye, in the land thou callest Khem,
Races shall rise and races shall fall.
Forgotten shalt thou be of the children of men.
Yet thou shalt have moved
To a star-space beyond this
Leaving behind this place where thou hast dwelt.'

When Mel read them, she had a different interpretation.

'This is from the Emerald Tablets. I had to learn them when I was at school in Atlantis with Mintaka. These lines are from the Eleventh Tablet. There are thirteen altogether and I had to recite them all off by heart at King Atlas's final banquet in front of all the guests. I had no idea that it was Tehuti, Atlas's chief adviser, who had written them.'

-*He didn't write them, Mel. The Black Sun brotherhood wrote them and Tehuti was taught them when he was a young giant living in Agartha. Then he was sent back to the surface by Black Sun, who told him to make the Emerald Tablets a central part of Atlantean religious lore. They did it because they wanted humans to think they were powerless. That's what the giants say, and I believe them.* Leon paused.

'Go on,' Mel urged, 'but say it out loud. I know you can, Leon.'

Leon looked a bit embarrassed, then smiled and took a deep breath. When he spoke with self-belief and from the heart, his voice was deep and strong, just like you'd expect a lion to sound.

'Mel, don't you see, Tehuti was controlling Jenti and his friends, making them think they were carrying out King Atlas's orders, when all the time Tehuti was planning to get rid of Atlas and take charge of New Atlantis himself when the time came for Atlantis to be evacuated. He is only loyal to Black Sun. Now we've trapped him under the statue, he will most likely drown, or, if he survives, return to the Black Sun brotherhood down in Agartha where he belongs. That means En.Ki's project is now over. You should rewrite the Emerald Tablets, Mel, to consecrate New Atlantis and to celebrate the fact that we've saved the Atlanteans from eternal domination! We might not have prevented Earth from experiencing death and destruction, but we are the reason there are survivors. Just like them, we are one consciousness – you, me and Kam – born into three modified human bodies, and we should write down what happened to us so that others can learn from our experience.'

He stopped, a little out of breath.

'Bravo, Leon! You're right. Let's write a brand-new Emerald Tablet to read aloud at dawn tomorrow.'

Leon and I both nodded vigorously.

'I have the perfect thing to engrave it onto, Mel.'

'What is it, Kam?'

'It's a piece of green rock I picked up off the ground in Libia after we were ambushed.'

I reached inside my drenched clothing, pulled out the fused rock and handed it to her. Mel turned it over in her hands.

'Yes, it makes perfect sense to use something from the place where Mintaka died,' Mel said thoughtfully, 'Because then she will always be part of our message.'

Disk XXVIII

CONSECRATION

T HE ATLANTEAN AND DOGON people went down
to the River Khem to bathe in preparation for the
heliacal rising and Mel's coronation. The giants gave us
some beautiful unused white linen that they'd found, and
Saha'Ra set about making coronation robes for Mel. Mel
couldn't wait to get out of the red dress Meth had made
her wear.

'It freaked me out when Meth made me to put it on,
because ages ago I had a dream it would happen, and the
Queen's soothsayer once gave me a strange doll with a
dress like this, to try and stop me drifting out of my body.'

'I'm glad the soothsayer's doll didn't work, because that skill of yours got you out of a lot of trouble earlier,' I remarked as I combed Mel's hair and attempted to get it into some sort of style. 'You know what, I think Saha'Ra is better at this than me,' I said, handing the comb back.

'You're just out of practice, since you haven't any hair of your own at the moment,' Mel joked.

'That's a bit mean. I think I'm the one who needs a crown, to cover up my baldness.'

I pretended to make a sad face, and then spotted Pa stroking Aum and went over to talk to him. Pa seemed to be looking for something in Aum's fur behind his neck.

'Has my fox got fleas or something?'

'Erm, no, he's perfectly fine. I was just removing his Blocker.'

'Aum has a Blocker too?'

'Aum has a lot of things, Kam. He and Babi were among my earliest and most successful creations – apart from you three, of course.' Pa rubbed his chin thoughtfully.

'Wow. I had no idea Aum was genetically modified. Did you make him to be a healer?'

'Yes, without Aum our whole family would have got sick in Relegation a long time ago, Kam. I created him to protect all of you while I was away. I created Leon's baboon for the same reason.'

'I see. But doesn't that mean, since I brought Aum with me on the mission, they'll all be getting sick back home?'

'Uncle Jainko has access to plenty of anti-radiation medicine at Black Khanus. I'm sure they're fine.'

'Do you miss them, Pa? I mean, did you miss us?'

'Every day, Kam. It was the only thing that kept me going.'

He looked at me with his head on one side and took my hands in his.

'I'm sorry about my harsh words earlier, Kam. I am really proud of all you've achieved – you, Mel and Leon. You've done Askew and me proud. No, forget I said that – you've done *yourselves* proud. This is the beginning of a new era, and it wouldn't even be happening if it wasn't for you.'

'How did you... make us?'

'It was very complicated. Askew and I worked on the designs for many years. The blue eyes were technically his idea, but the shapeshifting was my invention. I spliced together a segment of Atlas's second chromosome with that of a rare Sirian reptile that can change its form and colour at will. I had no idea of the incredible variations it would lead to – you're all so talented at shapeshifting. I just hope that...'

He faltered.

'Hope what?' I pressed him.

'Well, Askew was secretly planning to sell your innovative gene sequence.'

'Didn't you try to stop him?'

'I tried reasoning with him, but he was my boss and I...'

'Go on.'

'I just wanted to get home to Sirius, Kam. If I'd reported him to the En.Ki board, there would have been a lengthy investigation and it would have been years before they'd have let me go home. You and your sisters – especially Yuri – would have been grown up.'

'Yuri is not my real sister, is she? I mean, I love them all to pieces, but I know none of them is actually related to me. Pa, why did you take me home to Sirius for Ma to bring me up and leave Leon and Mel here?' I was crying now.

'Kam, please don't get upset. It was not an easy decision for me, I assure you. I became very attached to you when you were a baby – you were our first prototype, and En.Ki wanted me to do all these tests on you that I couldn't bear the thought of. So, I thought it best to take you somewhere out of harm's way. I told En.Ki that you'd died during one of our experiments.'

'And they believed you?'

'The board did. But Askew knew I was lying. He said he'd let it go if I turned a blind eye to his wrongdoing.'

'How did you smuggle me out of the lab?'

'One night, on an impulse I took you to the Dogon tribe in the mountains. They took care of you until my next period of leave, when I came to get you and took you back to Sirius.'

'Wrapped in blue silk.'

'Indeed. Wrapped in blue silk.' Pa gave me a wry smile.

'Last question, Pa. What did you make us *for*?'

'I had no idea at first that there was a purpose. I was just a genetic engineer employed by En.Ki to invent new things. But around the time we lost Leon, it became clear to Askew and me that you were Atlas's failsafe project. Atlas somehow knew that Atlantis was about to be destroyed by forces that lay outside his control, and he masterminded elaborate plans to make sure his people survived the catastrophe. One of them was New Atlantis and the whole evacuation protocol, and the other was you.'

'Me?'

'All three of you. You're a flagship project, Kam. The new and improved version of the human body type. A superhuman, in fact. Homo chameliensis. You're resistant to illness, you're stronger and fitter than any other hominid, you'll live a good deal longer than normal folk and, as you know, you have some unusual powers that humans aren't usually born with. I suspect there are a few things you three can do that I don't even know about.'

'You're right there. We discovered today that we can all telepath with each other.'

*

The giants were sweeping the platform around the now finished pyramids while the rest of us were preparing food and decorations for a dawn ceremony in front of the Great Lion statue. Just after the Sun went down behind the three pyramids and the stars came out, I looked up for a moment and saw something strange. The constellation of Orion, which looks like a man holding a staff, was now visible above the western horizon and the three stars that make up his belt sat in the sky in a horizontal line, one above each of the three pyramids like beads on a necklace, exactly as if it had been planned that way from the beginning.

'Look at those stars, Saha'Ra – they're exactly lined up with the pyramids!' I called her over to show her.

'Min's is the littlest one,' she said, squeezing my arm.

'Yes. Let's call that star Mintaka from now on.'

Just then I heard a strange noise coming from over by the steps. I realised it was Zep, who I'd stood in the sunshine to dry off properly after rescuing him from the flood.

-*Zep? Is that you? Have you finally decided to work again?*

-*Yes, Kam. I seem to be back. What did I miss?*

-*Quite a lot, actually!*

-*Did the world end as En.Ki predicted?*

-*Not entirely – some of us seem to have survived to tell the tale.*

-*Well, that's a relief. Now can I get back to my farm on Nyan Tolo?*

-*Funny, I was also thinking it was maybe time to return home. With Pa.*

-*You found your Pa?*

-*Like I said, you've missed a few things, Zep.* I laughed out loud.

Everyone was too excited to sleep, so we sat up all night discussing the wording of the new tablet while the Dogon passed round gourds of their potent tea to the Atlanteans, who sang songs and recited poems. Leon and Nazar did a sword-fighting demonstration, Pa told us a couple of Sirian sagas, and one of Jentilak's brothers did some magic tricks. They got Leon to sing particular notes, and then they picked up different sized rocks and when they let go of them, they stayed up in the air until Leon stopped singing. Everyone found it hilarious.

'I think this is going to make a great little starter community for New Atlantis,' I said to Mel, as we both threaded together a crown of palm leaves.

'Yes, and if any other refugees want to stay here with us, they are welcome to become part of it too,' she said, humming softly. 'Of course, that offer includes you and Leon,' she added.

Shortly before dawn, we all gathered by the river next to the Terraformer. Nazar washed the elephants and decorated their trunks with intricate patterns and put garlands around their necks. Meanwhile Saha'Ra went to help Mel change into her white linen robes inside the Terraformer, and when they emerged everyone clapped and cheered. Pa and the Dogon Elders anointed each other's faces with white tribal markings and put on their cloaks. Then Pa came up to me and anointed my forehead with the markings too. He noticed I was wearing the blue tunic that Ma had made for me.

'I recognise that silk,' he said with a smile, patting me on the back.

Mel asked Leon if he would walk out in front and lead the procession. She handed him the Dogon staff that she'd been given by the Chief.

'This is for you, Leon. You don't need Meth's sword anymore.'

When everyone was finally ready, Jentilak picked up Mel and put her on Elisha's back and Leon led the way slowly up the riverbank with Elijah following, to stand in front of the Great Lion and wait for Sirius to make its appearance.

I'm not sure what I was expecting to happen at that moment, but it was a bit of an anti-climax. Our bright blue star rose above the horizon, and slid gracefully up and across the inky sky, followed by a deep pink blush as the Sun prepared to appear. It was only when Aum started barking that we all turned around and saw that the real event was taking place behind us. Maybe it was an after-effect of the celestial alignment the night before, or perhaps it was due to the water that now filled the chambers beneath the plateau, or just that the pyramids were now complete, their white casings and gold capstones gleaming in the dawn light. Whatever the reason, the pyramids seemed to be alive, humming away as a beam of plasma streamed out through the apex of each one. I could sense something shift as my heart began to synchronise with the energy field of the pyramids and then with everyone around me. It grew and grew until it felt as if everything – the past, the present and the future – was one coherent whole, as if time and space weren't relevant anymore.

Mel stepped forward, and in her beautiful Atlantean voice, recited the words of the new Emerald Tablet that we'd carved onto the fused rock the night before:

For Atlantis to return requires us all,
those souls who lived those times before,
to meet again, to recognise, to face
and turn about, and work as one
to build Atlantis here.

I send my words to you,
and I expect that you shall send them on
till I receive them back, charged up
by such another citizen of time
who still remembers how the world should be.

So many left, and now so few return;
we must remain the core of those who know,
rebuilding links to beauty with our minds.

After ten thousand years we've come
to reinvent Atlantis in our time.

When Mel finished speaking, Pa stepped forward and placed the palm-leaf crown on her head, I put the new Emerald Tablet in her left hand, and Leon put the Dogon staff in her right. Then the giants lifted Mel up onto the Great Lion's head, so that she could make her first speech as Queen of Khem. She gazed down at the crowd below and smiled.

'On this day, we consecrate a new civilisation, the New Atlantis, and mark the beginning of a new era, the Age of Leo. I dedicate this new Kingdom in the valley of Khem to the memory of Atlas and his Queen, God rest their souls!' Mel kissed the Emerald Tablet and held it aloft for a moment before continuing. 'I welcome the survivors of Atlantis and the surviving Dogon people, whose wisdom and fortitude has taught me so much and brought us safely to this place, so I also dedicate this place to the Dogon

Chief and to Mintaka, God rest their souls!' She kissed and held up the Dogon staff and gazed at all the faces below her. 'And finally, I dedicate Khem to my new-found family, and especially to Kam and to Leon, brave pilgrims of this new world.'

I looked at Leon standing beside me, beaming from ear to ear, and at Pa on my other side, who was crying tears of joy and relief that his work here on Earth was finally complete. I linked arms with both of them and proposed a response to Mel's toast: 'To the Queen of New Atlantis and to all the brave pilgrims of this new world!'

'What's a pilgrim?' asked Leon.

'It's someone who sets out on a journey to try to change things and ends up changing themselves.'

'Like us?'

'Yes, just like the three of us.'

Disk XXIX

AFTERMATH

Under Queen Mel's direction, the giants wasted no time building a modest palace and homes for all the inhabitants of New Atlantis, large and small. They even built an elephant house in the palace garden, just as Mel had planned back in Atlantis with a sign to hang over the door: 'Elisha and Elijah live here'.

Leon and Nazar will stay until everyone has settled into their new lives and to help plant seeds in the fields beside the river. Then they plan to head off in the Terraformer to look for any other survivors and bring them to New Atlantis. As for Pa, Aum and me, Zep has put in a request to the Sirian High Kouncil asking them to arrange transportation to take us all back to Nyan Tolo.

Pa did as he promised and disabled and removed all the devices and programmes he'd put into Mel, Leon and me, and, although it felt a bit strange at first, I'm getting used to the feeling of being free from En.Ki's control. Of course it means I can't telepath with Zep anymore, but I'm fine with that. I never did like the fact that my thoughts got tangled up with his AI. I can still telepath with Mel and Leon, but I can't hear what they're thinking any more. It's our first taste of privacy, as well as freedom.

'What are you looking forward to about going home, Pa?' I asked him, as we walked along the River Khem early one morning.

'Seeing Ma and the girls, obviously. I also want to end the feud with my brother. And I'm thinking about starting an algae farm.'

'That sounds like a great retirement project, Pa. But won't you still have to work for En.ki?'

'I've got news for you, Kam. Since Tehuti's disappearance, En.Ki has folded. We heard it on the Terraformer's comms, so I no longer work for them,' Pa remarked with a satisfied smile.

'So you really can retire, Pa! Maybe once I've finished my astrobiology course, I can help run the algae farm with you.'

'That would be great,' Pa said, putting his arm round my shoulder.

'I did consider taking a course in genetic engineering, but...'

'But what, Kam?'

'I don't think we should be interfering with our DNA.'

'You're quite right. And I should know.'

'By the way, did I tell you? The first thing I'm going to do with all the mono I've earned is get us all out of Relegation.'

'Ma would love that, Kam. But I think you can do even better.'

'What do you mean?'

'You should persuade Nommo One to improve living conditions for everyone on Nyan Tolo. It's not just down in Relegation that Sirians are suffering.'

'You're right. There's hardly any clean water and the radiation levels are off the chart. Do you really think she'd listen to me, Pa?'

'No one is too small to make a difference, Kam.'

What on Earth can Atlantis teach us?

Kitty Carruthers interviews
Dr Camille Warden and Professor Ian Clyffe

29 February 2024

It's abundantly clear that we are struggling to cope with the effects of climate change on our planet, not least because we are still arguing about its root cause. We urgently need to focus instead on how we are going to cope with the devastating impact of climate change. To do this, we need to open our minds to what has been staring us in the face for a very long time.

Two brave researchers, archaeologist Dr Camille Warden and climate scientist Professor Ian Clyffe, whose controversial work earned them a Nobel Prize in December, have done just that. Apart from 'The Book of Revelation', their 'Atlantean Climate Change Hypothesis' is probably the best roadmap we've got, in terms of showing us what we're in for.

I caught up with them last week at the Climate Summit in Cairo to ask them what's to be done if we're living through the same extreme climate change that led to the fall of Atlantis.

> KC: Dr Warden, what's the context for your discoveries, and why are people finally taking notice of the

idea of Atlantis, long considered merely a myth?

CW: Yes, it's true, for centuries people have written about the myth, the meaning, the location, and the fate of Atlantis, beginning with Plato's 'Timaeus', which inspired many others after him to propose alternative theories about Earth's mishaps. For example, books like 'Earth in Upheaval' by Immanuel Velikovsky, which was seen as heresy in the 1950s, and the work of Ignatius Donnelly, 'Atlantis and the Antediluvian World', which was regarded as historical fantasy long after it was published in 1882. Many researchers have tried to link flood myths with the fossil record, and we're still in the process of piecing together the evidence provided by geological strata, ice cores and impact craters. We now know for sure how and when the dinosaurs were wiped out, and the public is well aware there have been other mass extinction events, but so far experts have been reluctant to say that humans were virtually wiped out too. I believe that's the real reason we've ignored Atlantis for so long: we have been in denial about what took place 12,000 years ago, but we're finally waking up to the fact that, back then, we almost became extinct too.

KC: *So, is this the conclusion that your work has led you to, Professor Clyffe?*

IC: Well, it's not all doom and gloom. The

Atlanteans were smart people, they saw it coming and made a plan to not only survive the calamity but miraculously also save much of their culture and technological know-how in the process. We have long known there were sudden advances in human civilisation, when we went from being primitive hunter-gatherers to having the kind of highly developed systems of writing, engineering, medicine, mathematics, et cetera that you see in ancient Egypt and Mesopotamia, but this massive shift has never been properly accounted for. The truth is, the Atlanteans probably seeded many survivor colonies; 'New Atlantis' was really a legacy project, not a place, and we now think it led to the emergence not only of Egyptian culture, but also the Guanches, the Basque people, the Mayans, and possibly many others.

KC: *Professor Clyffe, I understand you were initially sceptical of the extra-terrestrial aspects of Dr Warden's findings. Have you come to a new understanding of other forms of intelligence as a result of your collaboration?*

IC: I have to admit, the 'aliens and outer space' factor challenged my credulity for a long time, given that we had no visible evidence, but the moment Camille's intern showed me how the Sirian Disks had been encoded, I knew this was no terrestrial technology. I had to expand my thinking to realise that the Dogon people were not making it up: their ancestral stories about having contact with beings from Sirius had always struck me as possible from a mathematical probability point of view, but, seeing those disks for the first time, I knew it had to be true.

KC: *Camille, your research team, led by Major Jonathan Edwards, now includes many other disciplines, including astronomers and paleo-linguists, quantum physicists, even shamans and spiritual mediums. To what extent has your willingness to overcome the boundaries of academic disciplines been the secret of your success?*

CW: It's all about putting our heads together and being open-minded. That should be the approach of all scientific enquiry if we are to discover something we didn't know before, something that only our combined knowledge and perspective can shed light on. It's been very exciting and at times challenging to work across our various disciplines, since we all have our own ways of doing things, but it's taken us somewhere new, for sure. The work we are presenting here at the Climate Summit, for instance, has meant that even the most stubborn Egyptologists are changing their minds about pre-Pharaonic culture, and are finally coming to accept the antiquity of the Sphinx, the proof that it was eroded by water, and the real reason for building the Great Pyramids. By holding the summit here in Cairo, we have been able to open up the Hall of Records and various other chambers beneath the Giza Plateau for the first time, so that delegates can see for themselves what is described in the accounts of Kam, Mel and Leon.

KC: *Ian, your work is now the subject of a major touring exhibition entitled 'The New Atlantis', and soon people all around the world will be able to see the Dogon Scrolls, the Sphinx Codex and the Sirian Disks first-hand. What impact would you like these ancient documents to have on modern human consciousness?*

IC: They have already had considerable impact. I thought at first their main impact would be to silence the people who accused us of conducting pseudoscience. But now that we have unearthed the documents, translated the words and shed light on their meaning, the real impact will be measured by how quickly we as a species act. We know we're in the midst of a global catastrophe, but our findings show it is not unprecedented. We have faced climate change on this scale before. It is now up to the Intergovernmental Committee on Climate Change, as well as lobbyists and activists, to re-orientate their agendas to take into account our Atlantean Climate Change Hypothesis, and secure enough funding to make 'The New Atlantis' a living, breathing legacy project for today.

KC: *And what would that entail, exactly?*

CW: Like the Atlanteans, we need to evacuate our people permanently away from vulnerable coastal locations; we need to build hundreds of new cities in safe locations and find novel ways to ensure our survival. There is already a seed vault in Svalbard, north of Norway, containing the means to grow food again should all our plant species be wiped out, and many museums have created watertight, impact-proof vaults to store important artworks and artefacts, but without our survival this is all somewhat pointless. As individuals, we are not as resilient as we would like to think we are. We do not have the practical life skills that our predecessors had. Many of those who survived climate change back then did so by virtue of being at high altitude with access to fresh water and natural shelter. We can do better than this. We have the insight and the intelligence to secure an even better outcome than the Atlanteans. Our survival doesn't have to be a case of being lucky enough to be in the right place at the right time.

KC: *Lastly, what do your findings have to teach us about the future of renewable energy?*

IC: We can all do our bit individually, sure, but really, it's down to the big energy companies doing more than simply committing to becoming carbon neutral in the next quarter-century. It's going to take something a lot more visionary and joined up. First and foremost, what the Atlanteans can teach us is not their strategic level of foresight, but their mastery and understanding of renewable energy. They were far more advanced at this than we are. The pyramids are not just extraordinary feats of construction, they were skilfully designed and built to harness, attenuate, balance and distribute energy within Earth's atmosphere. We don't need to burn fossil fuels to obtain energy. According to our most radical scientists and engineers who believe we're living in an 'electric universe', we don't even need solar panels or wind turbines. We just need to tap into the flow of plasma and electrons in our upper atmosphere. If we do this, we can also boost Earth's magnetic field – much like boosting our own immune system – and protect ourselves from solar flares, mass coronal ejections and EMPs. We might even reduce the likelihood of anything impacting Earth and causing the sort of worldwide climate mayhem the Atlanteans had to contend with. The maths and the science have all been done. It's all up for grabs; we just need to implement it. I say 'us', but really, it's the next generation; they're the ones who are really fired up and angry about our governments' and industries' inaction. They've got the right idea – we just need to step aside now and let them get on with it.

GLOSSARY

Agartha	a mythical place believed to lie deep within the Earth
Atlantis	an advanced civilisation described in detail by Plato
Atlas	leader/king of Atlantis and son of Poseidon
baboon	a type of monkey which the Egyptians associated with Thoth/Tehuti
blue eyes	a genetic aberration that appeared suddenly among humans over 10,000 years ago
Black Khanus*	a secret underground organisation based on Sirius
Black Sun*	an underground priesthood that brought up Tehuti
Blocker*	a device inserted into the brain to avoid being tracked or traced
chameleonoid	a human bred to have shapeshifting characteristics
Chintamani	a special stone or jewel likely to be of extra-terrestrial origin, much prized in Buddhist and Hindu traditions

Dogon	a tribe of people from West Africa who believe their ancestors were visited by beings from the Sirius system and who knew about stars that are not visible to the naked eye
Draco	a reptilian being originating from Alpha Draconis
Emerald Tablets	a set of 13 tablets reputed to have been written by Thoth-the-Atlantean
EMP	electro-magnetic pulse
Enesidaone	the Minoan name for the god Poseidon, used here as his Atlantean name
En.Ki*	a scientific organisation engaged in research into genetic modification and developing AI-based technology
etheria*	an intoxicating substance that is produced hormonally when a chameleonoid steps out
Europa	a moon of Jupiter from which Commander Nazar comes
exo-mission	an intergalactic search and rescue operation
Fennec fox	a small mammal with long ears found in parts of North Africa
Gobero	an archaeological site in the Tenéré Desert in West Africa where extensive ancient mass burial sites have been found
Great Year	the period of one complete cycle of the precession of the equinoxes, which takes 25,772 earth years

halfling*	a Sirian dwarf
Hall of Records	an Atlantean repository of ancient documents thought to have been brought to Egypt for safekeeping beneath the Giza Plateau
Heliacal rising	the rising of a celestial object above the horizon at the same time as, or just before, the Sun
Homo chameliensis*	a species of genetically modified human with shapeshifting qualities
Jasper	an opaque red crystal
kamelan*	a collection of musical instruments similar to the Indonesian gamelan, played in Atlantean times
Khem	the ancient name for the area now known as Egypt
Koiak	the fourth month of the season of flooding in the Coptic calendar, during which the flood-waters of the River Nile abated
Lemuria	an ancient civilisation that predated Atlantis and is thought to have existed in the Pacific Ocean
Libyan Desert glass (LDG)	a vitreous impactite rock found in desert regions thought to have formed millions of years ago under conditions of immense localised heat
melanin	the pigment that gives human hair, skin and eyes their colour

Mintaka	the smallest star in Orion's Belt
Misra	also known as Mesori, the fourth month of the season of harvest in the Coptic calendar
monatomic gold	a refined white powder made from pure gold thought to have a rejuvenating effect on the body
New Atlantis	an incomplete utopian novel about a city state by Sir Francis Bacon, published posthumously in 1626
Nyan Tolo	the name given to the planet which orbits Sirius C, according to the Dogon people
O Nommo	the name given to the extra-terrestrial visitors from Sirius by the Dogon people
obsidian	a black vitreous rock formed from molten lava
orichalcum	a high-grade form of copper ore which the Atlanteans mined and traded
Paoni	the second month of the harvest season in the Coptic calendar
Petrie Museum	a museum in London that holds many of Flinders Petrie's Egyptian archaeological finds
Po Tolo	the Dogon name for Sirius B, the small dense planet around which Sirius A is thought to revolve
pre-cuneiform	one of the earliest forms of writing that predates the wedge-shaped marks in wet clay created by the Sumerians in 3200 BCE

Proteus — the second-largest of Neptune's moons

scalar weapon — a lethal directed energy device which uses sophisticated microwave technology

selenite — a gypsum-based mineral believed to have healing qualities

Sirius — the brightest star in the night sky, whose heliacal rising was used by ancient Egyptians and other cultures to set their calendars

Sothic cycle — a period lasting 1,460 years that starts when the heliacal rising of Sirius coincides with the start of the Egyptian solar year

Sphinx — the gargantuan statue on the Giza Plateau that faces east and is thought by many to have originally been carved with the head of a lion to celebrate the start of the Age of Leo in 10750 BCE

stadion — a unit of measure used in ancient times, equivalent to 190 metres, a similar length to a furlong

stasis giants* — a breed of very tall beings who retreated into the Earth and put themselves into long-term hibernation

Tehuti — another name for the ancient deity Thoth or Tut, the god of wisdom, writing, hieroglyphs, science, magic, art, judgment, and the dead

Terraformer* — a vehicle with tunnelling capabilities capable of traversing rough terrain

Third Eye*	a device inserted into the middle of the forehead to allow remote access to the wearer's line of sight
Toga Na	a thatched, open-sided meeting hut built by the Dogon
Trojan fleet*	a class of paramilitary space craft that patrols the asteroid belt
Urdinak	the Basque/Euskarian word for blue, which may have been derived from the equivalent Atlantean word
Valle Marineris	a major feature on the surface of Mars, most likely formed by cosmic electrical discharge
vimana	a small anti-gravity spacecraft referred to in several ancient Indian texts
zep	ancient Egyptian word meaning 'first', as in 'Zep Tepi', the first time

*asterisked entries have been entirely invented by the author

Credits

Excerpt on pages 79 & 301 taken from Tablet XI of 'The Emerald Tablets of Thoth-the-Atlantean', translated and interpreted by Dr Michael Doreal, reproduced with kind permission of Source Books Inc., Goodlettsville, Tennessee.

(https://www.sacredspaces.org/)

Excerpt on page 207 from Plato's 'Timaeus' obtained online and reproduced under fair use.

Excerpt on page 312-3 from 'Dialects of Light: Atlantis in Poetry' by Linda Pearce, reproduced with kind permission of the poet and Island Blue/Printorium Bookworks.

(https://eternalplanet.com/).

About the author

Having been a postman, an architect, a university professor and a development consultant, Sarah Holding is now a full-time author. She lives in Surrey in a funny old house with a leaning tower with her husband and her three children. She loves vegan food, good coffee and modern jazz. Her previous three books, *SeaBEAN*, *SeaWAR* and *SeaRISE*, which together form the *SeaBEAN* trilogy, are a middlegrade/young adult time travel adventure that also falls into the genre of cli-fi, or climate fiction.

sarah-holding.com